WHAT I'D DO FOR LOVE 2

What I'd Do For Love 2

K.F. Johnson

One Ironwoman Publishing

For information contact :
One Ironwoman Publishing
Grayson, GA 30017

Cover Design by Christina N. Davis
ISBN : 978-1-954469-05-1

Contents

Prologue - Greer   vii

1 Greer   1

2 Greer   9

3 Greer   20

4 Greer   29

5 Greer   40

6 Greer   52

7 Greer   62

8 Greer   72

9 Greer   83

10 Greer   94

11 Greer   106

12 Greer   116

13 Greer   126

14 Greer   139

15 Greer   150

16 Greer   163

17 Greer   176

18 Greer   189

19 Greer   200

20 Greer   211

21 Greer   221

22 Greer   232

23 Greer   242

24 Greer   252

25 Epilogue   259

Enjoy This Book?   261
About The Author   262

Prologue -Greer

I'm immersed in total darkness. Unable to see. Unable to move. I'm certain my attempts to scream are only being heard in my head. The silence is unbearably deafening. Silence, except for the slow, incessant, whooshing sounds of something I can't identify.

The last thing I remember is crying and gasping for breath in Race's arms. Blood oozing from the heart tattoo on my chest. I don't know what hurt more. The debilitating pain that stunned my body and buckled my legs before I eventually blacked out. Or the realization that my own father, shot me.

Christ. What if that's why I can't see or move? What if this was what being dead is like? What if my corpse is lying on a cold slab in a morgue somewhere? Or worse. What if all of that is true, and this is... purgatory?

I can't tell if the tears welling in my soul have actually manifest on my face. The face I can't feel. I've never been so afraid. I mentally recite every prayer I know. Pleading my case to the almighty between words. Hoping I haven't fallen so far from grace that God no longer hears my prayers.

In truth, I hadn't been much of an angel this past year, but there were arguably worse people in this world, my father in particular, that deserved to die over me. I'd been through so much. Hadn't God punished me enough?

This place between here and nowhere is claustrophobic. I'm on the verge of hyperventilating at the thought of spending an eternity in this... this abyss, when the silence is broken.

"Oh my God! She looks so... so helpless."

I instantly recognize the panicked voice of my best friend, Shan. I can't see her, but I don't need to. Her thick New York accent, and the fact that no other woman alive cares enough about me to shed tears, is a dead giveaway.

I can tell she's close enough for me to reach out and touch her. If I could move. I imagine her pretty face screwed into an ugly snarl the way Kerry Washington's always is when she's overacting on an episode of Scandal. My best friend. The one person I can always rely on. I love her so much.

"I just, I didn't expect to see her like this. On a ventilator, with all these tubes coming out of her. When they said she was out of surgery, I thought she would be awake."

A ventilator? Okay. On the upside, I'm not dead. Corpses don't need help breathing, but the fact that I'm not doing it on my own, isn't good either. Exactly, how bad are my injuries? After all, Daddy Dearest did shoot me in the back, like the coward he is. Twice.

My body went totally numb before I blacked out, and I remember fearing paralysis even then. If I am, I'm formally rescinding my prayers to live immediately. Shan has her own family in another state to worry about, my siblings don't care about me, my husband is dead, and my father is as good as dead either way.

There's no one to take care of me if I'm permanently immobilized. I'd rather be dead than trapped in an eavesdropping shell of myself for the rest of my life. That would be worse than purgatory. I imagine it would be hell on earth.

"I know her appearance is shocking, but it probably looks worse to you than it is. The ventilator and chest tubes are necessary to minimize the stress on her lungs until we're sure her body is strong enough to handle it on its own," a Caribbean woman replied.

She made me think of that old TV fortune teller, Ms. Cleo. She was supposed to be from Jamaica, and she would holler, "Call me now!" on every commercial. It was quite comical.

"I'm sorry. I'm just a little tired and a lot emotional right now. I've been trying to get here for two days from New York, ever since I heard what happened. The blizzard has practically everything shut down up north. I was scared she was gonna die before I got here."

"I completely understand. Would you like some water?"

"No. I'm fine. Thank you. I'm sorry. What was your name again?"

"Dr. Powell. I'm the resident physician assisting Dr. Chen on Ms. Patterson's case."

"Yes. The lady at the front desk told me Dr. Chen was in surgery. Would you be able to answer questions about her condition?"

"Certainly. I'll be happy to answer any questions I can. I hope you don't mind, but I'm just going to check her progress and vitals while we talk."

"Please, do what you have to do." She sniffled, inhaling deeply to calm herself. "I've just been so... scared. But she's going to be okay, right?"

"We're very optimistic. She did suffer some complications because of her injuries, but we're monitoring her very carefully. If all continues to go well, her chest tubes may be removed as early as tomorrow evening.

Once we've confirmed that both lungs are fully functioning, we can take her off ventilation and move her out of ICU into a hospital bed."

"How long will that take?"

"Within the next 48 to 72 hours. If there are no further complications."

"This might be a stupid question but, why does she have a chest tube? I thought she was shot in the back. I don't understand."

"She was. One of the bullets entered here..." I assumed she was demonstrating. "...and exited through her chest on the opposite side, breaking a rib, puncturing her left lung, and missing her heart by mere millimeters. The internal damage was severe and required invasive surgery in her chest cavity. Which is why she needs a chest tube.

"There was also a second bullet lodged in her T5 rib, here, in her upper back, that was fractured. Thankfully, Dr. Chen was able to abstract it."

"I was told she was rushed into surgery straight from the ambulance. Is that not true? Because if she was, I don't understand why she needed another surgery yesterday?"

"Yesterday evening, her lung collapsed. It was likely caused by the fractured rib in her chest piercing or widening the existing gash. Dr. Chen had to reopen to repair the lung, then align and reattach the rib with titanium plates. She's a very lucky lady to be alive."

Damn. I was in bad shape. I hoped my chest didn't look like a surgical jigsaw puzzle now.

"Oh my God. Well…Wh…Is there any permanent damage?"

Finally. The million-dollar question! The doctor was taking longer than I appreciated to answer though. Or maybe it just seemed that way to me. I prayed it wasn't a sign of more bad news to come.

"The bullet also damaged the trapezius muscle on her right side, which will limit her range of mobility in that arm. The permanency in that area is dependent on her progress with physical therapy, and her resilience."

"So, she's not paralyzed or anything?"

"Noooo. There was no contact with her spinal cord. She may struggle to walk initially due to pain management, but that will not be long term. Dr. Chen can provide a more in-depth explanation of expectations when she's out of surgery if you like. Otherwise, with continued treatment and physical therapy, her ribs should heal in six to eight weeks. Her other injuries may cause periodic pain for several months as they slowly mend, however."

Shan audibly sighed her relief, mimicking my own. I felt like a fly on the wall, listening to them talk about me like I wasn't in the room. Stupidly, I still wonder if Daddy knows my condition. If he even cares.

Is he happy or sad I survived? I bet he hadn't spent more than a night in the hospital for that flesh wound I gave him.

Here I am fighting for my life, and he's probably home being pampered by my ex-mother in-law, watching episodes of Snapped from the comfort of his own bed.

That man tried to kill me. Once as a child when he set the apartment my mother and I lived in on fire, killing her; and again, when he shot me in cold blood for confronting him about the first time. If anybody needs to die sooner rather than later, it's Charles "Chuck" Foster. Not me.

I may sound hypocritical, given my own murderous past. But y'all know I had good reason for every life I took or altered. They aaaall crossed a line that shouldn't have been crossed, or did something to me, first. Daddy doesn't have the same excuse. He was simply a coward who tried to kill his side-chick and their offspring to hide us from his wife.

I was an innocent little girl, and I have been nothing less than a doting daughter. Say what you want about me, but I worshipped the ground my daddy walked on before that night. Even my hateful ass half-siblings would agree I was a Daddy's Girl. I was a great daughter. There's nothing I wouldn't have done or didn't do for him when he needed me to. Even when he didn't need me to.

To find out he's been playing me my whoooole life, was like... like being told the God you've been praying to since childhood, is really Satan. There's no greater deceit. I thought I knew my father. He was the first man I ever loved, and the first man who was supposed to love me. But he didn't. He didn't love me. As it turns out, he was just good at pretending he did.

The thing about me is, I'm a true believer in speaking things into existence. I didn't see it before, but now everything is so clear. Every time Daddy affirmed, 'Nobody'll eva' love ya mo' than me.' He cursed my ability to find another man who could. Who would, love me more than him. He literally, spoke it into existence.

Even in the last moments before he shot me, he tried to turn my man against me. Blurting out that I killed Michael as a distraction from his own indiscretions was nothing less than a calculated ploy to destroy my chance at true love with Race.

But you see... I changed. I stopped being the demure, docile, door-mat of a human being I let people take me for, the day I slit my cheating husband's throat and framed his side-whore. I became a new woman. A butterfly. The days of people taking my devotion, love, and loyalty for granted, are over.

I deserve love. Pure, unconditional, authentic love. I've earned it. No one will ever prevent me from having true love, ever again. Just like Marlene, Song, Kendrick, and Michael, may his soul rest in hell; and anybody else who gets in my way, Daddy will soon learn what I'd do for love... too.

1

Greer

December 4th 2015

"I don't know who Detective Proctor's trying to impress with this overzealous arrest…" my attorney started as she dragged a chair near my bed. "…but he's about to have a rude awakening."

I expected her to sit in the chair, but she sat her purse and briefcase in it as her slim fingers scrolled the screen of a tablet. Sylvia Brass was a minimally attractive, tall, slender, coffee brown woman, with a short black bob. Her cheekbones were highlighted in the same shade of red as the pumps extending her height to nearly six feet.

The minute curves beneath her impeccably tailored navy-blue suit, screamed androgyny. Surprisingly, a thin gold band on her left ring finger implied she was married. Whether it was to a man or not, I didn't know. What I did know, was that her reputation as a top defense attorney in Atlanta was impressive. Hence why I hired her.

She graduated from my alma mater Spelman College, we crossed paths a few times at school events and parties. After Michael's murder, I secretly vetted her during a time when Marlene's lawyer's investigative team, coupled with police investigations had become particularly grueling.

My nerves were getting the best of me, and I wanted a shark on hand in case my original plans fell through and I ended up being charged. Thankfully, my husband's trifling sidepiece was convicted without my ever needing to book more than a consultation. But this time, was different.

I couldn't have been awake more than an hour before Detective Proctor with the Cobb County PD was at my bedside, interrupting Shan's visit. She'd been the first face I'd seen when I awoke before she called the nurses. Once it became clear that the detective was interrogating me, rather than questioning me as a victim, I lawyered up faster than a Gambino crime boss.

"He said I was going to be transferred to the prison hospital." I tattled to Sylvia fearfully. I'm built for many things. Jail is not one of them.

She exhaled annoyedly.

"Scare tactics. The hospital has not authorized a transfer into their custody, and they won't before I can stop it. The level of treatment you require exceeds what the jail facility can provide now anyway.

At worst, they may transfer you to another wing. Which I doubt will happen either. Especially if bail is granted at your arraignment, which I expect it will. If you pay it, or at least 10% of it with a bail bondsman, you won't spend a day in lock up. Although you will still have to be fingerprinted and booked."

"I don't understand why I'm being arrested at all. He tried to kill me. How don't they see that?"

She pursed her lips and shifted weight from one leg to the other.

"Greer. You don't mind if I call you Greer instead of Ms. Patterson, do you? You can call me Sylvia. Since we already kind of know each other."

"Greer is fine," I half smiled.

She nodded. Softening her previously hardened expression.

"What they see, is a drunken woman who drove across town with a handgun, entered her father's home, and shot him."

"That is not how it happened. I mean… not exactly."

Her hand raised to stop me.

"Those appear to be the base facts. I'm simply explaining how *they* see it. Not stating how it is. You shot a man in his own home and were shot in return. They could have charged you with attempted murder and a cluster of other things given the circumstances. And they still might if this goes to trial.

The critical nature of your injuries postponed your arrest, but an arrest would have been unavoidable in this case either way. The police rarely allow a case where there's gun violence resulting in the injury of one or more persons to go without charges being filed against one or more parties.

On a good note, a lot of the case information I would typically have to wait on, is already available for that same reason."

"Okay. Alright, but they're charging me with attempted murder *and* a DUI. How can they charge me with a DUI, after the fact? It's not like I was pulled over."

"They can. In fact, there are several other charges they could trump up if the D.A. is so inclined. Alcohol was a major factor in the crime and your blood alcohol level corroborates the charge. The legal limit is .08. Your hospital records show your blood alcohol ranked nearly triple that."

"I was distraught. I'd just found out my father was a murderer. Can anybody blame me for being drunk?"

"They can blame you for driving drunk."

"I wanted to confront him face to face. To get him to confess. To explain to me *why*. I… I wasn't rational. I was hurt."

She straightened, her long nails strumming the screen of the tablet as she gazed at me.

"Alright. Explain it to me. What made you think he killed your mother?"

"My brother's diary. It was right there in black and white."

"And how did you come upon his diary?"

"I was looking for something in my father's garage and it was in a storage box. Shawn is my older half-brother. We're not close. I'm not close with any of my father's kids."

"Why is that?"

"Because he was married to their mother when I was conceived with another woman. They've always hated me because I'm half-white and all bastard. So, when I saw Shawn's diary, I read it. It was from his teenage years. I wanted to see if there was any way I could maybe…connect with him.

I read the entry from the day my mother was killed the night I confronted my father. Shawn witnessed him drug us, then set our apartment on fire with fireworks on the fourth of July. My mother burned to death. A neighbor saved me through my bedroom window."

Her brows furrowed and she brushed at the bangs feathering her left eye.

"Was your father ever investigated or charged for the fire?"

"No. My brother never told anyone what he saw that I know of. Daddy didn't think anybody knew who my father was back then. My mother was an immigrant. But a neighbor knew his truck and told social services, who tracked him down. He took me in out of guilt. Not love," I lamented.

"And you're sure this information wasn't fabricated? How old was your brother at the time?"

"Fabricated! It wasn't fabricated," I answered defensively. "Shawn was 14. And my father *admitted* it. When I confronted him that night, and told him all the details I read, *he admitted it.* What more do you need?"

I had to calm down. I was getting angry, and I knew that wasn't helping my case. Sylvia moved her purse and bag to the small table and came back to sit in the chair.

Licking her lips quizzically she asked, "Did you record his confession?"

I swallowed hard and shook my head. I wished I had been thinking clearly enough that night to record him with my phone, but I wasn't in my right state of mind. It would only be my word, and the diary, against his.

"No. I wasn't thinking."

She sighed.

"Where *is* the diary now?"

"It's at my house."

"Is there anyone you can ask to bring it?"

I dropped my eyes. Four people had keys to my home. Daddy, Ms. Nina, Shan, and Race. Asking Daddy to retrieve it would essentially be me, asking a murderer to bring the smoking gun to convict him. Ms. Nina being Daddy's bed buddy, ruled her out.

I hadn't seen Race since I was admitted. Both phone conversations we had were awkward, short, and unemotional; leaving me confused about where we stood. I would have to ask Shan.

"Uh… yeah. I, I think so."

"Okay. We're going to need that diary. Do you think your brother will corroborate your story?"

I folded my lips, then blew out an agitated breath.

"I doubt it. He hasn't said anything all these years. He chose my father then, and I'm sure he'd choose my father now. It shouldn't even matter though. Whether he does or doesn't, he wrote it. It's what happened," I affirmed. "Daddy said my mother threatened to tell his wife about us. So, he tried to eliminate the problems."

"Is that when you shot him?"

I rolled my eyes up to the ceiling and brought them back to look at her with indignation. Was she even listening to me?

"I shot him to protect myself."

"The report says he claims to have shot *you* in self-defense. After you shot him."

"Self-defense?" I screeched incredulously. "Explain to me how you shoot someone in the back, *twice*, and still call it self-defense? I shot him when he was reaching for the gun in his nightstand to shoot *me*. I told him I was going to take the diary to the police, and that's when he lunged for his gun in the nightstand. If anything, I shot *him* in self-defense."

I was lying of course. That wasn't exactly how it happened. But it was close enough. Sylvia's expression was unreadable. I bet, as a defense attorney, the ability to appear unaffected worked well for her. She was probably a hell of a poker player.

"Why did you bring the gun if you didn't intend to shoot him?"

I wanted to say, "Because I'm not some Lifetime movie idiot. That's why. A man desperate enough to burn his mistress and their five-year-old alive, is capable of anything."

But what I said was, "For protection. For Pete's sake, who would be stupid enough to confront a murderer about a murder, unarmed? And look what ended up happening anyway. I have a license to carry. It's not like I only had a gun for the sole purpose of shooting him."

As practiced as I am with a firearm, even drunk, I could've pegged his forehead instead of giving him that measly little flesh wound. Now I was regretting that I hadn't. If I was going to go to jail for something, it might as well be for *committing* murder, rather than *attempting* it.

"The report lists Horace Banks as a witness. What is his relationship to you?"

"He's my… he was my boyfriend."

"Was, your boyfriend? Are you no longer together?" She adjusted her position in the chair once more. It did look a little uncomfortable.

"I don't know," I answered honestly.

I feared the things Daddy said to sabotage our relationship had worked. Or maybe, this whole thing was simply too intense for him. I didn't know what to think, and I hadn't made any attempts to call or text him to find out. Frankly, I was more worried about myself.

"Mr. Banks' witness statement somewhat supports your assertion that you were no longer presenting a threat. Although he says he didn't witness your father being shot, he says you lowered your gun when he arrived. He also states that Mr. Foster shot you as you turned to leave. Which does imply that you were no longer a threat to him."

I appreciated that I looked more like the victim and less like the aggressor in Race's version. Maybe there was hope for us yet.

"I think I have enough information for now to start my team off with. I have a copy of the warrant and I'll work on getting you a speedy arraignment and bail arrangement. You don't have any priors and from this report and what you've told me, I don't think a judge would hold you.

Also, I got word on my way here, that Mr. Foster has a restraining order coming down the pike."

"For me?" I balked.

If my right arm hadn't been in a sling, I would have clutched my proverbial pearls. How dare he!

"For you. Now. Let's get Detective Proctor back in here so we can get this interrogation over with. Keep in mind that although you haven't been removed from the hospital, you are still legally under arrest.

An officer will likely be stationed in or just outside of your room until you're arraigned and bailed out. Now, when Proctor asks a question, only provide the answer to *that* question. Please do not expound or provide any additional information.

The most important thing I want you to remember is that I am here for a reason. If I tell you not to answer a question, don't answer it. If I tell you to stop answering a question, don't say another word. If you're unsure how to answer a question, turn to me. I'm here to be your legal voice of defense, and I'm very good at my job. Okay?"

"Yes. I understand."

This wasn't my first rodeo. I'd been interrogated before, so I wasn't really as nervous as I led on. I was confident I could pull off any role that was necessary to be played, especially with my attorney in tow. I needed to appear intimidated and distraught over the charges, as any victim, which I was, would be. And I would.

However, it was alarmingly more intense than I predicted. I had to control my emotions and abide by Sylvia's instruction to stop speaking when I wanted to say more in my own defense. Which was often.

The detective and Sylvia sat in opposite chairs stationed beside my bed. The whole thing took considerably longer than I expected, requiring a nurse's interruption midway, and another dose of pain medication, which, thank God, shorted the nearly two hours of questioning I endured.

Proctor mostly asked me the same questions in different ways and made incendiary accusations that caused Sylvia to shut him down like school on Sunday when he got out of line.

It was hard to mask my temper in defense of my father trying to portray me as a psychotic and delusional drunk. But I believe I did well. Carrying on through tears and feigning concern about Daddy's condition, despite my own.

Of course, my father had spun the story to fit his own narrative. Clearly anticipating my defense, he claimed Shawn's diary, *wasn't* a diary at all. Supposedly, it was my brother's juvenile collection of *fictional* short stories, in a diary format, that *I* mistook as real in my drunken stupor.

To add insult to injury, my punk ass brother corroborated Daddy's claims over mine. Especially, since I hadn't produced the evidence as of yet. As I feared, the police weren't taking my allegations seriously at all. Furthering my resolve that the only justice Daddy would be served, would have to be by my own hand.

2

Greer

December 6th 2015

"Greer Talia Patterson, the criminal complaints against you are as such. Count One, Felony Aggravated Assault, as defined by Georgia penal code: 16-5-21 (b). On November 30, 2015, the defendant Greer Talia Patterson did knowingly and intentionally shoot one Charles Foster in his residence on 1682 Fountain Ridge Rd.

Count Two, as defined by Georgia penal code: 40-6-391(a)(5), Misdemeanor Driving Under the Influence of Alcohol. On November 30, 2015, the defendant Greer Talia Patterson did knowingly and intentionally operate a vehicle while intoxicated with a blood alcohol rate exceeding the .08% legal limit.

I listened to the charges against me with a teary eyed, somber expression on my face. A smoldering hatred for the man that caused them in my heart. The very heart he attempted to put a bullet through.

"Ms. Brass, how does your client plead to these charges?"

"Not guilty to both counts, your Honor."

"A not guilty plea is so entered on both counts. Does the Prosecution have any Notices?"

"Yes, your Honor. The victim, Charles Foster is prepared to testify. There's also crime scene evidence and a supporting toxicology report."

"Is there a bail recommendation, Mr. Adamson?"

"Yes, your Honor. The prosecution recommends Ms. Patterson be held on $50,000 bail, and that an order of protection be granted on behalf of Mr. Foster."

My widened eyes darted to Sylvia; whose head instantly cocked in agitation. Neither of us expected such a lofty number. I felt like I was in an episode of *Law and Order,* that I somehow hadn't seen before.

It was standing room only for everyone but me and the court reporter. She was a mousy Asian woman who transcribed from the singular chair in my tiny room; while the judge, both attorneys, and the detective who arrested me, crowded around my hospital bed. The officer who'd been posted up in my room before arraignment, stood stealthily by the door.

Honestly, this all could've been done without my presence from what I could tell. They talked amongst themselves as if I wasn't there anyway, and I was barely spared a glance. Detective Proctor, however; silently observed *me,* as much as he did the proceedings.

I pretended not to notice, taking an occasional sip from my water cup, and focusing only on the litigators. It was humiliating enough that I was arrested at all, let alone, being scrutinized by this gum shoe.

"Your Honor," Sylvia huffed. "Fifty-thousand-dollars is excessive, and Mr. Adamson knows it. My client hasn't had as much as a traffic ticket in nearly 10 years. She's never lived anywhere outside of Georgia and has had steady employment her entire adult life. She doesn't even own a passport to be a flight risk.

Furthermore, she's being arraigned from the hospital." Her hand swept over the bottom of my bed in reference. "She's *still* recovering from injuries sustained during this incident. At the hands of Mr. Foster, I might add. If anybody needs an order of protection, it's my client. Ms. Patterson shot Mr. Foster, in self-defense. *She's* here because he shot *her* in the back."

The prosecutor scoffed. His blue eyes narrowed.

"Mr. Foster is not being arraigned today, *Miss Brass.*"

"The defense requests Ms. Patterson be released on her own recognizance, your Honor." She continued as though he hadn't uttered a word.

Her stature alone was intimidating, and it was obvious the shorter prosecutor was affected by it.

"An ROR for attempted murder? Your Honor, Ms. Patterson is far from an angel. She shot her father in cold blood in his own home in a drunken rage. She's lucky she isn't being arraigned on murder charges right now.

Additionally, her blood alcohol level was at .17%. She could have killed herself, let alone someone else in route to kill her father."

"Your Honor!" Sylvia tattled.

"What? Are you going to argue self-defense on *that* as well, Ms. Brass?" Adamson squawked. Hands held up in mock defense.

"Clearly, if you were able to predict what I was going to argue, you wouldn't have lost every case you've ever had against me."

They exchanged disdainful looks; I forced myself not to smirk at the beet red color that burned his cheeks and neck. I liked her fire. Her confidence quelled some of my anxiety about the future of my freedom, and I yearned to be as brazen as she.

"Alright. Alright," Judge Renfro raised a mediating hand as a frown captured his face. His salt and pepper eyebrows nearly connecting in frustration. "Save your arguments for the pretrial hearing. Now, I tend to agree with Ms. Brass on the amount of your bail request Mr. Adamson. However, I certainly do not intend to release a defendant with an attempted murder charge, on her own recognizance, Ms. Brass."

"I understand, your Honor. Then, the defense respectfully, requests a lower bail as my client is a working-class citizen; who does not present further threat to Mr. Foster, or society."

He paused thoughtfully. A deadpan expression as he glanced between attorneys.

"Bail is set at $20,000. Per the prosecution's request, a temporary restraining order is also granted to Charles Foster." He paused, turning his attention to me. It was the first time he'd looked directly at me since proceedings began.

He was an old Orville Redenbacher looking man, who made me crave the popcorn his lookalike was famous for. It felt like he was looking through me, none the less. One of the worst days of my life, was probably just a necessary cog in the wheel of justice to him.

"Ms. Patterson, should you obtain bail, you will not be permitted to come within 1500 feet of Mr. Foster, or his home for the extent of the protective order I am granting here today.

You also may not communicate with any witnesses..."

"Your Honor. I object. The only witness was Horace James Banks, who is also the defendant's current boyfriend. He has already given his statement, which supports my client's version of events. I believe restricting them from contacting each other is unnecessary in this case."

"Your Honor, there may be witnesses to other incidents that will support the prosecution of this case. Who's to say she won't corrupt them if given the chance?"

"Does the prosecution have other witnesses?" Judge Renfro asked.

"Not currently, your Honor. But that doesn't mean we won't come across more during our investigation."

"The prosecution is reaching, your Honor. Any witnesses they could come up with would likely be a close relation or family member of Ms. Patterson and Mr. Foster, as they are father and daughter. Such an order would possibly isolate Ms. Patterson unfairly from the people she is closest to.

Given her current state of hospitalization, it also may prevent her from obtaining proper care once released. Again, my client has no history of violence your Honor."

"No *documented* history," Adamson chimed in.

Judge Renfro exhaled annoyedly.

"Very well. The only no contact order will be specific to Mr. Foster. Ms. Patterson, you also may not associate with known felons, participate in the use of drugs or alcohol, be in possession of any weapons, nor leave the country, or the state of Georgia without expressed permission from the court.

If you are arrested, or violate any of the conditions as I've stated, bail will be rescinded. You will then immediately be taken into custody at the Cobb County Adult Detention Center. Do you understand?"

"Y- yes, your Honor," I eked out.

"Your Honor, in light of the upcoming holidays, my client's need for continued medical care, and your already full docket, the defense would like to request pretrial be set for January 6, 2016, at 10:00 A.M."

Sylvia swiped the screen on her tablet, then looked expectantly to the judge. Judge Renfro adjusted the frame of his glasses and turned to the court reporter.

"Amy, check the docket. Mr. Adamson, does the prosecution have any objections?"

The Prosecutor was already checking his schedule.

"No, your Honor. January 6th works fine for me as well."

Everyone waited as Amy searched his calendar from her tablet. It was all so high tech. I hadn't known court could be held in one's hospital room prior to this arrangement. Then again, I didn't know I could be charged with a DUI without actually being pulled over for one, either. Though Sylvia assured me, both practices are fairly common.

"Yes. That date is open, your Honor."

"Very well. The pretrial hearing is hereby set for Wednesday, January 6, 2016 at 10:00 A.M. Anything further from the prosecution?"

"No, your Honor."

"Anything further from the defense?"

"No, your Honor."

"Alright. This meeting is hereby adjourned."

Nearly four hours later, I was under the watchful eye of yet another Cobb County officer. I recalled him being on a previous shift the day before. I'd been through six changes of the guard since my arrest two days ago. He was the second repeat babysitter.

Officer Ratcliff, was his name. He was a large dark skin man with a muscular build, a thick mustache, curly hair, and more bags than Marc

Jacobs under his eyes. I guessed he was in his 30's but the bags indicated he wasn't aging well. Much like the officers before him, he remained primarily seated across in a chair by the door, minced few words and predictably ignored me.

I was thankful I wasn't physically in jail, but three of the four rotating officers made sure I didn't forget I was supposed to be under arrest. They didn't allow me to use my cellphone, have visitors or even watch television under their watch.

"You're under arrest Ma'am." One redheaded cop with the last name of Dwyer nastily reminded me. He was the first officer to invade my space since Detective Proctor initially placed me under arrest. "You can't just do what you want. Please put the remote-control down and just… just lay there."

"Just lay here? Don't they get to watch TV in jail?" I retorted.

"Please put the remote-control down," he'd repeated sternly.

My attorney later said it was at the discretion of the individual officers what they allowed and didn't. Though she agreed there was no specific rules against my watching television, or even using my cellphone. I hoped this would be the last time I would see this officer, or any other before my bail came through.

At least this one let Shan to visit for a few hours before my arraignment; after thoroughly frisking her like a rogue TSA agent first. I don't know what sort of contraband he expected her to be carrying, given I was still hooked up to an IV, a catheter, and my ankle was pointlessly zip tied to the bottom rail of my bed. As if I could flee, even if I wanted to.

My conversation with her was focused on things outside of the shooting. We had little privacy and I wasn't answering anything I hadn't *already* disclosed to the police, *in front* of the police. I hadn't decided how much of what happened I was going to disclose to Shan anyway. Certainly not everything. Best friend or not, I would never tell *anyone*, everything.

The diary she was supposed to retrieve for my attorney had mysteriously gone missing, which I was sure was orchestrated by Daddy. I guessed he was trying to cover as many bases as possible, even though he admitted the diary existed.

I kept a little over two thousand dollars in an envelope in my underwear drawer for emergencies and I asked Shan to put fifteen hundred of it on a gift card. I was adamant that she pay for the card in cash so they would have to give me cash back if I ever returned it.

It was a bogus excuse and she frowned uncertainly when I said why, but didn't verbally question it. I backed up my preference with a cockamamie story about how I was trying to cut back on my credit card use.

In reality, I didn't want a paper trail. If she charged the gift card purchase on her card, it could possibly be traced back to her. If it ever came to that. I asked her to use the remaining cash to purchase a cheap computer from Craig's List. That, she questioned.

"Why? Is something wrong with yours?"

"There might be. I just need a backup one and I don't want to wait till I get home and can't go anywhere to have to get another one."

She stood beside me with arms folded, head tilted and eyes squinting suspiciously.

"I mean... I can get your computer checked while I'm here if you need me to. Is that really why you want me to do all this?"

"Do all what?"

"Use cash. Purchase a computer from Craig's List? I'm not an idiot Greer. What are you trying to do under the radar?"

I felt like she was talking too loud.

"*Shhhh.* Nothing," I hushed her, perturbed. "For all I know, they planted a camera in my house or on my laptop."

"What? Who is they?"

"*They. They.* Whoever the *they* is that stole the diary."

She rolled her eyes. "Greer. Don't be ridiculous."

"You're not the one lying up in the hospital with two bullet wounds Shan. I am. And I can't really talk to you about everything the way I want to talk to you about it while I'm in here. In here under supervision," I gestured towards the officer.

She ruminated over my words, looking between the officer sitting in a chair just outside the door and I.

"Look, if you don't want to do it, fine. I know you're only going to be here for a few more days. They'll probably let me out of here soon anyway. If I have to wait until I'm discharged to do it, I will. Just le—"

"I didn't say I wouldn't do it."

"Thank you."

I thought about that conversation and the things I would use the computer and gift card for as I stared unseeingly up at the ceiling, contemplating future decisions. In wake, I was consumed with thoughts of anger, revenge and plans for retribution. In my dreams, which were often reoccurring and more like nightmares, I was totally helpless.

In almost every one, Daddy gave a heartfelt soliloquy, professing his fatherly love with the sincerest of expressions. Debbie would interrupt, spewing her usual venom, which led to us fighting. Just as I got the upper hand on her, I'd be shot. This time, in the back *and* the face. The shooter, was always Daddy.

It was jarring. I was heavily medicated, and still relatively weak, so I slept often due to that, and simply to pass the time. No matter how short my dream state, some version of the same dream was had. The last gunshot would wake me. It felt so real. So personal.

"You okay? You need a nurse?"

I dropped my eyes to frigidly meet Officer Ratcliff's concerned ogle. He would've been much more attractive without the porn-stache and a haircut.

"Why?"

"You were whimpering in your sleep. Now you're stiff as a board and crying. I thought maybe… maybe you were suffering. You need a nurse?"

My fingertips found the wet path of tears he spoke of leaking from the corners of my eyes. I hadn't felt them welling, nor falling. But the pain of being repeatedly murdered by someone I once loved more than myself, certainly warranted them.

I wiped my face with the heel of my palm and sunk deeper into the pile of flat pillows under my head. The medication thankfully kept the agony I felt in my body without it, at bay. If only it could do the same for my mind.

"Like you care," I murmured.

"I wouldn't ask if I didn't care."

"Right."

His thick lips pressed into a thin line before the sympathy drained from his eyes; replaced with chagrin. He leaned forward, both elbows on his knees and dropped his gaze back to the phone. He adjusted the firearm on his waist, then resumed thumb-surfing the screen of his iPhone with obvious irritation.

I observed him with a newfound curiosity. Other than nurses, doctors, my attorney, and the visit I had with Shan after my arrest, I hadn't had many basic human conversations. I was only allowed to talk at length with my attorney, and to minimize people finding out I was under arrest, I had visitation privileges for everyone else suspended.

The last thing I needed was the embarrassment of people I didn't want to know I was arrested, knowing I was arrested. Once I was officially bailed out, and able to converse outside the presence of legal watchdogs, visitation would be resumed. I still received flowers from my job and Lisa.

What ate at me was that the one person outside of Shan that I wanted to visit me, hadn't attempted. Race texted and made one brief call, but he had yet to visit. Once again, I was all alone and feeling lonely. Making Officer Ratcliff's sympathy, that much more welcome. Momentarily at least. It just felt good to be cared about.

"The other ones didn't care," I baited. "I apologize for being nasty. They've been crude to say the least. Assuming I deserved what I got, I guess. They didn't talk to me. Unless you count telling me, 'No' as talking to me."

He exhaled loudly but continued to scroll.

"I had a bad dream. I *keep* having bad dreams. I don't know if you've ever been shot before; but I'm finding that sort of thing is kind of hard to get over. Even subconsciously. It has me a little on edge. So… again. I'm sorry. Thank you for caring enough to ask after me. I'll shut up now."

After a long beat, he finally looked at me and sighed.

"We're not all the same. I'm not here to judge you or punish you. That's for the courts or a jury if that happens. I'm just here to make sure you stay in police custody, until I get word you're released from it. Or until the end of my shift."

He offered a small smile. I returned the gesture. It was a start.

"They sure are taking their sweet time to do it." I glanced at the huge clock on the wall. "It's been hours since my lawyer went to pay my bail."

"Sometimes it takes a while. Believe it or not, crime goes up around the holidays. It's a busy time of year for the courts."

"I can imagine."

I swallowed hard, looking at the pitcher of water on the end table, then back to him.

"Would it be against the rules for me to ask you to pour me a cup of water? Or do I need to buzz a nurse to do that?"

"I can do it for you."

"Thank you."

At closer inspection, he was maybe six feet tall, and kind of handsome. In a rugged sort of way. I did notice, his ring finger was bare. That was a good thing given the wanton once over he gave me before handing me the cup. I watched him over the rim as I slowly sipped. Assessing his interest in me.

I had to look like hell. My hair hadn't been combed since I'd been admitted, and I imagined my skin was as dry as desert sand. I might not be a relationship expert, but I've had a lot of experience thwarting off unrequited advances. They always start with a stare.

"You have beautiful eyes."

"Thank you. I'm sure I look a mess," I tittered.

"Not at all. Well… your hair maybe. But you got that naturally curly grade where it looks wild instead of messy. Sort of like how some models wear it on the cover of swimsuit magazines."

"I'm sure I don't look *anything* like a model right now."

He grinned as I leaned to place my cup down. Officer Ratcliff did it for me.

"Thank you."

"No problem. You good?"

I nodded, watching him amble back to the chair. A lightbulb lit as I noted the newly formed grin on his face. I didn't know where Race and I stood, but I needed as many ally's as I could manage for my future plans to manifest. Having a cop I could possibly manipulate could only be a plus.

"So, are you allowed to talk to me? Or is that against the rules?"

"It's not against the rules. I'm talking to you now, right?"

I smiled coyly. "Yes, you are."

3

Greer

December 9th 2015

"Really?"

I sighed, forcing my grimace into a weak smile just as Lisa's vexed voice and chastising eyes peered at me from the doorway. I didn't think she'd be back this soon. Her glossy lips twisted into a frown. Her head cocked to the side and one hand propped on her hip.

"You want to tell me why you're up here instead of downstairs getting some rest like you were supposed to be doing? I thought we agreed you were going to stay in the guest room on the first floor so you could avoid those stairs?"

She pointed in the direction of the staircase, as if I didn't know where they were in my own home. I shook my head sheepishly while adjusting my back between the mountain of pillows propped against the headboard and shoving my laptop between them, out of sight.

"No. You *suggested* I stay downstairs in the guestroom to avoid the stairs, but I never agreed to it. Look. I've been waiting to get out of that hospital bed and into my own *comfortable* one for three weeks. One flight of stairs isn't going to kill me. The doctor said I need to be active anyway. I got up the stairs fine."

Which was true. I climbed the stairs without incident. It was climbing into my high-mattress bed that had me wincing; trying to find a position where the broken rib in my back didn't feel like it was trying to impale me. At least I had the use of both limbs now that my right arm was out of the sling.

"Umm hmm. I can't tell. Your face is beet red. Where's that piece of paper you got with the doctor's instructions? I could swear it said you need to *limit* your activity and stay in bed."

"My face is beet red because I have a broken rib sticking me in the back. Not because I climbed the stairs."

My lips pursed as I rolled my eyes and she disappeared from the doorway. A few minutes later she was back in my room with a glass of water, the bag of prescriptions, and care directions I got from the hospital. She stood at the foot of my bed reading them carefully as I glanced the bedside clock.

Lisa meant well, but she was getting on my nerves. Nobody wanted me to get better more, or faster than I did. I'm not only a germaphobe, I also hate being sick in any capacity. Working in a family medical practice for nine years, I've seen some horrendous results of what happens when people don't follow doctor's orders. God gave me a second chance at life, and I wasn't about to botch it up before I could live my best one.

I had to remind myself that Lisa was still essentially a new friend. There was still a lot about me that she didn't know, and a lot that she would never know. I wished Shan had been the one to drive me home from the hospital, but she went back to New York after a week. I suppose my bestie was where she belonged. At least until they all moved back to ATL in the coming year. Fingers crossed.

If I was from a *normal* family, one of my siblings would've cared enough to chauffer me home from the hospital. It wasn't Lisa's fault that my family wasn't worth the sperm that made them. It wasn't mine either, but it was true.

"You don't need to read all of that. I *know* what the doctor's orders are, and I'm perfectly capable of following directions on my own. He specifically said *not* to lay in bed all day because that could cause fluids to build up in my lungs and lead to pneumonia.

I'm supposed to take my meds, move around once every two hours, avoid heavy lifting, ice my ribs three times a day, and practice breathing into that spirometer thing they gave me. I appreciate your concern, but I got this. I'm not helpless."

"You don't 'got this' Greer. You're gonna be in this house all by yourself and you can barely walk without flinching or pausing to take a breath. What if somebody rings the doorbell? How long is it going to take you to get out of bed and get down the stairs to open it? They'll be halfway home before you even reach the landing. You need – to – be – downstairs."

I twisted my position, instantly regretting it. The repaired rib in my chest didn't give me much trouble, but the fractured rib in my back was a nightmare. It hurt like hell. Some movements, no matter how minor, would aggravate it and instantly reverberate pain through my body.

"See! See," she held a palm toward me. Undoubtedly noting the pain-stricken expression on my face. "This is what I'm talking about. All you're doing is moving in the bed and look at the pain you're in. I'm telling you th—"

"Just… shut up for a minute," I muttered through clinched teeth. I might have been a tad bit fed up with her, and a good bit out of practice subduing my emotions. Unfortunately, the pain was temporarily clouding my need to care. I drew a deep breath, squeezing my eyes shut, to stave off the brewing tears I didn't want her to see. But not before witnessing the shocked look on her face.

"Okay. Okay. I can hear the irritation in your voice. I'm just trying to look out for you. I know you've been through a lot and I'm just trying to help. But if you want me to go, I'll leave. Since I'm clearly not needed anymore."

I sighed, taking in the frown on her practically blemish free mahogany complexion. She was a pretty woman, and for some reason, that's what I focused on when I opened my eyes. It was unseasonably warm for mid-December, so I understood her opting for a blue knit sweater and jeans, sans a coat.

Lisa looked as youthful as a college student, though she was every bit of 32 years old. I could only imagine the hot disheveled mess I resembled. She placed everything on the nightstand beside my bed and absentmindedly smoothed hairs back in the hill of her high bun before skulking back towards the door.

"Wait. I'm sorry," I eked out.

She stopped in her tracks, huffing loudly, and rolling her eyes towards me.

I wasn't really, but it needed to be said anyway. *I* needed her more than *she* needed me. For now.

Despite how it seemed, I did appreciate her. She got me from the hospital, picked up my prescriptions, and went back out to get groceries; since everything in my fridge was molded or expired. She was a lifesaver. But aggravating, none the less.

Our budding friendship wasn't as strong as my bond with Shan, but with her away, and Race being distant, my support system had dwindled down to a virtual party of one. Lisa.

I hadn't seen hide nor hair of my ex-mother in-law, Nina; who, was a fixture in my life after Michael's death, until this happened. Unsurprisingly, my wayward siblings were also MIA.

As evidence, not a one of them called or visited during my entire stay. Not that I expected Debbie's hateful ass to show any care, and Shawn had always been distant, but I expected more from my baby sister, Donna. She was the only living family besides my father that I ever thought I had a connection with.

Clearly, our relationship was all as shallow as a kitty pool. Her allegiance was not to me, and there would be no remorse if she, or any one of those *jackals* that shares DNA with my father, met an early demise.

Surprisingly, Debbie's husband Will, called with prayers and wishes for a speedy recovery. I'm sure his shrew of a wife, was not privy to the call. I appreciated the gesture. Why such a kindhearted man chose a heartless beast as his wife was a mystery to me. She was so much like her mother it was eerie.

It was okay though. I had my best friend. No one showed up for me like Shan. And for that reason, I've been just as compelled to avenge her pain as I have been my own. When Jahari fell weak and cheated with that throwback slut, Wendy Alexander, it nearly broke her. Though Shan's forgiven him, she hasn't forgiven Wendy; and when my bestie has a grudge, so do I.

Left to my own devices, while Lisa was grocery shopping for me, I powered up my new laptop and began executing as many tasks as I could before she returned. Using my alias Gmail account, under the name Jared Morgan, I purchased a lock picking kit and two tracking devices with my gift card. I only had use for one tracker in my plans, but who knew if another reason might appear?

Then, I set up a Gmail account for Wendy, and made a profile for her on Backpage. If you don't know what that is, it's a popular website for people in various states to buy and sell sex through classified ads.

Well, thanks to internet search engines, it was super easy to get Miss Wendy Alexander's home address, research the layout of her slum neighborhood house, and find out where she worked. Unbeknownst to her, she has a rape fantasy that she's willing to pay $500 to have fulfilled.

Of course, the ad specifically states that funds would *only* be paid, *after* the task is completed. Instructions required the ad responder to do whatever was necessary to take her down and penetrate her vagina and asshole in the process. Condoms were optional and the preferred hour was after 1:00am.

Both her home and work address were provided, and the responder was supposed to call her a "Sexy bitch" during the attack so she'd know they were answering her ad. They were also told to take a picture either before or after the attack to inbox as proof they were the assailant and to claim their $500.

I had no sympathy for side bitches. All their homewrecking asses deserved to be punished for the families they destroyed without a simple thought. Shan, did not deserve the anguish Wendy and Jahari's indiscretion caused her to remain unrequited. No worries. I would get justice for her. Hey, that's what friends are for right?

Lisa, was no Shan, but was a good friend, and I would treat her as such.

"I'm sorry," I repeated more affably. "I'm tired, I'm irritable, I'm in pain, and I'm taking it out on you. You've been so sweet, and so helpful today. Thank you."

She turned facing me, her arms folded across her modest chest. I could read the forgiveness she was trying to hide on her face.

"You're welcome. Are you hungry? Some of those prescriptions say you're supposed to take them with food."

Just like that, she was over it. Must be nice to be so carefree. Not a care in the world but her business, her fiancé, and whatever other trivial matters she tended to regularly. No pending charges. No family betrayals. No romantic limbo. No daily pain to relieve with drugs. Eff my life.

"I am. But I can get my own food now that I have groceries. Thanks to you. I don't want to hold you up any more than I already have today."

She sniggered, waving me off, sitting at the bottom of my bed.

"I have time. I mean, I know you probably have a slew of other people you can call on, but I can help you get situated while I'm here. What do you want me to make you to eat?"

If by "slew", she meant her and Uber, she was spot on. I still wanted her to leave, but there was no harm in letting her make me a sandwich first. Was there?

"A sandwich will do. I just need a nap, and something in my stomach. After eating that bland hospital food for so long, anything, other than that crap will do. I basically only ate enough to survive and keep my stomach from touching my back."

"Did you? Because you're looking pretty skinny to me. And you were already slim. You should have asked somebody to bring you something from outside. You know I would have. You're practically swimming in those clothes. Are those new, or did you drop *that* much weight?"

I looked down, self-consciously running a hand over the fabric of my joggers.

"I look that skinny? I had Shan bring them from my closet so I would have something to wear home."

I craned my neck to look in the large mirror over the dresser facing my bed, and barely recognized my reflection. I hadn't seen myself in a few days. Granted, nine days in the hospital would take a toll on anybody's aesthetic, but I literally looked like death warmed over.

My curly light brown hair held no shine, and outgrew the sassy hair cut I sported previously. It messily framed my face, hanging just below my shoulders. The dark circles under my green eyes made it seem like I hadn't slept in ages. My light skin was so pale that if I believed in vampires, I would have thought I was bitten.

Lisa's voice beckoned to me, but my haggard appearance had my full attention. I raised a hand to touch my flushed cheek and ran it slowly down the side of my thin neck. I did look too thin. Sickly even.

"Turkey sandwich okay?"

"Sure."

"I bought you a thing of pre-cooked baked chicken too. I thought it might last you a couple of days. I'll warm that up and make some rice and green beans to go with it before I go. For dinner."

"Don't you have to get back to work at the range?"

"No. Race didn't tell you we hired some new staff? You know, with everything going on, he's barely there anymore, and I was getting burned out doing it all by myself. I needed a break."

Whatever he had going on, must've been pretty important, since it didn't include me. My expression must've been telling, because her smile waned.

"You okay?"

"Yeah. Just feeling the pain starting. I think I need to take an Oxy."

There was no need to involve her in my and Race's problems.

"Oh. Here."

She rushed to the nightstand, looked through my prescription bottles and opened one. Handing me the glass of water, she gave me two pills, which I gulped down without even looking at them.

"What's hurting?"

"The rib in my back. Small movements can irritate it."

"I thought that was soldered back together."

"Just the one in my chest. The one in my back has to heal on its own."

"On its own? Is that normal? What good is seeing a doctor if they're just gonna *let it heal on its own?*" she mocked.

"Don't even get me started. Doctor says it'll take four to six more weeks."

"Wow. You might really need somebody here to help you out, Greer. At least for this first week while you get situated. Are you planning to have anybody stay with you tonight? One of your sisters, Race, your friend Angie maybe?"

"I'll call somebody," I lied.

She eyed me sympathetically, her bottom lip folded between her teeth with concern. I repositioned myself, very carefully, into the pillows as the pain began to fade. I was so glad I had a backrest pillow that used primarily to get comfortable watching television, propped behind the others. It made a big difference.

"Is that better?"

"It will be," I nodded slowly.

Out of nowhere, I felt like I had to pee like a racehorse. The thought of having to move from my comfy spot on the bed suddenly seemed as daunting as Lisa had warned.

"I need to use the bathroom. Can you help me?"

Her brow rose.

"Help you what?"

"Get off the bed, dummy. Not use the bathroom," I snickered.

"Oh. Cause I don't mind helping but, I wasn't prepared to be wiping your ass."

"Girl, shut up."

"You *need* to move to the spare bedroom, like I said. What are you gonna do when I leave?"

"Just help me down." I pouted, gingerly easing myself from position, using her shoulder as a crutch.

Once stable, I adjusted my sweatshirt and stood erect.

"I'm good from here."

"You sure?"

"Yep," I waved her off and approached the master bath.

I was closing the door when the doorbell rang. Cracking it back open, I met Lisa's confused gaze.

"You expecting somebody?"

"No."

The corners of Lisa's lips turned down, her palms turned up.

"*Soooo...* you want me to answer it?"

"Please," I replied reluctantly.

My bladder felt full as a ravine and I was relieving myself long enough to fill one. I was mid-flow when Lisa's knuckles rapped on the closed door.

"Hey, Greer. It's a Detective Herrera from Dekalb County Homicide to see you."

If I hadn't already been on the toilet, I might have pissed myself.

4

Greer

"Do you need help?"

"No. We're fine," I smiled at Detective Herrera as Lisa helped me down the stairs.

My anxiety level was high. I'd spoken to the other detective on Kendrick's case right after his body was found. His name was Moore, or Monroe or something. So, whose murder was Herrera here trying to solve? I hoped that little hit and run the night I hung out with Angie wasn't coming back to bite me in the ass. Seemed like when it rained it poured. And lately, I'd been in the eye of the storm.

"Ms. Patterson. I'm Detective Herrera with the Dekalb County Homicide division." He flashed his badge as I reached the landing in the foyer.

"I've been told. Who was murdered?"

"I'm investigating the death of Kendrick Spears."

"Kendrick? I thought what happened to him was an accident. Didn't he fall down the stairs?"

"Well. Whether it was an accident or not has yet to be determined."

"I thought there was a different detective on this case. I talked to him, I think, a few days after Thanksgiving."

"Yes. Detective Monroe. Unfortunately, he died two weeks ago. So, some of his cases have been reassigned to me."

"Oh. Wow. Then… can we sit down? I just got out of the hospital today. I don't know how long I'd be able to stand up and talk."

"She just took her medication a few minutes ago too," Lisa advised. "I was just about to go make her something to eat."

"I'm sorry to disturb you. I left a message on your cellphone yesterday. Hopefully, I won't take up too much of your time. I wouldn't be here if it wasn't important."

"I understand. I just hope I can stay awake. These meds do tend to make me drowsy."

He and his scrutinizing dark brown eyes followed me into the living room. He was an olive skinned brunette, with a slight accent, thin rimmed glasses, and a bulbous nose. His black leather coat was unbuttoned, revealing an ironed white shirt and a black tie. His black shoes were shiny, and his khaki slacks were perfectly creased.

Signs that he was likely a strait-laced, by the books type of cop. All good reasons for *me* to be on high alert.

"Thanks. We're good," I shooed Lisa, once Herrera and I were both seated.

He on the sofa, and I in the recliner facing him. She dawdled to the kitchen as I made myself comfortable and he placed a small device on the coffee table. Nosy Nancy was in no rush to get out of earshot. Lisa held secrets about as well as a colander holds water. I would bet my last dollar my sandwich wouldn't be ready until she was done eavesdropping.

"I like to record my interviews, so I don't miss anything. My memory isn't as sharp as it used to be now that I'm getting older; and recently, I developed carpal tunnel." He flexed his right hand. "My handwriting has always been chicken scratch anyway. Less room for mistakes with recording."

I propped my elbow up on the arm of the recliner and rested my chin in my palm. I wanted to appear relaxed, though I was the furthest thing from it. Besides, I was genuinely starting to get drowsy.

"I'm sorry to have to bother you when you just got home. Why were you in the hospital, if you don't mind my asking?"

Frankly, I *did* mind him asking. But behaving as such, probably wouldn't have been a good start as a person trying to avert suspicion. I didn't know yet whose murder this was about, but I was probably a suspect. I bowed my head and exhaled before raising my eyes to look at him.

"Long story. I got into it with my father, and he shot me. They say I'm lucky to be alive."

"Your father, shot you?"

I nodded.

"Is he in jail?"

"Like I said; it's a long story. I'd rather not talk about it if that's okay with you."

His inquisitive eyes swept over me from head to toe, as if he were trying to determine what kind of woman gets shot by her father. Hell, I would have been wondering the same thing, if I were him. I'm sure he would look into it once back at the station anyway. What cop wouldn't?.

"I see. Well, as I said earlier, Monroe's cases have been reassigned to me. Which means, I'm a little behind on some of the follow ups. I may ask some questions you've been asked previously. But please, bear with me. I'm just trying to be thorough."

I'd hoped this case would be closed before I got out of the hospital, but I suppose, *that* would've been too much like right. I'm sure that other detective kept notes. Why couldn't this detective just use those? Lord knows I didn't feel like recapping anything right now.

"I know I told the other detective I would get him the badge information so he could check it against the swipes on the doorway, but I haven't been back to work since it happened. I was literally shot the day after I got the call. I'm not sure when I'm going back to work yet."

I planned to switch my badge number with Kendrick's in the system, to wash my hands clean of suspicion. For obvious reasons, I hadn't been able to get back to my office. The new plan was for me to go in after-hours once I was able to drive again.

"No need to worry about that. Building management has provided that to us already."

My heart raced like a 55-meter marathon, but I kept my cool.

"Oh good. I hope it was helpful. Were you able to match the badges?"

"I'm hoping you may be able to help me answer some additional questions I haven't been able to pin down."

He dodged my question like a squirrel in a tree. A sign I wasn't a cleared suspect.

"Sure. Okay."

"Can you tell me what you remember from your interactions with Kendrick that day? Was he in good spirits? Agitated? Normal?"

"Honestly, nothing out of the ordinary sticks out. Except that we closed early for the Thanksgiving holiday. Almost everybody went home around two. I stayed a little bit later because I was still wrapping up some paperwork."

"You said *almost* everybody. Who else do you remember being there?"

I purposely looked to my left before answering. I read once that when questioned, a liar looks to their right before responding, because they're visualizing a "constructed" or imagined, event. A person telling the truth, is more likely to look to their left; because they're summoning information directly from memory. If *I* knew that, I assumed it was something detectives were probably aware of too.

"I'm not sure. There might not have been. I didn't check, but I do know Kendrick was there at least a half hour later than we closed. He was late, so he had to stay later to make up his time."

"Was that unusual for him?"

I smirked. "No. He was late a lot. Not usually by more than 30 min-utes though."

"Was he upset about having to stay late?"

"I doubt it. I don't remember him being upset, if he was. Like I said. It was kind of his norm."

"Did you see him leave?"

"No. But I heard when the exit door shut. It's not far from my office. Everybody else takes the elevator. He's all obsessed with his health and exercise. I mean... he was."

"He didn't say goodbye?"

"No. He usually would if he passed through the hallway on the side where my office is, but I don't think he came that way. If he did, I didn't see him."

"Did you hear him come back for anything?"

"*Nnnno.* I was finishing up and getting ready to leave myself. I was only a few minutes behind him. Except I took the elevator."

"What time did you leave?"

"I didn't look at the clock. Maybe 2:35... 2:40. I'm not sure. Sorry."

"You said he was late, so he had to stay late. You didn't look at the time to make sure he made up his time?"

"They clock in and out. I would see what time he left when I processed payroll. I don't bother to monitor it in real time. If they don't work enough hours, I just dock 'em."

"Do *you* clock in and out?"

"No. I'm on salary."

"Where did you go when you left?"

"My father's house and then home."

It wasn't a total lie. That was exactly where I'd gone. Right after I left my boyfriend's, ex-girlfriend's apartment, where I'd poisoned her things with bleach, added miscarriage inducing drugs to her juice, and tainted her lotion with crushed glass. But... he didn't need to know about those, less than endearing activities.

"Is there anybody who can corroborate that?"

"Yes. My father, Chuck Foster, my sister Debbie Manly and my mother in-law Nina Patterson. My sister and I had a fist fight not long after I got there. I'm not sure how cooperative any of them will be under the circumstances, but that's where I was. My family and I aren't exactly the Brady Bunch, I'm afraid."

He nodded and asked for their contact info, which I readily provided.

"Did you and Kendrick ever have more than just a working relationship?"

My head jerked back.

"Did somebody say I did?"

"Did you?"

"We never had a *relationship*. We talked on the phone after hours, and slept together a few times, but that was it. It wasn't serious at all. It only lasted a couple of months."

Nobody but Angie's jealous ass could've told him that. Nobody else he would have questioned, knew. I hadn't planned to keep it a secret, should it have surfaced organically. But I was sure the only organ that divulged my relationship with Kendrick was Angie's dick sucking lips.

"We both decided it would be too complicated to date in the office. Besides, he started dating Angie shortly afterwards. She's an NP at the office. And I started dating somebody else too."

"What's her last name?"

"Reardon. Angie Reardon."

"So, your relationship with Kendrick was only sexual?"

"Well, we were also friends. But, yes," I answered demurely. "Look, I lost my husband last year. I was just trying to get my feet wet. Date. See what it was like to put myself back out there. I wasn't ready for anything serious. Besides, Kendrick was way too young for me. That's what made him safe."

"Safe?"

"Safe for me to experiment. He just wanted to have fun. He was safe to play with. Without getting either of our feelings involved."

"You said you didn't want anything serious, but you started seeing someone else. Is that serious?"

I licked my bottom lip and swallowed.

"It was. I'm not sure what it is right now, but it was at the time. That just happened though. I didn't expect it to get serious. It just, *did*."

"What's his name?"

"Horace Banks."

"You broke up with Kendrick because you didn't want anything serious; but then you got serious with the next guy. Did that cause any tension?"

"Again, we didn't breakup. We were never together. And we stopped seeing each other because it wasn't worth complicating our jobs. Not because I didn't want to get serious.

As for tension, there wasn't any with *me*. Maybe with Angie. She questioned me about it once. I wasn't as truthful with her as I could have been. But him being the first person I... *shared* myself with since my husband's death; and the fact that he was my subordinate, made it something I didn't really want to get around the office.

I assured her things between us were over and that I had moved on. *Buuut...* she still seemed a little jealous. We were pretty good friends before she found out. Then she stopped talking to me, and I guess she had an attitude with him. He confided in me once that she'd threatened him, but I don't think it was anything serious. Not *this* level of serious."

"Threatened him how?" Oh. His interest was piqued.

"Just usual jealous girlfriend stuff. Warning him not to mess with anybody else in the office, *or else*."

"Or else what?"

I shifted in my seat; pretending to be uncomfortable throwing Angie under the bus. "I mean... I don't want to get anybody in trouble. I honestly can't say *what* she meant. I wasn't there. I didn't hear it myself. I'm just saying what Kendrick told me."

"What about Horace? Did he have a problem with you working with a guy you used to sleep with?"

I shook my head vigorously.

"He didn't know about that. I never told him."

"Could he have found out another way?"

"No. He didn't know anybody at my office, and Kendrick and I didn't talk after work anymore."

"You said you and Angie were friends outside of work. Could she have been upset enough to tell him?"

"They never met. Angie stopped talking to me before Race and I got serious."

Herrera observed me for a short beat, then rubbed his big nose with the edge of his index finger.

"How would you describe Kendrick?"

"He was a nice guy. He was good looking, funny, friendly, flirtatious; maybe irresponsible for his age, but a nice guy. I can't imagine why anybody at work would want to hurt him. Certainly not Angie.

He was an athletic guy. Angie's smaller than I am. He could probably have tied either one of us into a pretzel." A yawn surfaced, halting my conversation. "Excuse me. I think my medication is starting to really kick in now."

"I understand. I only have one or two more questions for you. Were you aware of any allergies Kendrick may have had?"

"Allergies? Like, to pollen?"

"Pollen, or anything at all."

"Uh... no. I don't believe that ever came up in conversation before. Why? Is that important?"

The effect of those crushed almonds I added to Kendrick's protein shake must've finally come to light in their forensic report. His throat was already closing before I sent him reeling down the stairs like a sack of dirty laundry. I wonder how long he suffered before he finally expired. The bastard.

"It may be. Was there anyone else in the office that Kendrick was particularly close to? Anyone else he might have shared that information with? Anyone other than Angie?"

"I honestly couldn't tell you. I'm friendly with staff, but being their superior, they typically stop the banter when I'm around and get to working. If Angie and I hadn't been friends first, I probably wouldn't have known about them at all."

"I see. Did Kendrick routinely eat or drink anything that you're aware of for lunch?"

I shrugged.

"I don't know. He drank a lot of protein shakes. Like I said, he was a fitness guy. I tasted one once." My face screwed in disgust. "It was nasty as hell. I don't even know how he drank that stuff. He was always talking about how good the crap he had in it was for your body.

Seaweed, kale, oat grass, I don't know. Healthy people's drinks. Looked like green vomit most of the time."

"Did he ever mention ingredients like peanuts, cashews, almonds, any kind of nuts?"

"Maybe. I really didn't pay attention to what he said was in them once I tried one and didn't like it."

"Where do most employees keep their lunch?"

"In the fridge in the breakroom, I guess. We don't monitor that. Everybody has their own desk with a drawer to lock their important personables in, if need be. I suppose *some* of them might keep their lunch in there if it doesn't need to be refrigerated."

"Everyone has a draw that locks at their desk?"

"Yeah. Not everybody uses them, but, they all have lockable drawers. You know, for purses, wallets and stuff."

"Do you know if Kendrick used his?"

"Sorry. I don't. Again, that's not something I would monitor as an Office Manager. I don't micromanage."

"Alright. I appreciate your time Ms. Patterson. Now, I may have to circle back with more questions, if anything new develops in the case. I hope you won't mind."

"Can I ask you something?"

"Yes."

"Am I a suspect?" I brought a cautious hand to my chest.

"These are routine questions I have to ask to gather as much information as possible about Kendrick and the events of that day. He was a young man who died under suspicious circumstances. Accidents happen. But murders happen too. Everyone who knew him has to be considered."

So, the short answer was, yes. He was good at not answering a question directly. Herrera stood, retrieving his recorder from the table and pulled a business card from his jacket; handing it to me.

"If you think of anything else that might be helpful, please let me know. Anytime. Day or night."

"Okay. Thank you. I hope you won't be offended if I don't see you out. It's a lot for me to keep getting up and down."

"Totally understand. It's okay."

"Lisa!" I called as Detective Herrera walked towards the front door.

"Yeah?" Her punk ass was way too close to have been in the kitchen. She was probably lingering in that little nook between the entrance to the living room and where the bottom of the staircase began. It's exactly where I used to stand when Michael was in here on the phone and I didn't want him to know I was listening.

"Detective Herrera's leaving. Can you walk him out please?"

"Sure." She locked the door behind him and came back to the living room, leaning against the doorframe with her arms crossed. "Is everything okay?"

"That must be one hell of a gourmet sandwich you're making."

"Huh?" Her brows furrowed.

"You were supposed to be making me a turkey sandwich. Since I don't see one, I'm guessing that got postponed while you eavesdropped."

She grimaced. Eyes fully revealing her guilt. "My bad. I did make the sandwich. I just didn't finish it before you called me in here to walk the detective to the door."

"Umm hmm."

"Okay. I'm sorry I was listening. I was concerned."

"Concerned?"

"Yes, *concerned.* Your dad tried to kill you, Race said you found out he's the one who killed your mom, and then a homicide detective popped up at your door. I thought... maybe he was here to tell you what's happening with that. Your mom's murder I mean."

I'm sure I *looked* as dumbfounded as I felt. Funnily enough, that hadn't even crossed my mind. Partially because the police hadn't given any merit to Shawn's diary. Mostly because Lisa assumed *that* was the only open homicide I was linked to. But I knew better.

5

Greer

My breaths came quick and rushed as I fought off Debbie's attack. She was bigger, but I was angrier. She tried to subdue me in a choke-hold, but my left arm and wrist prevented her from getting a good grip; leaving my right hand free to claw the acned skin off her malevolent face.

"God Damn it!" She shrieked at a deafening decibel.

But then I blinked.

The afflicted eyes staring back at me were filled with tears and tempered confusion. She stood back defensively. One hand glued to her cheek. The other outstretched to keep me at bay.

"Wake up," she cried.

Mildly disoriented, my eyes roved the room. This wasn't Daddy's house. *She* wasn't Debbie. I was still seated in the recliner in my living room; the television blaring loudly behind her. *I* had been asleep.

Lisa removed her hand from her face, viewing the small traces of blood on her palm, her eyes growing in horror. Three red welts scarred her otherwise smooth cheek, confirming that I had undoubtedly attacked the wrong person.

"Oh my God," she mewled, rushing to examine the damage in the mirror over the mantle.

I was sorry. What else could I say? No sooner had the words left my lips, than her sideways glare rejected it like an invitation to a Klan rally.

"Where's your alcohol or first aid kit?" She hissed, pivoting towards me with all the disdain I probably would have held too, had I been in her place.

"In the medicine cabinet in my master bathroom. I really *am* sorry. I was having a bad dream. The scratches really don't look that deep, if it matters."

My assurances fell on deaf ears as she marched out of the living room and up the stairs. I swiped both hands up my face and under my eyes to fully arouse myself. I'd never seen Lisa angry before. She's always been chipper, chatty and playful. The transformation was slightly unnerving. Reminding me that we all have another side. No one knew that better than I did.

I sighed, gingerly using both arms to hoist myself from the chair. I was fully awake now, recalling what happened before I'd slept. After eating my sandwich and taking the rest of my meds with apple juice, I must've dozed off, letting the television watch me as Lisa cooked dinner.

I was drinking a glass of water in the kitchen when I heard her hurriedly descending the stairs. She approached bullishly, with her bag on her shoulder, a frown etched into her face, and keys firmly in her grasp.

"Alright Greer. I'm gone. Call me if you need anything."

"Lisa, *wait*. Please don't leave like this. You know I didn't do it on purpose. I've been having awful dreams lately and I think the medication makes it hard for me to wake up from them. I truly am sorry. I didn't mean to hurt you. I don't know what else to say."

"I know that," she assuaged. "I should've just let you sleep. It was my own fault. I was just trying to tell you I was leaving. Then all hell broke loose."

"How long was I asleep?"

She placed her hand and keys on the island, leaning her body against its edge. Under the bright sunlight strewn in through the kitchen windows, the thin red lines on her cheek glistened with ointment.

"About two hours. I made dinner like I said I would, and a couple of meals for lunch or snacks tomorrow. Nothing fancy. Chicken, rice, and beans for dinner. Tuna salad and some chili you can heat up tomorrow. Dinner's in the microwave on a plate. I put the leftovers away in the fridge."

"Thank you so much. I feel terrible," I placed my hand over hers on the island, and hoped my eyes conveyed the extent of my remorse. It was genuine. "You've been so helpful, and here I've been a major bitch all day, and tried to maul you in my sleep. I know you have things to do and places to go, and I'm not trying to stop you. But I don't want you to leave angry with me. I *am* so sorry. Maybe I should put it on a sticker, so I don't have to keep repeating it."

"What in the world were you dreaming about?"

I exhaled, rolling the perpetual tension from my neck. These dreams were hellish.

"Fighting Debbie. You know that heifer hates me, even though I've never done anything to warrant it. I beat her ass once, so I guess she's gonna keep coming at me in my dreams until she redeems herself."

Lisa simpered; her body slightly relaxing.

"I'm worried about you. Are you sure you're gonna be okay here by yourself?"

"Yeah. I'm moving around just fine. Slowly, but fine. I'm not an invalid."

"Actually, by definition of the effects of your injuries, you *are* an invalid."

We laughed. She placed her other hand on top of mine and asked softly, "Why didn't you tell Race you got discharged?"

I snatched my hand from the sandwich we'd made and used it to comb through my messy mane; placing the glass in my other hand down on the island.

"And you know I didn't tell him, how? Because *you* did?"

"I didn't know it was a secret." She shrugged.

"It's *not* a secret. It's just none of his business."

Her head and brow cocked simultaneously.

"Why's that? Did y'all have an argument?"

I flanked her with narrowed eyes.

"If he was concerned about when I was getting out, he could have called me to do it. Now, I know you have to go, and I don't want to keep you from your errands."

She glanced her watch smugly, then swayed her eyes back to mine.

"You're not keeping me from anything. Now, spill it. If nothing else, I deserve to be thrown at least *one* bone after the abuse I endured today. You better hope these scratches are totally gone before me and Geo take our engagement pictures Saturday. I'm so serious too. Now, we're *supposed* to be friends. So, tell me. What's going on?"

"You were Race's friend before you were mine."

"And? I can be both of y'all's friend and still be impartial. I did it with him and Song for years," she balked. "Plus, I might be able to help."

The mention of his ex-girlfriend's name made my cheeks clinch. Face and butt. I wondered if Song was the reason he hadn't been to see me in the hospital. She wanted him back, and this would be a perfect opportunity for her to snake her way in.

"You can't help. How *is* Song anyway? Maybe *she's* been comforting him in my absence."

Her face contorted.

"You can't be serious. And how do you know I can't help? Try me. Even if I can't, I can listen."

I threw my head back and stared up at the ceiling. My go to place for answers never found. I was dead serious. When my chin dropped, Lisa's focused eyes were there to meet mine. The island supporting her propped elbows and clasped hands leveling her resting chin.

"I'm listening."

"Tuh. You're aggravating, is what you are."

"Whatever. Tell me what's going on."

"Why don't you ask *him* what's going on. He's the one who didn't have time for *me* in the hospital."

Her eyes bucked. "Uh… that's not true."

"It *is* true."

She shook her head. "He stayed at the hospital with you for two straight days after you were shot. I know because Geo had to make him leave that second night to go home and take a shower. Then the next day, his granny almost died."

My face blanked. "What?"

"Yeah," she shook her head. "I didn't think you knew. His Granny's a diabetic. She let her blood sugar drop too low, messed around and passed out in the kitchen. Nobody was home with her. If Geo's last client hadn't cancelled, he wouldn't have left early and decided to stop by to check on her."

My hand slowly cupped my now gaping mouth. Race loved his grandmother as much as, if not more than, his biological mother. Even though I'd resigned myself to no longer caring about him, as I assumed, he no longer cared about me, I couldn't help the sympathetic tears that welled my eyes.

As ornery as his grandmother appeared on the outside to some, she had proven to be a warm hearted and nurturing old woman. Two motherly qualities I missed in my own mother and wished my step-mother had possessed even an inkling of.

"We all love Granny. She's almost like my own grandma. At first, the doctors couldn't even say if she was gonna make it. Geo was a mess and Race and Ron rushed straight to the hospital. She ended up in a diabetic coma with a concussion and her hip broken in two places. They were speculating about brain damage too."

"Oh my God."

"She's doing much better now. You know, you can't never count that old lady out. She woke up 13 hours later, almost as good as new. Sort of. That hip replacement surgery took a lot out of her. I think they're keeping her another week or two. She's still bossin' everybody around like usual though. Complainin' about Geo's hair, Race getting too thin, Ron getting too fat, my jeans are too tight, and worrying about Mitsy."

"Who's Mitsy?"

"You know. Her little Shih Tzu. That mean little thing's as old as dirt. But she loves it. She tried to get Geo to sneak it in under his coat the other day. She cussed him out when he wouldn't do it," she chuckled.

I remembered the hairy ball of salt, pepper and gold fur running around the house behind Granny at their house on Thanksgiving, but didn't recall its name. I don't particularly care for anything that's hairy, dirty or messy, and pets usually fall into all three categories.

I wasn't sorry when Race's cat, Juney turned up missing a while back. The thing was friendly, but it was also a fur-baby tie between he and his ex that needed to be broken. Or poisoned. Getting rid of him was an easy fix.

"Anyway, Race took it really hard. He goes practically catatonic when he's grieving. It's been hard on everybody else too. Well, everybody except Carmen. I don't even think she knows what happened yet." Her eyes rolled in disgust.

"Why not? I thought Carmen lived with his grandmother."

"She *did*. Till she started back using, and robbed the house while Granny was at church. We haven't seen hide nor hair of her thieving behind, since."

I shook my head critically and half-heartedly wondered what triggered Carmen's relapse after more than a year of sobriety. I didn't care for her when we met over Thanksgiving dinner, and it was clear the feeling was mutual.

She was a short, overly petite woman, wearing too much makeup, a too thin lace front and tight clothes I thought more suitable for a teenager. She took smoke breaks like commercial interludes and scowled every time we made eye contact. Rudely interrupting anything I said all during dinner.

I didn't let her petty antics throw me off my square. Per my usual behavior in front of other people, I pretended to be oblivious to her ignorance with a perfunctory smile on my face at each infraction. But believe me, her actions were *duly* noted. She reminded me of my scallywag sister. Her and Debbie were two miserable peas in a pod. With any luck, she'd OD for good this time and save her sons the future headaches.

"Geo blames Carmen's new boyfriend for getting her hooked again. Personally, *I* don't think anybody is to blame for what Carmen does, *but Carmen*. She swore up and down they were wrong when he and Race said old dude was a dope head. But they were right.

I told Geo she was acting like she was scratchin' that itch again when I picked her up from work the day before she did it. She was antsy, snippy and chain smokin' Newports like a death row inmate. But, he didn't listen. 'My momma knows better,' he kept saying. Umm hmm.

Now, nobody ain't heard from her since, and she ain't even been to work. Ron found two of Granny's rings at a pawn shop by the house and the owner confirmed she was the one who brought it in. Probably off binging somewhere with her no-good boyfriend and a needle in her arm."

She spilled the tea with all the neck rolling, hand movements and enthusiasm of a Wendy Williams clone. Exactly why I would never share anything I feared didn't want exposed with her.

"A needle? I thought she was a crackhead. Don't tell me she's a heroin addict?"

"Yep. Smack, not crack. Yet and still, Granny didn't call the police on her either. I mean, true enough, Carmen's done *way* worse than robbing the house before, but if she keeps getting away with this kind of stuff, why would she stop? That lady's getting too old and fragile to be dealing with Carmen's mess.

All Granny did was have Race change the locks to the house. Like she won't just break in the same way she's done before. Or even more likely, Granny'll just let her back in. You know Race does everything for Granny, so Carmen stealing from her, is basically Carmen stealing from Race.

Anyway, he's been up at the hospital every day with her, or out looking for Carmen's trifling ass. I don't know why he didn't tell you, or hasn't been to see you since, but maybe he didn't want to add to your stress."

"That's ridiculous. So, he just... deserted me instead of telling me what happened? Telling me why he was being so short on calls, not coming to see me and ignoring my texts? Why didn't anybody tell me this before? Why didn't *you* tell me this before?"

"I didn't know you didn't know until today. Listen Greer, he's been distant with everybody. He hasn't been to the range or the tattoo shop for more than an hour at a time in weeks. Half the time, when I see him, he's in the same clothes I saw him in the last time. Kinda like how he looked at the hospital waiting on *you* those first two days."

I slid my empty glass around the island nonchalantly and avoided eye contact with her. Admittedly, I vaguely remembered awakening the time I heard Shan and the Resident while I was on the ventilator. I had no recollection of any other visits from anyone before the day I was taken off it, although I'm sure there had to be doctors and nurses in and out of my room.

"In my defense, I didn't know you didn't tell Race you got discharged. It's not like you told me *not* to tell him. My bad."

"How is it that you can blab everything else, but you managed not to tell me about his Granny and Carmen?"

"I do *not* blab everything. All I did was call my man to tell him where I was and what I was about to do. I knew he had me on speaker phone because he was driving, but I didn't know Race was in the car with him."

"Umm hmm."

I moved to sit on a stool tucked under the other side of the island. What if Race wasn't avoiding me because he didn't love me anymore? I would've been understanding about what he was going through if he had taken the time to tell me. Last time I check, ghosting, wasn't an effective form of communication.

"Whether you believe me or not, my point is, my future brother in-law loves you. Now, I don't know if there's more to why you're not talking or not, and you don't have to tell me if you don't want to"—she paused for a beat as if I was going to refute her statement—"but I know he loves you."

My heart thumped like a thousand little rabbits pitter-pattered inside of it. Did he still? Could he?

"How do *you* know he loves me?"

She sucked her teeth incredulously. "Because he told me."

"Before or after I was shot."

"What difference does it make?"

"A *huge* difference."

"I know you don't think what happened to you would change that, do you?"

I sighed.

"I thought you said you had errands to run."

"Stop trying to rush me off. My errands can wait."

"They don't need to. There's nothing to wait for over here. Whatever happens between us, will ultimately be between us. Okay?"

She snatched her keys up with a huff and adjusted her bag.

"Okay. If that's how you want to be about it, I'm gone then." She turned and headed to the door. "I'll turn the bottom lock and you lock the top one behind me. I saw on the news there's been a lot of break ins around here lately."

I gave her a curt nod.

The rest of my day and most of the night was spent following doctor's orders, sleeping, eating, sifting through mail, email, and lamenting over my life the past year and a half. There had been some ups, but it was mostly filled with downs. Hell, *plummets*. And now, Daddy's restraining order, and my limited mobility, presented formidable obstacles for *any* schemes I planned to execute in the near future.

My mind and body needed to relax. Midnight crept up quickly, but time was irrelevant when I didn't have anywhere to go or anybody to see. I turned every light off in the house, lit my master bathroom with candlelight, and prepared to bathe my miseries away in cherry scented bath bombs and solitude.

Waterproof adhesive surgical tape protected the dissolvable stitches sealing my wounds. Still, I kept the steamy hot water in my garden tub below my navel to ensure they stayed dry, as the doctor ordered. I closed my eyes and let my head rest on the back of the tub as Maxwell crooned about us doin' a little somethin' somethin' through the speakers of my portable radio.

My fingers traced along the ovular shaped porcelain as I recalled my last time soaking in Race's beautiful Clawfoot tub. Our relationship was getting better every day before his unresolved feelings for his ex, threatened our serenity. His excessive care for Song after she lost their *maybe* baby, resulted in us having a huge argument, which led to me storming home to drink myself under the kitchen table.

When Race hadn't made any attempts to make up with me the next day, I entertained myself with more of Shawn's diary to keep my mind off of the jealousy fermenting inside. At the time, I had no idea that diary held the key to the history of my life, and how I *really* came to be a part of the Foster family.

I've had zero recollection of my five-year-old self being saved from the fire by a neighbor that 4th of July. Daddy later told me about it, but neither of us knew Shawn had been an eyewitness to it. Nor did we know he'd seen Daddy's stealthy escape as my mother's passed out body burned to death inside of our apartment.

Tears rolled down my cheeks as I rotated the golden coiled snake bracelet with ruby eyes on my wrist. It was the only wearable thing I had of my mother's. I'd worn it daily since discovering it in a box of her belongings that Daddy gave me this past summer. Until then, I had nothing of hers and knew very little about her besides her Romanian heritage.

The small shoebox containing two pictures, a green card, her bracelet, and my own hospital bracelet from the day I was born, satisfied a lifelong yearning I'd had to feel a connection with her. When my stepmother Stephanie, was alive, asking about my mother or even speaking her name, was grounds for whatever torture she deemed necessary.

Being so young when my mother died, I'd retained few, but cherished memories of our time together. I remembered her kind, smiling face when she tickled me awake in my princess bed. Her long blonde hair framing her porcelain face and big bluish-green eyes staring lovingly down at me.

We often ate Captain Crunch cereal straight from the box and watched "Sesame Street" on the PBS channel as I learned new words, and she improved her English. The recollection made me smile. We'd mimic the vampiric laughter of The Count while reciting the featured numbers the puppet taught that day.

Ironically, her birthday fell on the very day I was shot. I would never have known that if I hadn't seen her date of birth on her green card. She would have been 56 years *young* on November 30th. Irina Amanar, my mother, was gone too soon.

A loud crash jolted me from my thoughts. My eyes popped open with a start. It came from downstairs, but nobody was supposed to be in the house except me. The hairs on the back of my neck prickled with fear as I listened intently for something else. If there was an intruder, I was totally defenseless against them.

The police confiscated my gun, I didn't own a bat, and the only weapon besides kitchen knives I possessed was a pink stun gun that required close proximity to be effective. I scrambled from the tub as quickly as my feeble body allowed. Hoping I was hearing things. *Praying* I was hearing things.

Loosely wrapped in a fleece robe, cellphone in my pocket, and stun gun in hand, I flicked on the light at the top of the stairs and peered down nervously. I could see the top bolt on the door was still locked. The windows were still shut and intact.

I crept down slowly. Cautiously wavering on each step. I inspected the living room and half bath first, taking longer in the spare bedroom. The bedside trashcan had an empty Vitamin Water bottle in it, the duvet was pulled back to expose the sheets, and the decorative pillows were piled on the floor by the bed.

I hadn't been in the room since returning home, but I keep a meticulous home. No beds are left unmade and wastebaskets are emptied daily on my watch. This room was in top order when I was home, but maybe Lisa did it in anticipation of my sleeping downstairs. I stood in there the longest. Pivoting in a circle, surveying the room, the closed closet door, and opening it to examine before exiting.

For a moment, I thought I might have imagined the whole thing. But proof came swiftly.

My hand swept the kitchen wall in search of the switch just as the moonlight illuminated a bulky figure darting from one end of the kitchen to the other. Startled, I jerked my hand back and shrieked. Stumbling backwards, my heart palpitated at the speed of light as I thrust the stun gun out in front of me.

"Oh my God! Get out!"

Scrambling into the foyer, my hands trembled as I fumbled with the locks on the door, finally flinging it open with a thud and bolting into the night air.

"Help! Please! Somebody!"

I moved as fast as I could; bare feet padding the pavement; frantically looking for the intruder behind me as I screamed and motored towards a neighboring home.

Bright lights appeared from nowhere. Blinding me as I clumsily reached the asphalt, and the deafening sound of screeching brakes pierced my ears.

6

Greer

I swear. If it wasn't for bad luck, I'd have no luck at all. Thank God, the teenage driver of the car saw me in time to swerve, missing a parked car on the curb by inches. He sat stunned, ogling the exposed flesh beneath my robe as I fled across the street to Karen's doorstep.

My fists banged on the door until lights flooded the porch and she abruptly swung it open. Her meaty frame filled the doorway, hair tied up in a scarf, dressed in pajamas, a housecoat, and slippers. An expression of both confusion and annoyance graced her face as her Pomeranian, leapt and barked incessantly like it was a Pitbull.

"What in the world?"

"Somebody broke in my house!" Tears drenched my cheeks as I gathered my robe together, and she quickly ushered me in.

"Who did? The guy in the car?"

She craned her neck out the doorway, just as the Kia Sportage peeled off into the night. He hadn't done anything illegal, but maybe he thought he had. Thank God he hadn't struck me, or it probably would have been a hit and run.

"No. It's not him. They're still in the house. Please. Call 911."

She closed the door, peeking out the blinds of the side window, calling from her cell, already in hand.

"Be quiet Sheba!" She scolded the yapping mutt who instantly hushed. "Hello. Yeah. Somebody just broke in my neighbor's house. She just ran over here half naked to get away. Y'all need to get somebody out here, ASAP."

She recited my address to the operator as I inhaled slowly, trying to control my breathing like in yoga class. I felt like a panic attack was coming. The operator asked to speak to me, and Karen held her phone in my direction. I felt my own cell in my pocket as I moved to put my stun gun away and felt like an idiot for not calling myself.

I handed the phone back to Karen when the call ended and stared at the closed door as if I could see through it. It would never feel like home to me again. My house was put on the market after Michael's trial, and a buyer had made an offer a couple of days before I was shot.

The deal fell through while I was still in the hospital, so, I'd taken it off the listing until I decided how I wanted to move forward. This break-in presented several problems for me; both as a seller and a homeowner. One thing was for sure. I wasn't going to spend another night in that house without an alarm system.

"Here baby."

Karen grabbed a blanket from the arm of the couch and wrapped it around my shoulders. The hug accompanying it surprised me. Karen and I had merely been acquaintances over the years. She was called as a witness during Michael's trial, since she'd witnessed both Marlene's exit from my home that morning, and my arrival later that day. But I wouldn't have considered us friends.

Our relationship hadn't changed afterwards either. She wasn't really, my kind of people. Still, a hug was exactly what I needed in the moment. It was loose enough to avoid pressure on my wounds while allowing me to weep softly into her shoulder. I remained in her warm embrace until the police eventually arrived.

Later, Karen and another neighbor whose name I didn't recall, talked and smoked in the threshold of her open front door, gawking out at the police activity across the street. I watched through the window as other nosy residents began to gather outside to question the goings on as well.

Karen and the neighbor were both black women in their 60's. She, newly divorced from a husband who left her for a coworker last year; the neighbor, wearing a red winter coat over pajamas and sneakers, was one half of a lesbian couple who lived two doors down on the right.

All I knew about them was that they kept to themselves and loved decorating their home for damn near every holiday. It was kind of nauseating. They even put up decorations for Valentine's Day one year.

I wrapped the wool blanket tighter around my frame, peering across the street at my home. I was tired, but I knew what awaited me in slumber wouldn't be any better than the nightmare I was experiencing in wake.

"*Chiiiiiile*, and here they come. Empty handed," Karen announced, removing the cigarette from her mouth. "Not nair *one* negro or white man in handcuffs. They never catch 'em when they do a crime against one of us. Took 'em long enough to get here. They should've been puttin' out one of them APB's or whatever they call 'em on TV."

The neighbor nodded, toking on her cigarette as Karen stepped aside to allow the two officers she was referencing, inside.

"Ms. Patterson," the older looking of the two officers addressed me. "We did a full sweep and cleared the premises, both inside and out. It looks like they broke in through the basement door and left out the same way.

We did find large footprints in your yard that look fresh. I assume they aren't yours," he looked down at my bare feet. "Does anybody else stay with you whose footprints those might be?"

"No. I live alone, and I've been in the hospital for two weeks."

"You might have already heard, but there's been an increase in home invasions in the neighborhood. Since that new gas station went up, it's made the communities around here that aren't used to this type of crime, a target."

"I saw on the news just last night they beat an elderly man for a couple of TV's and credit cards. That's why I keep a shotgun ready for any of them bastards wanna come break up in here," Karen asserted.

The officer resumed speaking with a tinge of agitation in his voice.

"We're gonna call in for the crime scene guys to come down here and dust for prints and all that. Myself and Officer Gascow here are gonna take you back across the street to walk us through what happened, and you can take a look see for yourself and tell us anything that might have been stolen.

I suggest you put in a call to your insurance company the first chance you get too. Your homeowner's policy should cover a lot. Maybe even help you get an alarm system installed."

"They usually work pretty fast with that kind of stuff. The faster they can get an adjuster out here to look at the damages and document what's been stolen, the faster they'll process your claim," Officer Gascow offered. Probably just trying not to look useless.

"Okay. Can I put some clothes and shoes on?"

"Yes Ma'am."

It was daylight by the time the police and crime scene team was finished doing what they do. Nothing was stolen from what I could tell. The diary was taken before I ever left the hospital, so I didn't bother to mention that as a missing item. I suspected Daddy as the culprit in that case anyway, and he had a key.

The crashing sound I heard must've been the intruder knocking the glass I'd left on the island to the floor. Its shattered remains were evidence across the kitchen tile. The whole thing was unnerving. Where could I be safe, if not in my own home?

Both Karen and Jacky, the neighbor whose name I finally learned, offered me use of their second bedrooms, but I declined. I appreciated their kindness, but they were still virtual strangers to me. Being the germaphobe I am, I would never lay my head down on just anybody's pillows. If I hadn't been so cold at the time, I would've declined Karen's dog haired blanket as well.

In the aftermath, I took care of my wounds, gulped down a combination of sorely needed pain meds and booked a room at the Sheraton Hotel. I redressed in the sweats I wore home from the hospital, packed everything I needed into a carryon sized roller suitcase and summoned an Uber.

By the time I got there, I could barely keep my eyes open and crashed on the bed as soon as I entered my room. I might have slept all day, or at least until the pain woke me, if not for the ringing of my cell. I searched the bed blindly until my fingers found and answered it.

"Hello?"

"Hey girl. I was just calling to check up on you and see how you got through the night," Lisa's, too happy voice irritated my exhausted sensibilities.

"Hmph. Don't ask."

"*Weeeeeell* that doesn't sound good."

"It wasn't."

I sighed, groggily and opened my eyes to view the time on my phone. Two thirty-four. The afternoon sun dimly lit my room through the huge window as an overcast threatened to rain on the city.

"I hear you. It's only the first night. I'm sure it will get easier as you get better. Did you decide to sleep in the spare bedroom like I *suggested*, or keep tackling those stairs?"

"I didn't sleep there at all. Somebody broke in the house."

Her loud gasp almost startled the phone from my hands.

"What? Oh my God! When? Did you call the police? How did they get in? Did they hurt you? Are you okay?" She rattled off so many questions, I didn't know which one to answer first.

"I'm as okay as I'm gonna be, I suppose. After midnight, they broke in through the basement door; I wasn't hurt; and yes, I called the police."

She asked more questions, and I ran down the events while rising and beginning to unpack my things.

"So, where are you if you didn't sleep at home?"

"The Sheraton Atlanta."

"You know you're welcome to come stay with me, right? Why didn't you call me?"

"Thank you, but no. I've imposed on you enough. I wasn't going to call you in the middle of the night. As long as I've got a television, room service and elevators, I'll be fine."

"Alright. I'm not gonna push. We don't have turn down service or a continental breakfast over here, but the offer still stands if you change your mind."

"Speaking of turndown service, even though I didn't sleep in it, thanks for prepping the spare bedroom for me."

"*Huh?* What do you mean?"

"Taking the pillows off the bed and pulling the sheets back."

"*Umm...* I looked in there when I came back from grocery shopping for you, but that's it. I thought you did that, then changed your mind and went upstairs. I didn't touch anything. Maybe Shan left it like that. *She* probably thought you would sleep down there when you got discharged *too*."

I rolled my eyes at her little dig about me choosing to go upstairs. Shan likes order, and is as much of a creature of habit as I am. It was one of the reasons she and I got along as roommates in college. There was a place for everything, and everything was in its place. That included making our beds every morning before leaving the house.

I insisted she slept at my house the last four of the seven nights she was in Atlanta. She'd already shelled out enough money to be by my side and since she had a key, I trusted her to stay there alone. Still, she stayed in that room every time she visited and never left it with an unmade bed. Maybe it had been Ms. Nina?

"Well, let me go. I knocked out as soon as I got here. I just want to shower, eat, get myself situated and relax."

"Alright, call me later."

"I will."

I put my items away in drawers and took what I needed into the bathroom with me. My reflection was a perfect representation of what

I'd been through. The ugly scarring around my bullet wounds and the incision from the lung repair, assured I'd never wear a tank top or spaghetti straps in public without coverage again.

After a careful shower and re-treating my wounds, I brushed my hair back into a smooth ponytail and dressed in a long pink sleeve night shirt with matching boy shorts. I wasn't going anywhere but from the bathroom to the bedroom, so I might as well be comfortable.

I turned the TV on to some reruns of *Seinfeld* and grabbed the room service menu to order. It didn't have much of what I wanted, but I settled on an Indian River Salad with Chesapeake Crab Cakes and got comfortable on the bed.

I was a few minutes into a second episode when there was finally a knock at the door. About damn time. I eased from the bed and opened the door, glancing back at the show with a smirk when George Castanza said something funny. When no one pushed a cart through the door, I turned back to see dark brown eyes gazing down at me.

Black bomber, black jeans, and curly hair with an inch of new growth on his head and face, a somber expression darkened his handsome countenance.

"Race, what are you doing here?"

"I came to see you."

"Why?"

Head cocked; the tongue I yearned to have in my mouth swept his bottom lip in consternation.

"You don't want me here?"

I swallowed my feelings and shifted my attention to the person pushing a food cart behind him.

"Room service?" A middle-aged white man in hotel uniform asked.

"Yes."

I stepped back to give the man entry, and Race took it upon himself to follow behind him. I frowned but said nothing as the waiter positioned two trays onto the small table.

"Thanks." Race took his wallet out and gave the smiling man a Hamilton before I could get to my purse.

"I didn't ask you to do that," I said once we were alone.

"I know you didn't. It was only 10 dollars."

"What do you want, Race? I'm the same person you've been ghosting the last two weeks, so why are you here now?"

"Lisa said you got attacked last night. Are you okay?"

"I wasn't okay *before* I got attacked last night."

"I know. I'm sorry I haven't been more present."

"It doesn't take much to be more present than, not present at all. You haven't even had time to text. How am I supposed to feel when you kick me to the side?"

"It wasn't like that, Greer. On top of you being shot, my Granny has been in the hospital and Carmen's gone missing. My mind has been all over the place. When I'm not by Granny's bed, I've been out lookin' for my mother." He pulled out a chair from the table and sat. "I think I'm done with that though. If she wants to be out there getting' high and whatever else, that's just gon' have to be what it is. She's grown."

I watched him expressionlessly, but my insides were melting with a mixture of love, lust, and anxiety. I wanted to present an air of nonchalance, but I just wanted him to show that he cared as much for me as he did for them. Didn't he love me too? I was sick of the men I loved taking me for granted. *Somebody* needed to fight for me.

"Why didn't you tell me about your grandmother and your mother? I would've understood if I had *known*."

He ran a hand over his lips and chin.

"You were already dealing with enough. The thing with my mother happened the day before you got shot anyway. I don't know why she fell off again after over a year sober, but she robbed the house and took off somewhere. I didn't tell you, because we weren't talking after our argument about Song.

Then, while you were in the hospital, my granny fell into a diabetic coma and broke her hip. I didn't know if she was gonna come out of it alive. You know Granny is my heartbeat. I know she's old but, I don't know what I would do without her. I've just been in my head a lot.

Honestly, I didn't want to talk to *anybody* about *anything*. I haven't even been keeping up with my businesses. I couldn't give anything my attention until I knew for sure, my grandmother was gonna be okay. So, it wasn't just you. Besides, you needed to focus on your own recovery and staying out of jail. That detective was really trying to get me to turn on you."

"So, knowing all of that, you thought abandoning me when I barely had anybody else would be better?" I asked. Head cocked with hands akimbo.

He bowed his head in thought, then looked me in the eyes.

"No. That wasn't my intention at all. I didn't realize the impact my absence would have on you. I was just trying to cope the best way I knew how. In hindsight, I can admit it probably wasn't... nah, *definitely* wasn't, the best way. I should have handled it better.

You know, they say bad things happen in threes. First Carmen, then you, then my grandmother. I'm a strong man, but it was a lot all at once. It just triggered a lot of memories and feelings I haven't had to deal with in a long while. I don't feel like I abandoned you though. If I didn't call, I texted."

I rolled my eyes.

"Really? 'Just thinking about you. Hope you're good,' in a text, isn't saying much for someone who claimed to love me. Or did you only say that because I was drunk, and you didn't think I'd remember?"

He squinted incredulously, shaking his head and rested his elbows on his knees. His usual tell that he was about to say something serious.

"I said I loved you, because I meant it."

"Meant? As in past tense?"

"If it was past tense, I wouldn't be here right now. But, Greer, we *do* have some things to talk about. I'm not sure that you, and the woman I think I love, are the same person."

It was my turn to squint incredulously.

"What the hell does that mean? Are you back with Song?"

"Song? What... we're talking about us, and you're asking about Song?"

"Well, you're talking in circles and I'm tired. I don't have the time or energy to figure out your love riddles. If you loved me before, you should love me now. You do or you don't. If it's not Song, then what?"

Taking a deep breath, his lips folded, hands now steepled in thought, he peered into my eyes for a long time. Making me nervous for the words about to come.

"Did you kill your husband?"

7

Greer

"Get out."

He didn't flinch.

"Did you hear what I said? Get out! If you can sit here and *insult* me like this, after everything I've been through, you need to leave."

"Listen, your father said…"

"My *father*! My *father* said? The father that tried to burn me and my mother to ashes and covered it up for 25 years? The father who shot me in the back, in cold blood, right in front of you? Is that whose word you're weighing against mine? Against the verdict of a judge and jury who already convicted the *actual* murderer?

Are you really accusing me of doing something so heinous, on the word of the person who shot me in the back? The god damn audacity! Please. Race, just get out."

I was livid. More because he confirmed that my father's rant impacted his view of me than the fact that his accusation was true. Tears rolled down my cheeks as I marched toward the door. He stood, grasping my wrist.

"Wait a minute. I'm not accusing you. I'm *asking* you if it's true. Judges and juries don't always get it right. You didn't deny it when he said it."

"I didn't think I had to. He was obviously saying anything he could to deflect from the fact that *he* was a murderer himself. How was that *not* obvious to you? The fact that you even feel the *need* to question if I'm a killer is problem enough? Clearly, you don't know me at all."

He looked shameful but continued with his line of accusations as if I hadn't just dispelled them.

"I had to ask. I heard y'all arguing before I came in the room, Greer. He said you were just as bad as him right before you shot him."

"He reached for his gun."

"Okay. But then later, he said, point blank, you killed your husband. You didn't dispute it." He shrugged. "I keep replaying everything that happened that night. Everything that was said on the phone; when I got there. The helpless look in your eyes when he shot you. I'm just trying to make it all make sense."

"And you don't think I'm doing the same thing? Trying to make sense of everything that happened that night and replaying repeatedly what I could have done differently? What I should have done differently?

I was drunk out of my mind, Race. Maybe I didn't react to his crazy accusation the way you *thought* I should have. But I didn't react to a lot of things the way I should have. I was traumatized. That doesn't suddenly make me a murderer. How did I become the bad guy when everybody else is killing people? I'm the victim! I can't believe *you're* turning on me too," I cried.

"I'm not." He stepped closer, my wrist still in his grasp, his other hand now caressing my jawline. "I'm not turning on you, Baby. I swear I'm not. Even if you did it, I'm not sure I could let you go. I'm just trying to understand."

Well, that made me feel better.

"Understand what? What's confusing you? The fact that the people I love keep betraying me? Turning on me? Just go then."

"Okay. Alright, I get it. I'm sorry. I'm sorry for questioning you. You're right. I should know better. But I love you. And I swear I'll *never* betray you."

His six-foot frame towering over me, he lifted my chin and placed his soft lips on mine. I closed my eyes and allowed his tongue to part my lips. My tears salting our kiss. Our tongues dancing a waltz of apologies, love, and longing. I missed him so much.

Our kiss broke without warning, and he pecked my forehead softly.

"I'm here now. I'll take care of you. Can I take care of you?"

I nodded timidly. My heart swelling with love as the single dimple in his left cheek exposed itself in a doting grin. I was kidding myself, pretending I would let this love go so easily. I wanted him as much as I wanted air to breathe. He didn't have to do much to get back into my good graces. All it took was those three words, and all was forgiven.

"Did he hurt you? The man last night?"

"No. He scared me. Broke a glass in my kitchen and my basement door, but that's all. I only caught a glimpse of him before I bolted out the front door. I almost got hit by a car running across the street to Karen's in my robe, but other than that, I'm okay."

Cupping my face, he wiped tears from my cheeks with his thumbs and stared at me. "And they haven't caught him yet?"

"Umm mm. Not yet. The police said there's been a lot of break-ins lately. I guess I'm just unlucky."

"Break-ins with people home? You got a Yukon and a Corolla in the driveway and they picked *your* house? Of all the houses in your subdivision? Seems like they'd try a house with less risk."

"I don't know," I answered maneuvering around him to the table and uncovering my food. I was ready to eat. "I hate to be rude, but I'm hungry. Do you want to order something to eat too? I don't want to stuff my face while you watch." I broke off a piece of crab cake with a fork and put it in my mouth, sitting in the chair he previously pulled out.

"What I want to eat isn't on the menu."

He hung his coat on the back of the other chair, revealing his sinewy chest in a black Henley shirt. My god he looked sexy in all black. I watched him with a smirk while chewing, until he removed his shirt too. My eyes widened at the sight of the chiseled abs, large tattoos, and bulging biceps. His body was beautiful.

"What are you doing?"

"Getting ready to eat."

"Eat wha—" he was on his knees between my legs before I could complete my question.

One massive hand gripped my thigh and he moved the fabric of my boy shorts aside with the fingers of his other. His head dipped below my hips and his wet tongue pressed, then licked my exposed lips.

"Ohhhh my god," I whimpered. My legs trembling.

Race's mouth latched onto my bud and sucked His tongue periodically lapping at my slit in a French kiss. He moaned into my sex, sending shivers through my core, and making my head swim in bliss.

I don't know when he pulled my shorts off, but they were on the carpet, my naked ass in his grasp; his tongue sucking and slurping me to orgasm. Once, then twice. I ignored the ache in my back for as long as possible as he licked a fervent trail from my slit to my chocolate star and back again.

"Race… Baby… oh my God it feels so good but… my back," I finally conceded when the pain began to exceed his oral pleasure.

"Oh shit. I'm sorry," his apologetic eyes, glistening mouth, mustache and beard rose above my hips, as he gently rested my bottom back down in the chair.

I smiled. Then giggled.

"What's so funny?"

"You face. It's drenched."

He grinned. "When I'm hungry, I eat."

"I see. I'm hungry too. For *food.* You only let me eat one bite before *you* started eating. I'm surprised my stomach isn't grumbling."

"You complaining? You got food right there. I didn't stop you from eating."

"I'm *not* complaining," I chuckled, reaching back, breaking a piece of cold crab cake off with my fingers and popping it in my mouth. It was still delicious. "I'm just stating facts. There's no way I could eat, while you were eating me like that. Do you want me to choke?"

"Not on a crab cake." He stood, his erection evident through his jeans.

"And you want me to choke on it?" I raised a brow.

"Maybe just gag a little bit," he smirked, unbuckling his belt, and dropping his jeans. The prominent imprint in his black boxer briefs made my mouth water. "But I can wait until after you finish eating."

I popped another piece of crab cake in my mouth with my fingers and licked the remnants of it from the tips.

"You *do* know I'm still healing right? I still can't sleep on my back and one of my ribs is still not set completely. I'm popping pain meds like Tic Tacs every few hours and I don't even know if I'm capable of having sex like a regular person."

"Regular people sex is boring. There are a lot of other positions than on your back, Baby. If you're not ready, I can wait until you are. I don't want to, but I will. At least I got a taste to hold me over for a while." He licked his lips.

"Have you always been this nasty?"

"Probably."

I shook my head. "*Aaaaaaanyway*, I might be willing to try if you promise to be gentle. After I finish eating. I've got a salad here too if you want it."

"Nah, I'm good. I ate a couple of hours ago on my way from the hospital."

"How is your granny by the way?"

"She's good. Might be able to come home by the end of next week. I bought her one of those Hoveround's so she can still be mobile when she gets out. Doc said it will be a long while before she can walk without assistance again. If at all. I know she's gonna hate it."

"Her floorplan looks pretty wide. Those wood floors should make it easy for her to maneuver around in there good."

"Maybe. I don't like the idea of her being in that house all alone. Carmen wasn't ever a big help, but she was there enough that I felt like Granny could make do if Geo or I didn't see her for a day or two. I'm thinking about moving her in with me."

"Hmm," I nodded, smiling phonily.

I wasn't a fan. On one hand, I loved that he was so invested in his family and treated his grandmother like gold. But on the other, being formerly married to a momma's boy for seven years, I knew the downside of playing second fiddle to the matriarch. I wasn't keen on it.

"Hey, can you get me a bottled water from that little hideaway fridge in the cabinet over there please?"

He retrieved it, twisting the cap off the bottle before handing it to me.

"Why don't you come stay at my place?"

I took a swig and cleared my throat.

"Sounds like you're already gonna have your hands full with your grandmother."

"You got jokes. If she does move in, I'm sure it won't be for a while. I'll have to get her to agree to it first. Anyway, I'm talking about tonight. And maybe for a week. Maybe more."

"For what? I only booked the room for a night. I have an alarm company and a door repair guy coming out tomorrow."

"You'll still be in that house by yourself though. Lisa said you can barely make it up the stairs."

"Lisa, talks too much."

"I was serious when I said I want to take care of you. You said I haven't been there for you, and you're right. So, I want to be here for you now. And since somebody broke in, I'd feel better knowing you were safe with me at my place."

As enticing as his offer was, I was hesitant. There were a lot of things he didn't know about me and it would be harder to keep them covert if I were under his thumb 24/7. Still, the idea of being doted on by the man I loved for at least a week and having unabridged access to his domain was equally alluring.

"I'll think about it."

"You do that."

"Can I ask you something?"

"Shoot."

"Have you seen Song since I've been in the hospital?"

Bad timing? Perhaps. But it was eating at me and I had to ask.

His lids lowered disconcertedly as he sat on the edge of the bed facing me.

"Why do you keep asking about Song?"

I shrugged. "She was an important part of your life for a lot of years. You even shared a cat. I know you still care for her *soooo...* I was just wondering."

He sighed. "I've seen her twice at the hospital. Visiting Granny."

My brows furrowed. "Interesting. You told Song about your grandmother but not me?"

"I didn't tell Song anything. Lisa did. You have to understand, my grandmother is loved by a lot of people, Greer. She didn't just take me and my brothers in while Carmen was running the streets. She saw to it that all the kids in the neighborhood had a safe place to go if they needed it. Her house.

She fed, nurtured, and mothered a lot of my friends when their parents weren't around to do it. Her relationship with Song is separate from me. Like most of us, Song's upbringing wasn't sweet either. Granny intervened on her behalf many times when we were kids. Not to tell her business, but Song's mother was a super hoe.

Ms. Barbara kept men coming in and out of her apartment like a turnstile. Song had all the best clothes, and jewelry, but she was an inconvenience to Ms. Barbara's lifestyle. Song got locked out or snuck out a bunch of times so her mother could entertain her "company." Or kicked out for whatever reason after Ms. Barbara got fed up with something and put hands on her.

Song stayed some of those nights at Granny's. She'd stay in Granny's room with her of course. No way was she gonna let Song loose in a house full of "man boys". That's what Granny used to call me and Geo." He smiled at the memory. "I'd hear them talking into the late hours sometimes. They shared things *I* don't even know about. So, I'm saying all of that to say, their relationship is their relationship. Our relationship, is ours."

I nodded. Not wanting to beat a dead horse. But I would beat Song into a coma if I found out she was still sniffing around my man.

"What ever happened with her situation? I know she lost the baby, but didn't you or Lisa, say she was… poisoned?"

"Yeah. By her roommate Chelsea. They're still trying to prove it though. Everything is circumstantial, and Chelsea swears up and down she didn't do it. For obvious reasons, they don't live together anymore, but the police haven't been able to charge Chelsea with anything."

"And this was the girl whose boyfriend she slept with when she cheated on you, right?"

"Right. Also, her cousin."

"Hmm. Messy." I ate the last morsel of my crab cakes and got up to get my prescriptions. Water bottle in hand. "I hope she's learned her lesson about sleeping with other women's men. Karma's a bitch."

"Poisoning someone is a lot more extreme than just being a bitch. Ingesting bleach could have killed her. And she caused her to have a miscarriage. That's criminal."

My back was to him, so he couldn't see the satisfied smirk gracing my face. Whatever. A little bleach and crushed up abortion pills never killed anybody. Except that unwanted baby. There was no way I was going to let Song prance her pretty little ass back into my man's life and become his baby-momma.

I placed the pills in one hand and tossed them back, washing them down with water.

"You're right." I turned to face him sympathetically. "I don't agree with doing anything that drastic for revenge. Especially bringing harm to an innocent baby. I just wish people would be more considerate of the other people they hurt. And loyal.

It's hard enough to open up and love someone freely without having to worry about them crushing your heart frivolously for pleasures of the flesh. You can get sex almost anywhere. But love…" I walked to him as he sat on the bed and placed my arms around his shoulders, straddling his lap. "Is so hard to come by. So precious when obtained. I just want you to know that I would never betray you in such a manner. I know too well how it feels to ever put that kind of hurt on someone else. I hope you feel the same about me."

His hands rested on my hips. His manhood awakened. Our eyes linked.

"I do."

I wished a pastor or judge had been there to make it official, but there would be plenty of time for that.

"Is *this*, a good alternate position to being on my back?" I whispered sensually.

"It is," he spoke in my ear; his tongue tracing the lobe before sucking it.

My head lolled back, exposing my neck to further kisses. His hands creeping slowly under my shirt.

"Be careful with me," I whimpered.

"Always," he answered, lifting my shirt, and helping me ease it over my head.

My wounds now uncovered, he stared wordlessly at them in solemn fascination. The pink, crystalized heart tattoo with our initials, G and R, was little more than an abhorrent scar now. The bullet meant to kill me, the reason for its demolition.

"I can't believe I almost lost you."

"But you didn't. I thought I was dying that night. This might sound crazy, but if I had to die, I was happy that it was going to be in the arms of the man I loved." I caressed his cheek with the back of my hand. "Your handsome face; is the last thing I remember before blacking out. Not the pain. Not fear. Just feeling your love."

Our lips melded as he held me in place with one hand and shimmied his underwear down with the other. Seconds later, I was impaled with the girthy culmination of his desire.

Time sauntered on as our moans penetrated the walls of my hotel room. Our mouths consuming each other between breaths. The impending rain suddenly battered its arrival against the window, and thunder clapped an ovation. It was almost a metaphor for the slick welcome my body was giving his dick.

My walls tremored with every thrust, his hands gripping my thighs. Every inch of his thick and veiny muscle, plunging in and out of my gyrating core. Race's lips volleyed between my neck and suckling my hardened nipples, taking care to avoid my wounds.

"*Ohhhh fuuuuck*," he murmured. Softly biting my shoulder. One hand firmly gripping the back of my neck.

I could feel him growing inside me. Want and need manifesting itself in lust. My own orgasm at the precipice of erupting as my hands held onto his shoulders for dear life.

"Cum with me Baby. I don't... I don't think I can hold it much longer."

"I am. I am. I am," is all I could utter in repetition. I was coming up on my third. "Give it to me," my tongue and lips ordered in his ear.

His arms tensed and the passionate pounding he was giving my pussy sped up with ferocity. His lips crashed against mine. His tongue demanding compliance as he plowed deeper inside of me. My essence milked every stroke. My own orgasm building and erupting singly as he roared in rapture, flooding my hollow with his pulsing seed.

Spent and speechless; we remained in each other's listless embrace. His head lightly pressed against my chest. My hands stroking, coiling, and recoiling the curls atop his head. Both, listening to the downpour of the storm outside, having no idea of the true turmoil awaiting us.

8

Greer

"It's the best protection you can have next to a firearm."

"I hope so," I replied as the alarm company guy showed me how to activate and deactivate the new system from my phone.

He was an average height white man with sandy brown hair and bright blue eyes that didn't fit his otherwise gaunt appearance.

"You can arm, disarm or set it off from the panel like I showed you, but you can also do it from the app. Just press selections from anywhere you are. In or outside of the home, no matter how far. You can also set up a duress pin number."

"What's that?"

"If somebody ever forces you to disarm the alarm, just enter your duress pin number instead of your normal pin number. It *will* deactivate the alarm, but also silently alert the police that you're doing it under duress. It's an extra layer of personal protection IMD Security prides itself in providing for its customers.

I know you already have cameras for the front, back and basement doors, but are you sure you don't want to add a couple cameras to the interior as well? The sensors on the doors and windows are great, but cameras allow you to see what's going on in live view. You can set them to monitor and record on a timer or by manual selection, just like you can the door cameras."

"No. That's too invasive."

"Well, nobody but you and whoever else you may give access to will be able to see it."

He glanced at Race, watching, arms folded across his chest from the archway between the foyer and kitchen.

"What about the police? Won't they see it?"

"They would only have access to it if you give it to them. Or if God forbid something happens and they have to get a court order to view it because you're unable to. Even still, they would only see whatever you set the video to record or didn't erase from the cloud. That way, you can keep videos longer, and safer for storage and view."

"I'm good, but thank you."

"Just remember that you can upgrade your current security package anytime you want, and we try to get somebody out within 24 hours of every order."

"I'm only gonna be here a few more months, or until I sell the house anyway. I'm gonna put it back up for sale next month right after I get some things squared away. If you know anybody who might be in the market, please keep me in mind."

He handed me back my phone, adjusted the matching cap to his IMD uniform atop his head and nodded with a smile.

"Sure thing."

Jacky waved a hello from her front yard as I let the security guy out to his van. It was still damp and chilly out, causing me to wrap my arms around myself after returning the gesture and shutting the door. I hoped she didn't consider us friends now.

Friends in this neighborhood were the drop by unannounced type, from what I knew. I didn't need any friends like that. Especially nosy ones that lived across the street. The watchful eyes of Chain-Smoking Karen and her porch bound habit were bad enough without adding Jacky to it.

"I still think you should stay with me."

I smiled at my protective man.

"I'm a big girl Race. It *was* scary, but now the door's repaired and I have a brand-new security system in place. The police said they almost never try the same house twice. And anyway, I'm tired of being a victim. I feel like things keep happening to me, and I don't have control of anything. I need to take control.

It may not seem like it, but I'm tougher than I look. If I learned to stay here and sleep in the same room my husband was murdered in for over a year, I think I can manage to stay in this house alone for a few more months. If it sells."

"You don't have to be alone. At least not every night."

"That's good to know."

I ambled to him and pecked him on the lips.

"You didn't get your gun back huh?"

"No," I dropped my head.

"I wanted to ask you yesterday, but since we were busy making up, I decided to wait. What's happening with that? They got my statement and said I might have to testify in court, but did they charge either of y'all with anything?"

I sighed. Already hating this conversation.

"They charged me, not him."

"With what?"

"Aggravated assault and a DUI. According to my attorney, I'm lucky it wasn't for attempted murder."

He leaned off the frame.

"Whoa. And they didn't charge him with anything?"

"Nope. Because everything happened in his house, and I came there with a gun, they just pinned it all on me. I can't prove he killed my mother, so..."

"But, you said it was in your brother's diary? Are they at least investigating it?"

I shook my head.

"Nope. The diary went mysteriously missing, but even if it hadn't, it wouldn't matter. Shawn's punk ass is backing up Daddy's claim that it's all fiction."

"What do you mean it went 'mysteriously missing'?"

I ran a hand through my mane, which was becoming my own nervous tell. I truly didn't want to talk about this, but the conversation would need to be had eventually, so I might as well get it out the way now.

"I asked Shan to bring it to my attorney and when she came here to get it, it was gone. Unless it grew legs and walked away on its own, somebody stole it."

"Maybe it's in your car. You might have brought it with you in and forgot?"

"No."

"Greer. You were really drunk. You might—"

"Race! I know what I did. I don't care if I was drunk. I was lying in my bed reading it, and I left it right—there—before I went to Daddy's. Even if I hadn't, Shan got my car out of impound for me before she left. It wasn't in there. You see the car in my driveway. You wanna check?"

He held his palms up defensively. "Okay. Alright. I hear you."

I shouldn't have snapped on him, but how stupid did he think I was? I knew where I left it. Even still, Shan searched the whole house for me. There weren't but so many places it could have been. I softened my tone and placed a hand on his arm.

"I know you're just trying to help. I'm frustrated. It's hard knowing he's going to get away with what he did to my mother, even though I'm not the only one who knows he did it. Hell, he even admitted it to me."

"Wait. What? He admitted it?"

"Yes. Before you came, he admitted it. Why do you think I was so riled up and he was throwing out wild accusations about me? Why else would somebody... like my father... steal the diary? You know what? Let's not talk about this right now. I really don't want to."

"Okay. Hold on. I know you don't want to, but we need to talk about this for a minute. You said he admitted to you, that he killed her?

Now you're saying you think he came in here and stole the diary? You should've changed the locks on all the doors. You can't trust him anymore. What if he comes back?"

"He won't or he'll be violating the restraining order."

"When did you put a restraining order on him?"

"He has one against me. Same rules apply either way. I can't be within 1500 feet of him. According to the prosecutor, Daddy's afraid of me. So, now that I'm home, I'm sure he won't be popping up."

He ran a hand over his face.

"Alright. You got me paranoid now. All this talk about him murdering your mom and trying to kill you too. How am I supposed to process that? The man is clearly a danger. I don't like you staying here with locks he has a key to. Why didn't you have the guy replace all of them when he was fixing the basement door?"

I shrugged. I suppose I should have, but I honestly hadn't thought about it. I knew Daddy, even with his murderous history, wasn't an imminent threat to me. I couldn't say the same in reverse. I hoped he hadn't thought about changing his locks either. I was going to need easy access to his house again, eventually.

"Look, I'm about to head to Home Depot. I'll change the locks myself. I've gotten kinda good at it at Granny's. I wish you'd stop being so stubborn and just come stay at my place, but since you won't, I also have a bat I keep in my trunk for emergencies. I'm gonna leave that here for you too. You know. So, you'll have a weapon if you need it."

"What kind of emergency requires a baseball bat?"

He smirked, kissed me on the forehead, and moved around me toward the door. The stress of needing to protect me etching new lines in his face.

"The type that come up when you don't have a gun or don't want to use it. I'll be back. Go lay down and relax for a little while. You've been doing a lot already today. Aren't you supposed to practice on that breathing thing?"

"How about you let *me* worry about what I'm supposed to do, Mr. Banks," I quipped.

"If I'm gonna take care of you, like I said I would, I'm gonna have to make sure you're following the doctor's orders too."

"I'm perfectly capable of doing that myself. But thank you. Are you sure you're not related to Lisa by blood? I feel like I had almost this exact same conversation with her."

I didn't mean to quibble. I loved that he wanted to take care of me. That's what a good man was supposed to want to do for his woman. Right? It could however, easily become an inconvenience for my future plans. I was going to need some private time away from him and everybody else after my healing improved. A lot, of private time.

He retrieved the bat from his trunk, as promised, and left it behind my front door. When he left, I soon found myself standing at the threshold of the spare bedroom. Everything was exactly as I discovered it two nights earlier. I wondered if Shan really had left it in this condition before she left. Then it dawned on me that I hadn't heard from her since my release. Odd.

I texted her.

Greer: Hey girl. Haven't heard from you. Everything okay? Also, did you turn down the bed in the spare room for me before you left?

I walked around the room, examining it more thoroughly than I had before while waiting for a response. It had to be her. Ms. Nina hadn't stayed overnight for weeks before I was shot. Who else could have done it?

Rather than texting back, she called. Figured.

"Hey."

"Hey. I kept meaning to call, but then things kept happening and I didn't want to text. I'll tell you about that later. My bad friend. I meant to see how your first day home from the hospital went. And what turn down are you talking about? Leaving the bed unmade?"

"Yeah. The pillows were off the bed and the sheets were back."

"When have you ever known me to leave a bed unmade? I don't even do that at the hotel."

Ice pricked at my spine.

"Did you have a Vitamin Water while you were here?"

"What's that? I didn't go in your refrigerator if that's what you're asking," her tone was becoming one of offense.

"It's not what I'm asking. The duvet on the spare bed was pulled down, the decorative pillows on the floor and an empty Vitamin Water bottle in the trash can.

Lisa said she didn't do it. I know I didn't do it. So, I was hoping you did. Somebody broke in my house the other night. And if they did it, that means they were in the house longer than I thought."

She gasped. "Are you fucking serious? Greer! And you didn't think to call me? What the hell? Are you alright?"

"Yes. He didn't harm me."

"For Christ's Sake. What else is gonna happen? Were you home when they broke in?"

"Yeah. It was like, midnight. I was upstairs in the bath. I heard broken glass, came downstairs and he was in the kitchen. I ran out to a neighbor across the street, and that's it. He was gone by the time the police got there."

"This is bananas. On your first night home? What kind of idiot breaks a window in the middle of the night and doesn't think anybody will hear it?"

"He didn't break a window. He broke in through the basement door. Police said it might have been done days or even weeks earlier."

"Well, what glass did he break?"

"He knocked a glass on the floor in the kitchen."

She scoffed.

"And he was still in the kitchen when you got there?"

"Yes."

"Hmph."

"What?"

"It's just weird. What's there to steal in a kitchen? You don't have no TV's or anything in there. Believe me. I've got some relatives with severe sticky fingers, and the kitchen is the last place they looked to steal shit from."

"Maybe he was on his way back down to the basement. Remember, you have to go through the kitchen to get to it."

"Okay. Maybe so. I would just think that after he broke something, he'd be trying to get the hell out of there so nobody would wake up. What all did he end up stealing?"

"Nothing, that I can tell."

"Nothing? *Soooooo*, he broke in; messed up the bed and got what... busted while trying to get a glass of water from the kitchen? What kind of Goldie Locks wandering into The Three Bears mess is that? It sounds to me like you had a squatter. Especially if you found a Vitamin Water bottle or whatever in the trash. He was either there for a long time, or there before.

And for the record, I have never in my life put your pillows on the floor. I put them in that little chair you have by the closet. Only a man would do something so stupid."

I took in her words as I began to yank the duvet and sheets off the bed. I didn't know if the creepy intruder had slept on them or not, but I knew I never would again. A squatter? I shivered at the thought. I sort of regretted not telling the cops about the condition of the bedroom, but at the time, I thought Lisa had done it.

"Well, the police dusted for fingerprints, so if he's been arrested before, they'll know who it is."

"And if he hasn't? I don't like you staying there all by yourself Greer. What if your father sent somebody over there to finish the job?" Shan whispered.

"He didn't."

"You don't know that. You don't know where that diary is either. Which we still need to talk more about."

"You sound like Race," I grumped, stuffing as much of the bedding into the clothes hamper by the closet as much as possible.

"Race, obviously has some sense then. Did y'all make up?"

"Yes."

She chuckled.

"It must've been one hell of a make-up session. I can hear you smiling through the phone."

The smile I didn't originally know I was wearing, widened.

"I assume he had a good reason why he's been avoiding you?"

"He did. Multiple reasons actually. His mother's gone missing and his grandma fell into a diabetic coma. He's just one of those types that clams up when they're distraught. His mother's probably strung out somewhere in a back alley and Granny's still in the hospital." I sighed. "He didn't want to burden me."

"Burden you? How about informing you why his black ass wasn't visiting? Men. I swear. If it wasn't for that good schlong, they wouldn't be worth a damn half the time."

We chuckled.

"Enough about me. It's been all about me for the last three weeks. I'm perfectly fine giving the people I love the spotlight and being able to offer some sound advice to someone else for a change. What's happening with you? How's my godson?"

I was hoping she'd have some shocking news to tell me about Wendy being repeatedly attacked by random rapists. There'd been a few responses to the ad, and I encouraged each of them to show me, or Wendy, what they were made of.

I hadn't checked my messages for Backpage recently, but when I did, hoping for the proof that someone had gotten the job done. I knew Shan would never cosign the implementation of such a heinous form of revenge on her behalf. Hence why I never told her what I was doing.

"Shamari is fine. Not sick anymore, thank God and growing like a weed. He's been begging us for a puppy for Christmas and I can't believe Jahari actually wants to get him one."

"Who's gonna train it? I heard you have to spend a lot of time with puppies to get them housebroken and all of that. With the way y'all work, when would you have time to do that?"

"That's what I said. I mean, I love dogs too, but I just don't have the time to split between running behind Shamari and a puppy. Especially if the pregnancy test I'm taking right now comes back positive."

"What!" I screeched stopping to sit on a step as I passed the staircase on my way to add the Vitamin Water bottle to the kitchen garbage. "Shan! You think?"

"Maybe. With his momma finally giving us a little space, we've actually been having sex a lot. I thought my period was running behind because I was stressed about you, Shamari being sick and the BS I have going on at work; but now I'm thinking, it could be something else.

I always keep a few tests just in case. I just finished taking it when you texted me. I'm too scared to look at the results yet."

"Girl stop playing. You better look at that thing and tell me if there's a little Greer on the way or not. Remember, you promised you'd name your next one after me if it's a girl," I chirped.

I loved kids. If I could love them and send them back home to their parents, I was a child lover. The innocence and joy that children possess is like no other. I didn't want any myself, for the time being, but I could maybe see Race and I with one or two.

"I'm nervous. I don't know if this is a good time for us to have a baby right now. Don't get me wrong. We're doing much better since he ended that thing with Wendy; but we're not 100%. I'm not sure if adding another child would make us better or worse."

I pondered her words as I approached the door to look through the peephole and see who was ringing my bell. I was too new at using the security system to think to look at the camera feed from my phone, let alone to know how or if I could do it while a call was in progress.

A red-haired female in a peplum style blue coat faced the street with her back to the door. I assumed she was white, but with the way these black women wear wigs these days, I wasn't sure. I should've ignored her.

"Hold on a second Shan. Somebody's at my door."

"Talk about bad timing."

"I know," I replied unlocking and opening the door just enough for her to see my full body. "Yes?"

The red head spun to greet me with a face full of makeup, a big grin, and a microphone in her hand. Behind her, I noticed a Channel 11 News van parked at the curb.

"Mrs. Patterson. Donnatella Gladson from "Channel 11 News: Behind The City." Your sister, Deborah Manly, has recently accused *you* of killing your husband and framing Marlene Braxton for his murder last year, in the "Sleeping with the Enemy" case. We're told Deborah's now assisting Marlene's family and attorney in her upcoming appeal.

Would you like to give a statement addressing or refuting her claims?"

9

Greer

I slammed the door so hard it felt like the whole house shook. It took everything in me to suppress the rage-filled scream churning in my belly. Angry tears evidenced my feelings before I could stifle them. I squeezed the phone with the force I wished my hands were crushing Debbie's windpipe with. My teeth grit as I closed my eyes, taking a meditative breath to calm myself.

"Oh my God! What'd she say? Debbie's working with Marlene's attorney on her *appeal?* Oh hell no!"

I was too upset to reply. I didn't want Shan to hear me crying. Mostly because I didn't want to *be* crying. That conniving, too bored with her own life, beast of burden, was going to pay for besmirching my name this time. I hated to make Will a widower and take a parent from my niece and nephew, but they would be better off without The Wicked Bitch of The Southeast in their lives. I certainly would be.

"Greer? You there?"

I cleared my throat and wiped at my damp cheeks.

"Yeah. I'm here."

"*Ohhhh,* G. Are you crying?"

My best friend knew me too well.

"She's so hateful Shan. For no reason at all. Can I have one—single—day without somebody attacking me? Why can't she just let me live?"

"I don't know, honey. She's just… mean spirted."

"She's just like her evil ass momma is what she is. I thought when Stephanie died, I was rid of the unprovoked nastiness from my own family. I mistakenly thought Debbie would start acting *human*, without her mother as a catalyst for her depravity.

I was wrong. She's never going to stop finding ways to attack me. She's not happy unless I'm miserable. She's like a rabid dog. I just… I hate her so much."

"I know you do. I wish there was something I could do to make it better. Talk to Sylvia about her. Maybe you can sue her for defamation of character or something."

Or kill her.

"She's a troll."

"What do you think she's telling them?"

"Whatever bullshit she can think up. Who knows? She's crazy."

"Yeah but, for Marlene's attorney to b—"

"You know what? I don't care. She can do whatever she wants to do. *Say* whatever she wants to say. I know I didn't kill Michael and so does the jury that convicted Marlene for it. I don't know what she's supposed to be "assisting" them with on appeal; but it doesn't matter. Because it's not true."

"Right. Don't worry about it. It must be a really slow news week for that stupid show to show up at your door too."

"*Really* slow." I took a deep breath and tried to roll the tension from my neck. What *was* Debbie telling them? "Okay. I'm pulled back together. Now, where were we? *Shaaan.* Go look at the test."

"Oh, girl I'm already lookin' at the test. I was on my way to check it when the heifer rang your bell."

I sniggered. Impatient.

"Well, what does it say, fool?"

"It says… me and Jahari are about to have another mouth to feed."

I howled with excitement and danced around in a small circle as she squealed on the other end.

"Yes! Yes! Yes! Yes! Yes! I'm about to be an auntie again! Baby Greer! Coming to a hospital near me, in 2016!"

"You so stupid," she laughed. "Don't get your little feelings hurt if it turns out to be another boy."

"Greer is a good name for a boy too. I looked it up once. My name means, "watchful and vigilant." Any boy or girl would be lucky to have this name. If my mother didn't do anything else right in her life, she chose a great name for me."

"We'll see what Jahari has to say about it."

"Jahari loves me? Doesn't he?"

"Yes, but that doesn't mean he'll want to name his son after you."

I sucked my teeth as the call muted for a short beat.

"Oh hey, G. This is my mom calling on the other line. I didn't even get a chance to tell you about what's going on with Shalita yet. She's back from Philly, living with my mom and caught a charge for hitting Jermaine in the head with a paperweight."

"What? Damn. Your sister is so sweet. What'd he do? I thought they would be engaged soon."

"Doesn't look like it now. What else? Cheated. Anyway, le'me call you back later."

"Okay."

She clicked over and I hung up. If it wasn't one thing, it was another. I cared less about Shalita's drama. I was worried about Debbie and her shenanigans. I needed a drink like I needed air, but supposedly, I was banned from alcohol while out on bail.

Pshhhh. After the last couple of days I had, Judge Renfro and his rules could kiss my petite ass. Unless he was going to catch and cuff me in my kitchen, I was positive I was safe drinking in here.

I'm no dummy. I know mixing alcohol and meds can be dangerous, but I only intended on *one* glass of wine. I was about 20 minutes out from needing to take my next doses, and I could already feel the last ones wearing off. I would be fine.

I've never been a big wine drinker, but I can stand a glass or two sometimes. If I remembered correctly, there was a bottle somewhere in the back of a kitchen cabinet, originally intended for Michael's birthday, which he didn't live to see. Aww. Such a shame. Ha ha!

Bingo! Found it cozily tucked behind a big bag of popcorn in the cabinet over the fridge. By the time Race got back, I was stuffing my face with cheese popcorn and two glasses too many into a bottle of Pinot.

He admonished me like I was a juvenile and only partially yielded when I told him what triggered my need for libations. We argued about my mixing alcohol with my meds while he installed the new locks and I was forced to drink H2O to dilute my system.

Eventually, he lightened up. Becoming more of a comfort about the situation than my warden. Thankfully, the rest of the day, and the next two days were essentially uneventful. No uninvited guests graced my doorstep; I learned the ins and outs of managing my security system; and I was gradually healing and getting stronger every day. I was even driving again.

"I'll be back tomorrow afternoon around two."

Race stood at the bottom of the bed putting toiletries into a small bag. He, Geo, and a few other tattoo artists from Tat Life were flying to California for the grand opening of his friend Anthony's shop.

"Alright."

"You know you can stay here if you want to. The master's on the first floor, you wouldn't have to climb all those steps."

"I know I can stay, and I love that you want me to stay here. You've been making me feel very loved and taken care of. I probably won't though," I smirked, pulling the sheets further up my body. He made sure to leave me spent and exhausted before taking his shower. I was still lying in his California king recovering.

He jerked his head back and his thick eyebrows furrowed.

"Why not? What you got planned, Ms. Patterson?"

"Just some me time. I have some errands to run and paperwork to go through that I've been putting off."

"Errands to run like what? I'll be back tomorrow if you need me to drive you around."

"I don't. I told you I need to get back to doing things for myself. I drove over here just fine. I'm getting better every day. And my doctor's appointment tomorrow is *before* you get back. Stop worrying. What time does the opening start?"

"It's from two to six. Not too long. We'll probably go to this cigar bar Ant's been talking about taking us to afterwards."

"Cigar bar huh?" I gathered the sheet around me and rose to my knees in front of him. The clean smell of his body wash mixed with his cologne was intoxicating. "Don't you and Geo forget you have women waiting for you back here."

He smiled, leaning down, and taking my mouth in his.

"Why are you covering yourself up?"

I shrugged and said the first lie that came to mind.

"I'm a little cold. It *is* winter."

"You want me to turn the heat up?"

"No. I'm only cold because I'm naked."

In truth, I was still self-conscious about my scars, despite my attempts to pretend otherwise. I was constantly staring at the reflection of the raised and mangled flesh around my shoulder, chest and back. My body would never be the same again. I could only imagine what Race had to do to block out his repulsion while sexing me six ways to Sunday.

I didn't know if it would be possible to reconstruction the damage with plastic surgery in the future, but I was going to look into it. Race may have been sparing my feelings now, but he might not be as forgiving years from now. I wouldn't make the same mistakes with Race that I made with Michael. For Race, I would be perfect.

The doorbell rang and he zipped up the bag, placing it atop a blue duffle, also on the bed.

"Hell must've frozen over," he said looking at his watch on the way out of the bedroom. "Geo's early."

I picked up my discarded long sleeve pink pajama shirt with matching pants from the side of the bed and put them on. I was sure Geo would be coming inside, and I didn't want to be rude to my potential future brother in-law.

I had a bit of anxiety around Race's people. I hadn't had to impress anyone's family since I started dating Michael, and *his* mother was not easy to please. I felt like I was off to a better start with the Banks; however. Everybody that counted seemed to like me, and the only one who didn't, was hopefully overdosed somewhere in an abandoned house.

My phone rang and after seeing who it was, I promptly ignored it. Officer Ratcliff, or Nick, was the last person I was thinking about right now.

I straightened my appearance in the mirror and sauntered into the great room where they were talking. They were both standing under the long metallic light fixture that hung down between both floors of Race's grandiosely designed home.

Geo's dreads were piled up into a thick wraparound bun, exposing the shaved sides of his head. He was a lighter, younger, stockier, slightly shorter version of my man, but to see their faces next to each other, was to confirm they were kin.

He was more animated than Race and ran hot and cold easily from what I learned being around him. I felt like he liked me, but I wasn't sure how much. It wasn't uncommon for me to catch him watching me from the corner of my eye. Never in a lascivious manner, but more in a studying fashion. As if he was trying to learn me from a far.

Not having siblings that cared about me, I wondered if it was the common nature of people who did. Maybe it was a protective habit they acquired while trying to determine whether the person their brother or sister was dating meant them any harm. I couldn't fault Geo for that if that's why he was doing it.

"What's up Greer," Geo greeted as I approached, stopping at Race's side. "Pinky Tuscadero. I don't think I've ever seen you without something pink on."

"Good morning. I wear other colors. Pink is just my favorite."

"Sorry I haven't had a chance to see you since you've been home. It's been a little hectic at the shop lately and you know... with everything going on with Granny. Lisa said you've been doing good. How you feelin'?"

"I'm good, thank you. Your brother's been taking good care of me," I lightly touched Race's arm and smiled coyly.

On a side note, I was really starting to like my man's new curly haired look. Tapered, brushed and neat, it even snatched a few years off his age. Wearing blue jeans, sneakers and a long sleeve Orange shirt with a Tat Life logo, his outfit contrasted Geo's all green Nike sweat suit.

I wondered if his coat was in the car. I knew it would be warmer in Cali, but the weather forecast for Atlanta was only 41 degrees.

"I heard. I also heard you're not an easy patient to take care of."

"From Race or Lisa?" I placed a hand on one hip.

He shrugged and smirked. "Sorry, I don't snitch. Yo, Race, did Granny tell you they're releasing her on Friday?"

Race's lip curled. "Don't listen to her. That's what *she's* saying. The *doctor* said Saturday. *Maybe.* She be tryin' to lie to get what she wants. Like we're gonna take her out without them officially discharging her."

They snickered in unison.

"She's a trip. Me and Lisa was up there last night and she was telling the nurse what angle and grip to hold the needle when they drew her blood. Then gon' tell me when the lady left, 'These young hoes they let work here, hold the needle like they holdin' a dick for the first time. All light, and cautious. Ain't nobody got time for her to be pussyfootin' around tryin' to take my blood.'

Talmbout' 'Them older ones get in and get out. I barely feel it. But them young ones be havin' to do it more than once and when they get it right, it hurts like blazin' hell.'

Bruh. I 'bout fell out. You should've seen her face. You know I ain't wanna hear nothin' 'bout what she knows about holdin' dicks," Geo recounted animatedly. "Anyway, where's your stuff? I heard the TSA lines are bananas."

"I just have a carry on. We're only staying one night."

"Aiight. Go get it then."

"Man chill out. You're early for once in your life and now you wanna rush somebody."

"I don't want to rush *somebody*. I'm rushing *yo'* ass!"

Twenty minutes, a passionate kiss, and a bunch of reminders to be careful driving home later, Race and his brother were gone, and I was in my Yukon. I had a long day ahead of me and not enough hours in the day to do what I wanted to do.

Black coat, blue jeans, a dark blue shirt, and white sneakers on my feet, contrary to popular belief, I do wear colors other than pink. Especially when I want to be inconspicuous. I made myself a quick breakfast at home and checked in with Shan and Lisa, the only people who could predictably call my phone other than Race.

By 10:30 a.m., I had the black wig with bangs I wore as part of an old Cleopatra costume and a pair of Michael's black shades in a grocery bag as I headed back out. Without my phone. I learned a long time ago not to bring it with me if I didn't want anyone to be able to trace my movement. People existed just fine without cellphones before the 90's, and as much as I hated *not* having it, having it could be a hazard to my health, and freedom.

I didn't know who in the Nosy Brigade across the street may be watching, so I wouldn't put on the wig and glasses until I was closer to my destination. Mary J. Blige, Jill Scott and Beyoncé kept me entertained on Pandora for my little over two-hour drive to Greenville, South Carolina.

I wasn't supposed to leave the state. I know. But who was gonna tell? I had a purse full of cash to pay for everything, and the receipts were going in the parking lot trash as soon as I left. I was driving my Corolla, which was a different color than my registration since I had it repainted after I hit that rude driver.

I took a lot of side streets before I got to the highway and would do the same on my way home to avoid traffic cameras. I was going to put my car up for sale in the AJC as soon as I got a chance. I'd made a few mistakes before, but I wouldn't be making anymore.

I had weeks in the hospital to plan everything meticulously and had to revamp that plan each time a new threat made themselves known. I was better than prepared now. I hated to think of myself as a killer, because I'd also like to think of myself as a good person. But, the more people betray me, the less concerned I am about a label and the more I just want… revenge.

A few miles over the county line, I pulled into the nearest station with my wig and glasses on to get gas. I asked the cashier where the nearest drug store was and as luck would have it, there was a Walgreens just a half a mile on the left.

I only needed one thing from there; a six pack of dark color, non-prescription contact lenses. When you have green eyes like mine, people remember them no matter what your hair looks like. I asked a customer in line at the register if she knew where a Walmart was. I'm glad southern hospitality was still alive. She didn't know but looked up the nearest location on her phone for me.

Less than five minutes later, I perused the aisles with a cart purchasing rope, off brand sneakers, one size bigger than my actual fit, multiple pairs of long sleeve thermal underwear and a few pairs of cheap black sweats.

Add to that, two 20-pound adjustable weighted workout fitness belts, and a thick pack of socks. I noticed a beauty supply store on my way back to the highway and stopped in. Although very different from my natural look, I was self-conscious that the wig I was wearing wasn't inconspicuous enough to wear often.

I bought two more shoulder length wigs and foundation about two shades darker than my natural color. Being that it was winter, I'd be covered in clothes everywhere except from the neck up, so this darker foundation would be the perfect camouflage for me.

I would wear gloves to hide my hands, but the plan was not to be seen by anyone close up anyway. From a far at least, I knew I would look totally different if spotted in person, or by camera.

I began feeling inordinately drowsy on the way home, and I was late for my next dose of meds. I became even more paranoid about staying under the speed limit, knowing I couldn't afford to be pulled over.

I was ecstatic when I finally made it to my driveway without red and blue lights flashing behind me. I still wasn't in good enough condition to comfortably tackle multiple trips upstairs. So, I detoured to the kitchen, made myself a sandwich and brought a glass of juice with me to take my meds.

I left everything in their bags and stuffed them in the back of my closet before checking my phone. No calls, but Race texted me to say he got there safely. I hoped to make it back before he landed, but I didn't. It was barely past four o'clock, and Cali being three hours behind, I knew the event hadn't started yet.

"Hey babe," Race answered my call with a lot of chatter in the background.

"Hey. I'm just seeing your text. I had my ringer off."

"I figured. It's cool."

"Are you at the opening already?"

"Nah, it doesn't start until two. Me and Geo gettin' grub from the hotel restaurant right now."

"Aren't they gonna have food there?"

"We'll eat when we get there too."

I laughed. "How was your flight."

"I slept through it. We didn't crash and we landed on time. That's good enough for me. You get a lot done?"

"For the most part."

"That's good. So, how about Ant promoted me and Geo as guest artists without telling us."

"What's that mean?"

"It means we're supposed to be tattooing people at the opening. That's not something you just spring on somebody. I told his black ass no when he asked me, and he put me on the flyers anyway."

"*Ohhh.* Geo too?"

"Yeah. He *knew* he was doing it though. I told Ant I wasn't in the right head space to ink anybody when he asked, and this dude set appointments for me anyway. I don't even like using other people's equipment. And check who my first client is supposed to be."

"Who?"

"Jim Jamerson."

"Who's that?"

"He's an MMA fighter. Apparently, he follows Tat Life on IG and he's likes my work. Requested me specifically when he heard I would be here."

"Oh, that's real good, baby," I yawned. "Real good. Excuse me. I'm getting tired."

"It's cool. Yeah, it would be good for business, but I don't like being blindsided. Tattooing is therapeutic for me. I don't do my best work when I'm not focused."

"Why wouldn't you be focused? Granny's okay, I'm okay, and Carmen's probably fine too. Wherever she is, she chose to be there. You can't control her, or anybody else, baby. I know you weren't ready for it, but this could be a big opportunity for you. Embrace it."

He sighed into the phone.

"See, this is why I love you. Look at you, supporting your man."

I giggled. "Of course."

"You're right though. Like Granny says, 'God's will, will be done, whether you cosign it or not.' I'm gonna stop trying to drive and just let Jesus take the wheel."

Tuh! I hated to disagree with my man, and I wasn't going to do it aloud now, but I believe, the Lord helps those who help themselves.

I was going to do what I needed to and rely on his assistance, rather than his lead.

10

Greer

December 16th 2015

I hate Christmas time. The seasonal bliss that seemingly graces the faces and hearts of people on the streets each year has always eluded me. I never had a reason to adore the holiday that most of America celebrates as a time for family to come together, when mine treated me like a stray the other 364 days.

Oh, I ate at the decorated dinner table and got presents like everybody else. My father would never have allowed my stepmother and siblings to be so blatantly hateful in his presence. But the chatter was always around me, and not to me. I felt like an invader in my own home. My gifts were never what I wanted, rarely what I needed and inevitably delivered with feigned kindness.

My only comfort and joy on Christmas morning, was cuddling in my daddy's lap as a small child. I would watch the sparkling lights on the tree with one of the two or three gifts I would have received, clasped in my hand as the other kids ripped through the wrapping paper on theirs.

As I got older, seven to be exact, Stephanie insisted Daddy stop coddling me. She claimed it showed favoritism, making the other girls jealous, and of course, Daddy relented. In the future, I would sit on the floor beside his chair like a faithful little pup, invariably mute and timid.

I expected it to be a particularly miserable Christmas this year, even with Race in my life. As stupid of me as it is, I've never known life without my father's simulated affection. It was real to me, and frankly, I was going to miss my niece's grinning face frolicking through Santa's spoils on Christmas morn.

The street decorations and rotating jingles on the radio, only made my already delicate stomach roil as I pulled into the parking lot. Corrine was squealing before I reached the partition. Her plump brown cheeks housing a wide toothed smile.

"Greer!"

"Didn't you know I was coming? I should be on the schedule."

"You are! But I'm still happy to see you. You're early too. Come on and sign in, Miss Thang. How've you been?"

Maybe she had the holiday spirit, but Corrine was never this enthusiastic to see or work for me before. We were close in age and I'm sure she thought of us as equals since the majority of the staff, sans doctors, were younger than the both of us.

We were not, however.

"As good as expected. How have things been around here?"

She rolled her eyes, tossing her braids back from her face and leaned through the open window, speaking in a hushed tone.

"Chaos. We short-handed like a one-armed bandit. Don't barely nobody that's here know what they're doing half the time."

"Why's that? I haven't been gone *that* long."

"Long enough. Angie and Fatima been trying to cover your job and see patients too, but from how the doctors have been complaining, I don't think they been doin' too good. They already messed up payroll once.

Quincy's out on maternity leave and Nicky quit the week after they found Kendrick in the stairs. Did anybody tell you he died, or was you already in the hospital when they found him?"

"I heard what happened. So, Nicky just quit? No notice?"

She propped one elbow on the sill and dropped her chin in her hand.

"Not that I know of. One day she was here. The next day she wasn't."

"Humph."

There was one other person in the waiting room, likely out of clear earshot, but this conversation was inappropriate in front of patients none the less. Had I been on duty as the Office Manager, I would have checked her behavior. But seeing as I was interested in the goings on in the office in my absence, I would save her reprimand until *after* I got all the tea.

"Isn't that bizarre?" she whispered lower. "I heard it might not have been an accident. The police asked me a lot of questions about Angie and Nicky. I don't know, maybe Nicky quit for—a—reason." She over enunciated with raised brows. "Did you hear anything about that?"

"No. I can't say I have," I answered dryly, imagining that she gossiped about me as much as she was gossiping about everything else. I wondered if she knew I was one of Kendrick's bed mates too.

"Oh. *I* heard Nicky and Angie was both sleeping with Kendrick and Ni—"

"Corrine," Angie's stern voice startled her to attention. "Can you stop running your mouth and bring my patient back?"

"I was just getting ready to. I had to check Greer in. Did you see that she was here?" Embarrassed, she looked between us, then hurriedly disappeared from the window.

I nodded a greeting to Angie but received pursed lips and a cocked brow in return. Apparently, the grudge she had against me before Kendrick's death was still pressing. She icily pivoted on her heels towards the hallway of patient rooms and stalked wordlessly away. Seconds later, Corrine held open the door to the waiting room with a chart in her other hand.

"Dominique Martin?"

The other woman in the waiting room stood, looking between Corrine and I curiously. She gathered her bag and phone from the table and walked briskly through the door with Corrine in tow.

My appointment was one of the earliest of the morning, and I supposed other patients would be trickling in shortly. No sooner had I put my purse down than the waiting room door opened again.

"Greer. Come on back, Hun," Dr. Lancaster greeted.

Surprised, I tentatively got my things and rose to follow.

"Dr. Lancaster, why are *you* bringing me back yourself? Where is everybody?"

She shook her brown coiffed hair and aggravatedly fanned the air with the hand holding my chart.

"Oh, I didn't have to. I just did. I know you're early, but since I saw you out there, I figured I would. That Erica girl is never where she's supposed to be anyway. I have to get on her about *something* almost daily. These girls don't know *what* they're doing without you here to whip them into shape. We're in room four."

She smiled at me as I glanced past her at the empty intake desk and held in a scoff. At least one person should have been manning the phones and signing people in while another took patients back to their rooms. Scheduling staff wasn't rocket science.

"Before I forget, thank you for the flowers."

"You're so welcome sweetheart. I think everyone here that day signed the card. It's the least we could do to try to bring some cheer your way during these trying times. I'm more than ready for 2016 to get here. This has been a tragic couple of months for us all."

We stopped in the hall where she took my weight on the scale, then went into the room. I put my things down and sat on the exam table for her to take my blood pressure.

"It's good to see you. How have you been holding up?"

I sighed. Preparing to deliver the monologue I knew would be necessary during this visit. People would have questions. What happened to me wasn't a secret, but I needed to put my own spin on how it was portrayed in the media. I'm sure Dr. Lancaster would be sharing the non-medical parts of our conversation with her colleagues.

"I guess I'm fine. Things at home obviously aren't great. My father and I are now estranged after what he did to me, and now I'll probably be alone for the holidays. My family is… really screwed up. That long hospital stay, and the media back in my face again may have taken a bit of a toll on me too. You remember how vicious and relentless they were after Michael's death."

"I do. I've heard that a couple of them came here asking questions too. Of course, the staff has been instructed not to answer any questions from anyone other than the police, and reporters have been asked to leave. We're rattled enough here trying to get over Kendrick's death without being bombarded with questions from media piranha.

On another note, your blood pressure is a little higher than I would like, and you've lost a considerable amount of weight for your physique. Have you been taking your medication as prescribed?"

She removed the pressure cuff from my forearm and to a small stool, awaking the computer to begin entering my vital information in the system.

"I have."

"Are you experiencing a loss of appetite? Depression? Any side effects from the medications?"

"My appetite is better since I was discharged," I smiled. "I didn't care much for hospital food. I don't know if I'm depressed, but I might be. There's a lot to be depressed about. Then somebody broke into my house the day I got home. So, there's that."

She gasped, turning back to face me with her already light features paling.

"Oh! My word! Were you harmed?"

"No. Just scared. Makes it kind of hard to keep your blood pressure down when your bad luck just keeps increasing. First my husband is killed by his mistress, and now all of this. You probably think I'm a horrible person."

"Not at all. Greer, I don't pretend to know your personal business, and I would never want to pry, but in the years you've worked here, you've shown yourself to be nothing less than a kind, smart, loving person."

"I try to be Dr. Lancaster, but what do you do when it feels like the whole universe is against you? That night, my father called me saying suicidal things. Yes, I had been drinking, before he called. But my first thought, was my father and *his* safety.

I made a bad decision to drive over there instead of just calling the police. I just thought… I thought I could stop him if he actually tried to do it and ended up getting shot myself.

Somehow, the news got the story all twisted and…" I began to sob. "I'm suddenly the one who came over there to kill him."

She pet, then rubbed a light sympathetic circle around my shoulder.

"There, there now. Don't cry. I see the news like everyone else, but I know they don't always have the full story. I don't understand what happened, and I don't need to. What's important is that you're okay. Maybe you should speak to someone. A psychiatrist or therapist? We all need help sometimes an—"

Erica's reluctant blue eyes peered into the room as she slowly opened the door. One hand fidgeting with the blonde ponytail hanging over one shoulder, her enlarged pupils darting between the two of us tentatively. I wondered if she was high while I hastily wiped tears from my face.

"Dr. Lancaster. I'm sorry I didn't bring her back for you. I must've been in the bathroom when she came in. I'm here now. I can pick up wherever you left off and come get you afterwards."

Dr. Lancaster's previously benevolent disposition froze over.

"Never walk into a room occupied by a patient with a closed door, without knocking. We'll discuss where you were and why I had to bring my own patient back another time.

For the moment, I think you'd best serve the practice now by ensuring no other patients have arrived without being tended to. We're fine here."

"Yes ma'am."

Erica glanced at my damped face, then quickly shut the door.

"She may need to be replaced," Dr. Lancaster huffed.

"I'll get in touch with the staffing agency we use as soon as I'm back."

"Well, right now, I'm going to leave out and let you change into this gown," she handed me the folder paper garment from the counter and stood. "I'll be back in a few minutes to see if you're ready and give you a complete exam."

She winked, pat my hand empathetically and left. I exhaled and fingered my own bushy ponytail. My work would be cut out for me upon my return. Twenty-Five minutes later, my exam was over, and I was redressed in jeans, a blue turtleneck and boots, headed to my office.

I was told that for the most part, I was progressing satisfactorily. My breathing was good, my lung sound was strong, and my wounds were healing well. She did make minor changes, however. I was only to use the Oxy as needed rather than in scheduled doses to prevent gaining a possible addiction to it. She recommended some changes in my diet, mostly a higher intake of green vegetables, and updated my wound care advisement.

My next appointment would be in two weeks on the 30th. I was scheduled to return to work on the 4th., but I advised Dr. Lancaster that my court date was on the 6th and she okayed extending my return until the 11th, which I accepted.

I knew they needed me with the staff issues and all, but I wasn't sure if everything I had to do would get done before I had to work anyway. Doing what I had to do was already going to be tedious without having to juggle work on top of it.

Instead of going straight to check out, I detoured down the hall to my office. Something caught my attention as I passed Angie's station, causing me to stop. I ensured no one was in the hall on either side of me before reaching across her paper riddled desk and plucking the funeral program from the corner of her cork board. Kendrick Spears.

Not wanting to get caught red handed, I hurriedly strut to my office and sat behind my desk, holding the program in my lap. The heartfelt poems and kind words included by loved ones almost made me remorseful of his death. Almost. At least he was loved by many.

I quickly shoved it into my purse when Dr. Lancaster surprised me with a rapid knock on the door and a reminder not to stay too long as she passed. I recomposed myself and ran a nervous hand through my hair before plucking the Clorox wipes from my draw to wipe down my desk, computer, and keyboard.

My office remained in much the same condition as it was on my last day there. It was obvious that someone or ones rummaged through the paperwork on my desk. I assumed it was Angie, Fatima or one of the doctors in search of information while I was out.

I wasn't officially working, but I did tell Dr. Lancaster I would try to answer any pending voice messages, emails or notes on my desk before I left. Turning on my computer and seeing the abundance of pending emails, I was in the process of keeping my word, when I felt a presence looming from the door.

Looking up, my gaze met Angie's inhospitable one. She was leaning against the frame with her arms folded across the breast of her medical coat. Dark hair curled in ringlets hung down to just above her shoulders. She was pretty. In the basic sense of the word.

"Can I help you with something?"

"As a matter of fact, you can."

She entered, closing the door behind her, then proceeded to sit in the chair on the other side of my desk. Her smug expression instantly churned the bile in my throat.

"It must be fate that you were scheduled to come in here today. I was already going to call you."

"You don't seem too happy to see me. What were you going to call me for?"

"To ask you why you stole my prescription pad and to see if your explanation would be good enough to stop me from reporting you to the police."

I kept my outward composure but was far from it. My arms mimicking her previously crossed ones, I straightened in my chair.

"I beg your pardon?"

"Don't even bother to play stupid. As you know, PDMP reports generate on the 15th of every month. Every doctor and NP here is required to review and sign off on theirs and give them to *you*, by the end of the month to stay compliant. Well, I was looking over mine, and you'll never guess what I discovered."

I remained silently stoic. PDMP stands for Prescription Drug Monitoring Program. It's a state monitored database used to streamline prescriptions written by every prescribing doctor and nurse practitioner. Essentially, it's cross referenced with pharmacy filled prescriptions to prevent overprescribing opioids and other addictive medications by physicians.

I feared what she would say next but refused to voluntarily incriminate myself. She leaned forward with a smirk, and that's when I noticed the glossy look in her eyes along with the slight aroma of alcohol and mint wafting off of her. Was this silly broad drinking on the job now too?

I knew she drank heavily outside of work, and told me herself that she often used it to put herself to sleep at night. It was an unhealthy solution to what I deemed as some form of depression, but hey, she was the physician.

"No guess?" She smirked. "Okay. Funnily enough, I found a prescription that I don't recall ever writing, for Cytotec pills to one Charles Foster. When I looked in our patient system, I couldn't find him. No Charles Foster. The name seemed *sooo* familiar to me though. I couldn't for the life of me, remember why," her theatrical tone and Cheshire cat grin made me want to claw her eyes out. "Then, it finally dawned on me. Isn't Greer's father's name Chuck Foster? Hmmm. Chuck. Charles. Could they be the same person?"

I leaned my elbows onto my desk and steepled my hands in front of me. She met my father briefly, the day she was supposed to be helping with my yard sale, but merely showed up near the end. God damn her good memory.

"Your point?"

"My point is, that one of my prescription pads has been missing for a few weeks now. Ironically, a prescription I never wrote, for a patient I never saw, is now showing on my PDMP report. And that patient, is coincidentally *your* father. What are the odds?"

"Have you been drinking? Because you smell like it."

Her eyes grew indignantly and she sat back again.

"You must be part Bloodhound. I spilled some on my jacket last night and my other one is in the drycleaners."

It was a blatant and obvious lie, but she was wasting my time.

"Angie, what exactly is it that you want?"

"What do I want? You know, you're pretty fucking superior for somebody who stole my prescription pad and forged my signature. I'm sure you're aware that's a felony. A better question is, why would you do something so stupid?"

I suppose my cool demeanor was blowing her plan to intimidate me. Now she was exposing her fangs and showing her full, nasty colors.

"My father was experiencing a lot of side effects from the cancer treatments he underwent. He's also getting old, and as is with some old people, their joints aren't as strong as they used to be. What he was already prescribed wasn't helping and his doctors refused to prescribe anything else to help him. I was just trying to alleviate the pain for him. He was really suffering."

"Was he? So, why didn't you just come to me and explain what was going on, rather than stealing my prescription pad and writing it yourself? A simple appointment could have allowed me to assess him and see if there was some other way to help him. What if he would have had a bad reaction or died?"

"Well, he didn't. I didn't come to you about it because you were busy being mad at me over something that happened long before you should have cared about it. You were angry about something petty and I was worried about my father."

"*Excuse* me? Are you talking about you and Kendrick? Because if you are, please don't try to make yourself out to be the victim. You and he were screwing for... at least a month if not more. You knew he and I were seeing each other. Still, when I asked you point blank if something was going on with y'all, you lied to my face."

"It wasn't your business. It wasn't anybody's business. It didn't happen during the time you were seeing him. It wasn't serious, it didn't last long, and he was my subordinate. We both agreed that it would make things easier at work if no one knew."

"Alright. But I thought we were more than just co-workers. I thought we were friends. I shared my personal struggles with you. *Outside* of work."

"As did I."

"Not as much as I did. I was sympathetic and tried to keep your spirits up during your husband's murder trial. Like… were we not friends?"

I sighed, tilting my head in disbelief. I had more pressing issues to tend to than stroking Angie's bruised ego, but if appeasing it would prevent her from reporting me to the police.

"Of course, we were friends. I tried to explain it to you that day in my office, but you stormed out of here with your mind already made up. And for the record, I didn't *steal* your prescription pad. You left it on my desk. I just didn't give it back."

Her eyes rolled. "Greer, please. Cut the shit. *However* you got it, you shouldn't have had it and you damn sure shouldn't have signed my name on it."

"You're right. I apologize. I shouldn't have. I was desperate at the time. He was in a lot of pain and I didn't think that one prescription would be noticed. I made a mistake."

"Yeah. You made a mistake. I work too hard to have my license jeopardized by you or anybody else. I'm out here barely scraping by day to day and *this* is the position you want to put me in? We don't *all* have a cushy life insurance policy to fall back on if we get laid off.

I'm working two jobs now just to make ends meet. I've got debt out the ass, and my dad's not helping me pay them anymore since I refused to support his gay or bi-sexual… whatever it is lifestyle."

"I'm sorry. I thought you made up with your dad when you found out your mom already knew he was dealing with men too. I didn't know you were working a second job either."

"No, we didn't make up. She can accept what she wants, but I'm not accepting him putting up this façade my whole life and trying to act like

I'm in the wrong for being angry about it. And yeah, I work from 7:00 p.m. to 11:00 p.m. at East Dekalb Med, an *hour* away from my house, six days a week. Not five days. *Six* days. You know what day I have off? Tuesday. So, I never have a week where I get a full day off anymore."

"I was looking at the schedule. At least you have all next week off to relax and regroup. Are you going to spend the holiday with your family?"

She scoffed.

"I *just* said I didn't make up with my father, Greer. See, you're not even listening when I'm talking directly to you."

"I am listening. I know you usually take off Christmas to visit them is all. Are you going to visit somewhere else?"

"Me, myself and I are going to celebrate by the fireplace watching movies and keeping warm with as many bottles of Bacardi as my liver can handle. Probably the same thing you'll be doing unless you and your father made up?" She smirked.

I pressed my lips into a thin line and swallowed the urge to curse her out.

"Well, I hope you have a good vacation. If that's all, I'm gonna finish up what I'm doing here and leave."

"Greer. Darling. That is definitely, *not* all. You're not getting off that easy. Some of us, can't *afford* to make 'a mistake', as you called it and not reap the consequences. You shouldn't either."

If I had dog ears, they would have stood straight up at attention. I sensed the other shoe about to drop, and if she was eluding to what I thought she was, Angie, was going to become another problem for me.

"What are you saying?"

"I'm *saying*, I can either report what you did, which means you'll not only be fired, but you'll also be arrested. I heard you can get up to five years in jail for something like that. Or, you can give me a reason not to." She flopped comfortably back in the chair, eying me menacingly with her hands firmly clasped together. "Perhaps, a few *hundred thousand*, reasons."

11

Greer

If not for prescription drugs, I wouldn't have slept a wink. I locked myself in my bedroom with a knife and stun gun under my pillow. Alarm system or no, I felt like I needed a weapon at arm's reach to feel secure.

At least I hadn't dreamt of my father shooting me in the face. Instead, I had nightmares of being beaten to death by an intruder in the basement of my own home, who turned out to be Angie. Lucky me.

That wench had the nerve to try and blackmail me. Three hundred thousand dollars was the cost of her silence. It was easy for her to believe my counterfeit agreeance because I went to the bank after I left the office and withdrew $5000 from my bank, while wearing winter gloves. Then I had her meet me in the lot where I handed it to her as a deposit on the rest.

I didn't want my fingerprints on that money at all while it was in her possession. I reminded her that it would be in both of our best interests to be cautious to prevent anything we were doing from being traceable.

I promised her I would take out larger increments as soon as I made some transfers and I'd have another $50,000 for her by the following week. Little did she know, $5K would be the only money she was ever going to receive from me.

Her greedy little grin and warning not to try any tricks on her, all but solidified that her death day would be coming soon. The demise I planned for Debbie, would now be tweaked to fit Angie's undoing. STAT.

I hated not having the ability to outline and check off the multiple tasks requiring completion, but I risked a paper or computer trail discovery if I did. One too many episodes of "Snapped" and "CSI" included evidence of lists, computer searches and the like to aid law enforcement in obtaining solid convictions.

Fortunately, my memory has always been stellar, and I hoped it wouldn't suddenly fail me on things with *this* level of importance. I had *a lot* of important things to memorize. Anyhoo, the first thing I did after breakfast, was order an edible arrangement for Karen. I appreciated her kindness and hospitality the other night and wanted to say so in a noticeable way. I strategically set up delivery for Sunday, the 20th, that way she'd get it *after* Rolly was "sold".

Hair tightly wound in a top bun, thick black leggings, and a baby blue fleece sweater, I slipped my socked feet into black leather boots and placed the single pair of Gucci glasses I owned on my face. It was a warm 51 degrees for December, so I grabbed my purse, forewent a coat, and climbed up in my Yukon in the driveway.

Thirty-six minutes later, I arrived at *Will's Auto Experts* and pulled into one of the four vehicle service lanes. Leaving my keys in the ignition, I got out and went into the store side of the building. The storefront was maybe 500 square feet, connected to a large garage where they worked on cars.

"G-Greer?" Will's dark brown face lit up in a combination of surprise, ambivalence, and glee. His 6'2 teddy bear body rounded the counter with arms warmly outstretched. "What are you doing here?"

"I came to get my car fixed," I smiled, accepting the brief hug.

"Oh, wow. Okay. You drove yourself?" He looked behind me nervously.

"Yeah. I'm okay to drive."

"It's the Yukon this time I see. What's wrong with it?"

"Nothing major. I hope. I know for sure it needs an oil change, but my heat hasn't been working right either. It's blowing cool air on me when I turn the heater on. It doesn't matter if I turn it up high or low. You know, I don't pretend to know cars, and I didn't know if that was related to me needing an oil change, or what."

"Probably not," he rubbed the stubble on his chin and stood akimbo in thought. "Probably something to do with the coolant system or the antifreeze. I'll have the guys look at it. Umm… does Debbie know you're here?"

I reared back and pressed my lips into a tight line.

"Are you trying to be funny? Since when have I ever ran what I do through her? Why? Do I need to now?"

"*Noooo.* I mean… well maybe. Don't get me wrong. I'm happy to see you. I'm glad to see our prayers worked. You look wonderful. Uh…healthy! Healthy, is what I meant to say. You look *healthy.* Healed. But, Debbie… she's been on a rampage since your daddy got shot and… I just don't want to make any waves with her if she finds out I be—"

I held a hand up to stop his rambling. Debbie sometimes made accusations that the reason he was so nice to me, was because he was also attracted to me. It's a reach. If anybody knows Will's kindhearted, god fearing spirit, it *should* be his wife. But I believe Debbie inherited Stephanie's suspicious and often irrational nature, regardless of the benevolent man Will has proven himself to be.

The mere fact that he hasn't strangled her for the harsh way she talks to him and everybody else, on top of her selfish ass behavior, should have earned him the Nobel Peace Prize.

"Will. Calm down. I'm here to get my car fixed. Now, you've been my mechanic since you opened this shop. Are you telling me you don't want my business anymore because my deranged sister said so?"

"She didn't say so…" his head dropped shamefully before his regretful eyes met mine again. "But you know how she is. I can't even say your *name* anymore without her biting my head off. Now I know y'all have always had trouble, and I try to stay out of it, or keep the peace. But this is different. *She's* different."

"Tuh. Different than what? The pit bull in a bad wig she's always been? Now, I don't doubt she's meaner, because I just found out the other day that she's helping my husband's murderer with her appeal to spite me. So, she's clearly more venomous than usual. Has she told *you* what that's all about?"

He sighed. His broad, cowardly shoulders sinking lower as my eyes rolled behind my shades. He was such a punk when it came to Debbie.

"Boss Man? What are we doing on the Yukon?" A tall white guy in work overalls and a ski hat asked from the doorway to the shop area.

"Oil change and a diagnosis to see why the heat isn't working."

Ski Hat threw a thumb up and went back in the shop. Will looked like a deer in headlights when he turned back to me, then looked at the two people sitting in the makeshift waiting area that I hadn't noticed previously. One was watching whatever was on the hanging flatscreen TV and the other's face was buried in their phone.

"Hey, Greer, I've got customers. Why don't we pick up this conversation another time," he stated more than asked.

"When exactly is that supposed to be, Will?" I stepped closer to him and lowered my voice, trying to sound less confrontational. "I'm dealing with enough without Debbie adding to it. You're right. You *have* always tried to stay out of it, or mediate. I'm really not trying to drag you into anything, but a reporter ambushed me at my house. Can you blame me for being upset?"

"I'm sorry about that. I didn't know that happened."

"Do you know what she's telling Marlene's attorney?"

He exhaled exasperatedly, looking away from me guiltily.

"Will?"

"Hold on a minute." He picked up the phone behind the desk, pressed a button and spoke into the receiver. "Hey. Do me a favor and come man the front for me real quick. I gotta step away for a second... Okay."

He hung up, and we stood in silence until Rodger's creepy ass stalked through the shop door, pulling work gloves from his hands. He stutter stepped when he saw me, replacing his usual dumbstruck expression with a lascivious grin.

"Hey there Greer."

"Hi."

"I heard about what happened to you. Glad to see you're home now."

"Thank you," I smiled curtly, readjusting the purse on my shoulder, and taking a step back.

He had no respect for personal space and the first thing he did was invade mine. He was big and light skin with coke bottle glasses, wild acne, and a mouth full of crooked teeth he flashed at me too often. He made my skin crawl but was obviously as smitten with me as I was repulsed by him.

"I'll be back in a few minutes," Will told him, placing a friendly hand on Rodger's shoulder. "Come on back here with me, Greer."

I followed Will into his office, avoiding eye contact with the big oaf molesting me with his. Will closed the door behind me, and we both stalled in front of his desk.

"Alright. Listen. First, I want to make it clear that *I* don't condone what she's been doing or what she's been saying about you." One hand rested against his chest with conviction. "Debbie's her own person, and I can't control her."

I exhaled impatiently, awaiting news of something I didn't already know. He ran a nervous hand over his receding hairline, looked up to the ceiling, then down into my face.

"She's convinced you tried to kill Chuck because he knows you killed Michael."

"What? That's ridiculous. Did he tell her that's why I shot him?"

He shook his head emphatically.

"*He* said you believed he killed your mother because of some fiction story Shawn wrote when he was a teenager."

"It wasn't fiction, and that's not why I shot him. I shot him because he was going for his gun to shoot *me* when I came to confront him about it."

He held his palms up defensively.

"Okay. Well, I'm just telling you what *he* said. You was drunk and inconsolable and he had to shoot you to defend himself."

"You know what? I'm not even gonna sit here and explain myself, because I'm gonna have to do that in court. What I want to know is what *that* has to do with her malicious accusations about *me* killing my husband?"

"She doesn't believe that's why you shot him. She thinks you used Shawn's story as an excuse to kill him because he knew you weren't at the house when Michael was killed."

I chuckled satirically.

"Are you sure she's not back on drugs again?"

"Greer, come on now."

"What do you mean, *'come on now'*? She's around here making wild and unfounded accusations about me out of thin air, and you don't think anything is wrong with that? The case is closed. My phone records prove I was at the house the whole time I said I was there and traffic cams show me leaving and arriving at my house exactly as I said it happened. I was his wife for Christ's sake!" I wailed. "I was the first one they investigated. Who is she supposed to be, Olivia Pope now? The bitch that killed him has been convicted of it. Why is she trying to get her out?"

Hot tears fled my eyes as I quickly swiped them with the heels of my palms. That bitch made my blood boil. Did she really know something?

"Oh lord. Don't cry. I'm sorry. I tried to reason with her, but she won't let it go."

"If Daddy didn't think I was there, why didn't he tell the police that then? Huh? I mean, did he tell her he doesn't think I was there?"

"Naw. He told her to let it go too. I heard him say himself, that as far as he knows you were there."

I was surprised Daddy still had my back on this after his show of disloyalty in front of Race, but thankful for it.

"Still, she uh… has this theory that you took Stephanie's car and… I… I really don't know what to tell you, Greer. To be honest with ya', I don't even listen to her anymore when she gets to talking about it. I suppose that's why she went down to that gal's attorney and them news people. Trying to be heard.

Look, *you* know there's no truth to it. Other than kicking up bad press for you, it's not gonna do anything to hurt you or to get that gal out. Just… ignore her and this'll all die down soon."

I sniffled the last evidence of my tears away and was glad he couldn't see the rancor in my eyes. He was so God damned weak for that Wench. Ignore her. She'd been trying to destroy me virtually every day of my life since we were kids, and he wanted me to *'ignore her'*? The fuck I would.

I inhaled the calm back into my demeanor and exhaled all indications of my hostility through my nostrils. Correcting my posture, I held my chin up and placed a hand on the doorknob.

"I'm just gonna wait out there for my car to be ready. Thanks for talking to me."

I had the door open and was walking through it before he could say another word. Rodger's eyes were fixed on me as he finished a sports drink and tossed the bottle in the trash. He was closer to the office door than was necessary, which probably meant he'd been eavesdropping.

"Hey. They came back with the estimate on your car. I got them working on your oil change already, but we were waiting on your approval before doing the other work."

I stopped in front of him and rested an elbow on the counter.

"What'd they find?."

"Turns out it's just a leak in the radiator hose. Which is good news. Cause that's pretty simple to fix, and cheap. With the 99-dollar oil change special we're running on trucks, plus replacement and repair of the hose, your total's only gonna be $149."

"This one's on the house," Will interrupted looking over Rodger's shoulder at the screen.

"No. That's okay. I'll pay for it. I wouldn't want your wife to find out you're comping my car repairs."

Rodger looked confoundedly between us.

"*Weeeell,* I can pay for it if you want. It could be like a Christmas gift from me to you." He smiled big. Pleased with his gesture.

"Boy, you don't even have a steady place to rest your head right now. Cut it out," Will scolded.

Rodger's light face brightened with embarrassment.

"No. Thank you. I can pay for myself. Just let me know when it's ready."

Both men watched my back as I found a seat in the waiting area and sat. My car was having heating issues, but my primary reason for coming was to get intel on what Debbie had against me from Will. My mission was accomplished, but I was still steaming at the news.

My sister was a menace to my life. If she was alive, she would never let me live in peace. That would need to be remedied, STAT!

I waited another half hour for my car to be ready, paid and left without another word or glance in Will's direction. Nick called on my way home. The conversation was light, yet revealing early on, and I realized he would be far less useful to me than I originally thought. Not only was he still a rookie of less than a year on the force, but he lived with his girlfriend and their six-month-old son.

Not once had he brought *that* up in our lengthy conversations, but now that I was released, I assume he thought this was a good time to come clean. I initially thought I could use him to get inside information on my case, or at least, to entertain me in my singledom the way Kendrick had when I thought Race and I were over.

Alas, he dashed those prospects when he brought up the girlfriend and their child. I'm not a homewrecker and I would never be a side-piece. I told him I had another call and abruptly hung up while he was mid-sentence. Boy bye!

The man my heart really beat for called just as I walked in the door and brightened my frustrated mood. He let me know he was back from Cali and would be headed my way after he visited Granny at the hospital.

We bantered a few more minutes before hanging up, and I soon settled in front of my computer with microwaved stuffed peppers on my plate and a glass of wine in my hand. I was on task now to place an ad for my Corolla in the Atlanta Journal Constitution. I had no actual intention on selling good old Rolly. Not right now. But I needed to place the ad *now*, to authenticate the sale in the meanwhile.

I listed my home number, which I rarely, if ever answered, and Google searched a Bill of Sale form to download. I made up the buyer's name and South Carolina address from a combination of things I saw on my road trip. I also made sure to fill out the seller information with my right hand, and the fake purchaser information with my left. I was also very careful to change the way I typically wrote each letter.

Being thorough, I also postdated the sale to the 19th as I anticipated being able to dodge Race for at least part of the day to pretend I sold the car then. I intended to park it in a low traffic residential neighborhood I was familiar with for whenever I needed it. It was well within walking distance to a MARTA station, so I could easily walk from home to the train or bus, and be able to do the same back from my car.

I dug out an old license plate Michael had in our basement, taken off his very first car. It was totaled in an accident when he was 17, but he kept the plate because it ironically included the numbers from the date of the crash. He believed it to be some sort of divine sign. Of what, I had no idea, but his nostalgia turned out to be a godsend for me.

I would eventually switch it with the current one on my Corolla and put the GA sticker from my newer tag on it. My only constant concern would be making sure I never got pulled over and hoping the car never got towed.

Regardless, I believed I had all foreseeable bases covered. If my car were caught on camera, it would be a different color blue than what the DMV had listed for me. I never updated my records after Will re-painted it, and now, the license plate would be different too.

If I were photographed driving it by chance, I would also look very different with my disguise on. As always, unless I was in a particular rush, I would take as many back roads as possible to avoid being caught by modern day technology.

I don't think you can ever be too careful when doing something il-legal. Underestimating unforeseen circumstances and police investiga-tions sent many a clever criminal to jail. I had no desire to add myself to the many examples of convicts who weren't as smart as they thought they were.

I anticipated executing everything I needed to do in the next 30 to 60 days. Afterwards, I would sell Rolly for real, or bring it to a junk-yard to be compacted. Either way, it would be gone for good, as would the last link to my sins and every individual I had to eliminate in the process.

Just a few weeks ago, I would not have thought of myself as a crim-inal. I would have justified everything I was doing as retaliation for the terrible wrongs others have done to me. But now, as I traced the gnarled flesh resulting from thine's own father's bullet with my finger-tips; I accepted this one, pure, unadulterated truth about myself. I can and will unapologetically *end* anyone who threatens my love, happi-ness, or livelihood, *ever* again. Period.

12

Greer

December 16th 2015

My lips suctioned and swaddled Race's long, thick shaft as he greedily feasted on my engorged bud. Hips bucking against his dampened face, my orgasm churned strenuously beneath the surface, ready to explode.

"Cum for me baby," he garbled between my folds.

Already at the cusp, his wish almost instantly commanded the flow of all the juices he conjured to intensify and gush into his awaiting mouth.

I released his girth from my throat only to allow the squeals of ecstasy I could not contain to escape. His large hands clamped my thighs down around his head until my body had no more to give.

He lifted me off him and placed me on my stomach, slightly writhing, eyes closed in an abyss of pleasure. My pelvis was soon filled with his meaty mass, driving in and out of my vaginal walls like a piston.

"Oh! Oh God!" I wailed, clinching the bedsheets with every thrust.

Ding Dong! Ding Dong!

Whoever was at the door had terrible timing. I planned to ignore it. I was grown and the only person I might have even slightly felt compelled to answer to, was currently pole driving me. Race must've thought similarly as he hadn't broken his stride in the least.

Ding Dong! Ding Dong!

Unanswered, the ringing stopped. Race reached his climax maybe three or four minutes later, summoning one from me as well. We both lay splayed out on the bed. Me on my stomach. He on his back. A giggly lust filled conversation ensuing. Then it started again.

Ding Dong! Ding Dong!

"The fuck is that?" he questioned rising from the bed, putting on his T-shirt and sliding on his sweatpants, sans the boxer briefs he wore under them when he arrived.

I didn't ask him to answer the door, nor did I particularly want him to. Whoever it was could've rang until their fingers fell off for all I cared. But I wouldn't stop him from doing it if he wanted to. He was my protector, and I liked that.

"You know I can see who's at the door if I look on my phone, right?" I called behind him, making no real attempt to retrieve my cell from the dresser across the room to look.

He regarded me blankly and sucked his teeth before descending the stairs. Moments later, I heard him disarm the alarm, then turn the top lock and open the door.

"Where's Greer?" The nasty, uninvited guest spat.

Oh damn. I reached over the edge of the bed and gathered the long night shirt I wore the night before in one hand while pushing myself up with the other. This couldn't be good.

"Was she expecting you?"

"Listen, Geeves. Don't question me. Just go get the bitch. I know she's here."

"That's not what I asked."

"I don't care what you asked. I *saaaaid*, go get her," Debbie's loud voice carried like a bullhorn as I put on my robe and belted it closed on my way downstairs.

"Yeah, bring your ass down here so I can say what I have to say directly to your face, since you wanna be stalking my husband for answers."

Race remained a barrier between us as I approached, his eyes peering down at Debbie derisively.

"You can move now," she ordered.

"Nah. I'm good right where I am."

"For what? She don't need you to protect her. I didn't come here to beat her ass, *tuh-day*, unless she provokes me."

"Debbie, what the hell do you want?"

Her beady eyes addressed me with all the warmth of a rabid dog as I stood beside Race with my arms folded across my chest. As expected, she had on another one of her dollar store wigs. This one was auburn, curly and shoulder length with bangs. It might not have looked so cheap if it wasn't so shiny.

She wore a long black coat and her face was surprisingly bare of makeup, which was probably a sign that she came ready for whatever. I'd whipped her ass like a runaway slave during our last altercation at Daddy's, but I wasn't back in fighting condition just yet.

Her warm breath permeated the cold air as she moved closer to the threshold with her neck already beginning to roll.

"If you want your little boytoy to hear what I have to say, then fine. Quiet as kept, he probably *needs* to hear it so he'll know to watch his back."

I pursed my lips and shifted my weight from one leg to the other impatiently.

"First, keep your ass away from Will. You have other choices of mechanics you can go to out here where you live. You ain't gotta drive all the way over to our side of town just to get your damn oil changed, and he don't need your business."

I snorted and tongued the inside of my cheek, allowing her to continue, uninterrupted. She paused, eying me up and down in expectation of my response, but I had none. I knew she wasn't done, so I was gonna let her finish before I said my peace.

"Don't come by. Don't call him. Don't do *anything* when it comes to my husband. He ain't got shit to say to you and if you want to know something about me... you ask *me*," she poked herself in the chest with her index finger. "Lastly, I know what you did, and you're not gonna get away with it. You may have Daddy wrapped up in your spell, but I see all the way through you.

You ain't no innocent little flower. You a evil, green eyed devil, just like my momma always said you was. I know you killed Michael and framed that girl for it. I got proof."

"Are you drunk? High?"

"Fuck you."

"It's not like you haven't been in rehab before."

Her upper lip curled as she stabbed me with her eyes.

"Bitch, don't try to be cute putting my business out in front of your little boyfriend. I didn't come here to drag you, but I will. Then you'll be going to jail for murder with a speed knot on your head," she smirked.

"You're delusional. I didn't murder anyone, and you can't prove something that didn't happen."

"*Ooooh* it happened alright. I knew you wasn't looking for nothing you left in the shed that day. I couldn't figure out what the hell you would need Daddy's keys for. But then it hit me. Mommy's car keys were on that ring too," she smirked.

I shook my head, feigning confusion, but I remembered Debbie's surprise visit to Daddy's house the day I killed Michael. I'd forgotten to put Daddy's keys back in the bowl where he always kept them. Just my luck, Debbie and Will had come to get Daddy's car so Will could inspect an oil leak he complained about.

Debbie made a big stink about me having the keys and I said I needed them to look for something in the shed. Per usual, she questioned my truth. I thought she had let it go, but I thought wrong.

"And?"

"And, *Bitch*, I bet you drove my momma's car instead of yours. Soon as they're able to check traffic cams for it, they'll prove me right. And another thing. I knew your ass was lying when you said you told the police about your little phone surveillance on Michael. Marlene's attorney said there's nothing in the police reports about you admitting to videoing Michael and Marlene. You're just a liar."

I glanced at Race in my peripheral, and he was no longer staring at Debbie with the disgust he originally greeted her with. His expression was unreadably void. As if he were taking in what she said and processing it.

I yawned, pretending to be bored by her accusations, but I was anything but. Could Marlene's attorney still get traffic cam footage from two years ago? If so, how long would it take? If he did, would that be enough evidence to reopen the case or fuel Marlene's appeal? Debbie was a rat bastard if I ever knew one.

"Maybe you should find a job. Being a stay-at-home mom has apparently provided you with way too much time on your hands if this is what you're spending it doing. Pulling fake evidence out of thin air is not going to make me guilty. You really should see a therapist about your obsession with me."

"Girl bye," she waved me off with a cynical chuckle. "I am not obsessed with you. I'm just sick of people falling for your innocent victim act all the time. You ain't nobody's victim. You're a perp. I know you shot my daddy to keep him quiet, and you're gonna pay for it."

"Keep him quiet about what? You're the only nutbag claiming I'm a murderer. What happened between me and him is about what *he* did. He knows it, and I know it."

"He knows it's bullshit and so do you. You probably found that book while you were in that shed snooping around for God knows what and decided to make it part of your plan."

"Which is it? Was I snooping in the shed, or stealing Stephanie's car keys?" I tilted my head smugly.

"Both, Bitch."

"Alright. You said what you came to say," Race spoke up.

I'd almost forgotten he was standing there. Debbie cut her eyes at him, then back to me.

"Yeah, I did. If you know what's good for you, you'll get as far away from this one as you possibly can. Y'all men let them green eyes, light skin, and long hair fool ya', but underneath it all, is a rattlesnake."

"You're jealous of things I had no control over. Things I was born with. I can't help how you feel about yourself, but don't project your insecurities onto me."

"Insecurities? You don't make me insecure. You don't have anything I want. Believe me. I'm perfectly happy with what God blessed me with. My melanin is beautiful and comes straight from my momma. I'm perfectly happy with *alllll* of me."

"Are you? Is that why you're wearing that cheap ass wig? Is that why you can't open your mouth about me without talking about my eyes, my hair or my complexion? Cause I can't tell."

"You know my hair used to be just as long and pretty as yours. I told mommy you did something to my conditioner that time, but I couldn't prove it," her face tightened. "I don't wear wigs because I'm ashamed of what God gave me and you know it, you uppity whore."

"Tsk Tsk Tsk. Poor Debbie. It's always somebody else's fault, isn't it? I'm done. I'm not wasting anymore energy on you. You can shut the door," I told Race, pivoting towards the kitchen, leaving them both to watch my back as I left the foyer.

I knew that dismissing her as I had would spear her ego far better than sparring words back and forth. Being ignored or regarded as unimportant were huge emotional triggers for her. Hence why I did it. Bang! Bang! Beelzebub.

She continued ranting outside of my presence, but I eventually heard the front door close. Race soon appeared by the island as I leaned against it, drinking a glass of orange juice.

"Your sister's crazy."

I set the glass down.

"That she is. Crazy and vindictive. I'm so embarrassed. I guess you never had to go through stuff like this with, Song. Huh?"

"Song and her family aren't perfect, and neither is mine. Believe me, I have some embarrassing stories I could tell. Have you *met* my mother?" he smirked. "When did Debbie go to rehab?"

"Like, seven or eight years ago. Before she had Tamia."

"For drugs or alcohol?"

"Drugs, mostly. But she still guzzles alcohol like a fish when she doesn't think anybody's around, with her closet drinking ass. She'd rather people think she's just a raging bitch than think it's because she's high or drunk."

"Wait. Debbie's a stay-at-home mom, isn't she? You really think Will would leave her alone with two small children if she was back on drugs?"

"She finds a way to pawn those kids off on somebody almost every day until it's bedtime or Will gets home from work," I snorted. "Anyway, I was just trying to get under her skin. I don't know if she's back on drugs or not. I can't stand her, but probably not."

To my surprise, he looked relieved.

"Oh. Cause I was gonna say, Will ain't shit for letting a drug addict raise his kids when he knows she needs help. Carmen put me and my brothers through a lot when she was getting high all the time before Granny took us. I wouldn't want nobody's kids to go through that."

How compassionate. I loved that about him. I was sure he'd be great with Tamia and Willow on the weekends Will let me watch them, once Debbie was dead. I really did miss my nieces and I'm sure Will would welcome the moral support without his trifling wife nay saying my efforts.

"Speaking of Carmen. Have you heard anything?"

He rested both elbows on the marble and ran his hands over the top of his head with a sigh.

"Nothing concrete. One of my boys thinks he saw her at a gas station in East Point. By the time he swung a U-Turn to go back and confirm, she was gone."

"Well, that's good right? At least you know she's alive."

"*If* that was her. He wasn't sure. And if it was. She was probably out there trickin' again."

"Again?"

His eyes dropped shamefully.

"She does what she has to for money to get high."

"East Point is far from your Granny's though, isn't it?"

"She knows a lot of people in a lot of places. I just hope she doesn't end up in the morgue this time instead of the hospital before she decides to get clean."

I didn't. She was a liability in his life, and I could only imagine what a burden she would become in mine if we ever married. Ms. Nina was a meddling pain, but Carmen would be an added financial drain too. Plus, we didn't like each other. Her junky ass was better off dead in my opinion.

"Babe," I placed a sympathetic hand on his arm. "Let's think positive. Hopefully, Carmen will be home soon and in one piece."

"Anyway, let's not talk about all that. You sure you don't want to come with me to pick up Granny? I can swing back by here after I leave the shop and come get you."

"No, I don't want you to go out of your way."

"She would be happy to see you. She's even asked about you."

"I just can't. After spending all that time in the hospital, I... I just can't do it right now. I almost had a panic attack when I had to go up to Franklin Family Practice for my follow up the other day," I lied. "Besides, I'm supposed to meet the lady coming to buy my car today. I still need to call her and confirm the time, but she did request early evening."

"I don't like you meeting this person by yourself."

"Why not? I'm not helpless, babe. It's a woman."

"Women can be psychos too."

He didn't need to tell *me.* I had nothing to fear from this fictitious buyer, however. I just needed him to be out of my hair long enough for me to fake sell my car, find a good place to park it and get back to the house.

"Stop worrying about me so much. Don't get me wrong. I love that you're so protective of me. But if I'm honest, I sort of… need a little bit of time alone. You know, to process my feelings. I know Michael's been gone over a year, but with the holidays, all of this mess with Daddy, and Debbie and, Marlene's appeal coming up… it's dredging up a lot of pain I thought I'd gotten past.

Then being confined to that hospital bed for so long, not being able to do for myself, needing nurses to help me do everything. I need to feel good about being self-sufficient again. I'm doing so much better, just like the doctors said I would.

Now, I of course, I plan to be at the surprise coming home party for Granny, Race. With bells on. It's at six o'clock, right?"

He stared concernedly. Furrowed brows ruminating over my words.

"What are you saying? I'm smothering you?"

"*Noooo.* No. I'm not saying that at all."

"That's what it sounds like to me."

"Well, maybe I'm just not saying it right then. I love you. I love spending time with you, and I love how you take care of me. Especially when nobody else is, but none of that changes the fact that I have some demons to deal with that you can't help me with.

Guilt over how my marriage failed. Not being a good enough daughter. Not being a good enough person. Things I can't talk about with you. You don't want to hear me whining and working through the mistakes I made in my marriage. In my life. You shut down completely when you're processing. That's not what I'm doing. I'm just asking for a little bit… just a tiny bit… of alone time when I need it.

My therapist said it's healthier for me to take the time to compose my thoughts and let my feelings out, than holding them in or putting on a show. I'm being as transparent as I possibly can with you right now, Race. Please understand."

Tears welled on cue and I shamefully turned my head away, knowing damn good and well I neither had, nor sought the advice of a therapist. He cupped my chin, turning my face gently back towards his.

"I understand. I do. I didn't mean to push. I just want to make sure I'm here for you, and that you *know*, I'm here for you."

"I want you to know that I'm here for you too. I don't want you to think I'm so selfish that I can't see that you're also going through something. With your mom, even with dealing with what happened to me. I know it affected you, more than you let on. But I have to clean up my own mess before I can tackle anyone else's. Or else I won't be any good to either one of us. At least, that's what my therapist says."

"I didn't know you were going to a therapist."

I hung my head.

"I started seeing her on and off after Michael's murder. I hadn't seen her in months until the day of my follow up exam. I felt like I was on the verge of breaking down just entering the building, so, I made an appointment. I was lucky she had an opening."

He nodded slowly, then approached me for a hug, which I happily accepted. Resting my head on his chest.

"Thank you for being so understanding. I've put you through a lot in such a short time. We haven't even been together a whole year yet. Are you sure you want to ride this ride with me?"

I looked up with a slight smile.

"If you can promise to be 100% honest with me and give me the same love and respect, I'm giving you, I'll ride with you until the wheels fall off."

I lifted to my tippy toes to make my lips reach his and placed an assuring kiss on them. Of course, I could genuinely promise to love and respect him. Now, being 100% honest... that was going to be more of a challenge than I was ready to accept. Two out of three was still good though... wasn't it?

13

Greer

December 19th 2015

Race left around 1:30 p.m. to make a tattoo appointment, and I left shortly after he did to go stash my car in plain sight. I was back by three-ish, cutting through my neighbor's backyards and entering my house through the backdoor.

An hour later, out of my disguise, and debating what to wear to Granny's coming home party, the infamous doorbell rang, yet again. This time, I checked the app on my phone and saw Karen on my porch.

Hair loose around my shoulders, wearing a red, long sleeve onesie and red furry socks, I slowly made my way downstairs to answer the door.

"Hey!"

"Hey, Karen."

"I wanted to come over and say thank you for my gift. I would've come over earlier, but I saw your other car wasn't in the driveway, so I thought you wasn't home. But then, I come out to take a smoke with Sheba, and I saw the lights come on in your upstairs window, so I thought I'd take a chance."

She was as predictable as fireworks on the fourth of July. Her aged face held a huge smile beneath the black wool hat pulled down over her brows and ears. She wore a gray oversized sweater and baggy jeans, making it easy to mistake her for a man if you didn't know who she was. *I* only knew it was her on the camera because she was holding the edible arrangement in her pudgy hands.

"I only have the one car now. I sold my Corolla."

"Did you now? Wish I'd known you were selling it. I got a niece that needs a new car. What you sell that old thing for? A couple or three grand?"

"Something like that. Anyway, I'm glad you liked the arrangement," I said rubbing my hands up my arms to demonstrate how cold I was.

"Oh yeah. I love it. Fruit cut up all designer and fancy. Nobody never sent me nothing like this before. Not even my George. Course, he wasn't never the romantic type anyhow," she rambled.

"You're welcome. It's the least I could do to show my gratitude for the other night. I don't mean to rush you away, but I'm in the middle of getting ready to go out."

"Oh, okay. No problem. Thanks again."

She exited with a wave, and while I was headed back upstairs, Nick's name popped up on my phone. This negro was persistently ignorant! How many times does someone have to ignore your calls before you stop calling? His messages were getting increasingly thirsty and demanding, which was not persuading me in any way to call him back. Ugh!

By 5:20 p.m. I was dressed in an ankle length, pink, ribbed, turtleneck dress and beige, low heeled, bootie styled boots. I left my hair down, put on a light coat of makeup, and was looking pretty good, if I did say so myself.

I arrived 11 minutes early for the party and parked in the first available spot, two houses down. I watched a few people enter the house, but I didn't know any of them. I texted Lisa at five minutes to six to see how long it would be until she and Geo arrived and was glad when she said they were already inside.

I knocked on the reef covered door and Ron answered with his youngest daughter in his arms. Even though he was the youngest of the three brothers, he looked like the oldest. In a too fat to be younger than thirty kind of way.

A married pastor with two daughters under three and a six-year-old son at the age of 27, might have been more difficult than he anticipated. His close-cropped fade was already receding, and his forehead always seemed to be creased with dismay.

"Greer, good to see you."

"Good to see you too. Hi Sweetie. She's adorable. What's her name again?" I smiled at the pacifier sucking, red, frilly dressed wearing, little ball of beauty in his arms.

"Malia."

"So cute."

"Thank you. She looks just like her mother. Everybody's in the living room waiting for them to get here. Race texted when they left the hospital. They'll probably be here in another 10 or 15 minutes. There's hors d'oeuvres, lemonade and tea on the dining room table if you want to grab something on your way in there."

"Thanks."

It looked like Santa vomited Christmas all over the house. Poinsettias, tinsel, and various ornaments, accentuated tabletops, door frames and shelves, highlighted by the six-foot Christmas tree in the corner of the living room.

I made my way to the table and placed a few skewered meatballs, pineapple slices and strawberries on a saucer sized plate. Lisa saw me first and called my name from a spot by the fireplace. Her hair was piled up in loose curls, with ringlets framing her countenance. She wore an off the shoulder, black, faux-fur shirt, with tight black leather pants and black calf high boots.

"You look pretty. I love the fur shirt."

"Isn't it cute? I saw it in this little boutique in Little Five Points and I had to have it."

"I was worried I might be a little overdressed for a house party, but *you* make me look underdressed," I smiled, biting a meatball off the stick.

"Girl please. You look great. And we're both overdressed for this party," she giggled. "Almost everybody has on jeans. Me and Geo are going to this new 30 and over spot in Sandy Springs after this. I look too good in this not to be seen by more people who can appreciate my fashion sense."

"I can't argue that. Where's Geo?" I craned my neck to search the throng of people in the quaint sized area.

"In here somewhere. Their cousins Algernon and Lance are here from Alabama. I don't know if Race told you about them, they lived here for a few years when they were kids. They're two of Geo's grooms-men too. I think my sister Lana got a little something-something going on with Algernon. Her face lights up whenever his name comes up."

"Is that the oldest or youngest one?"

"Youngest. Lora's the oldest."

"Are they both gonna be in your wedding?"

"Yeah, of course. My cousin Aaliyah, you know the one I told you was on American Idol, she's gonna be my maid of honor."

I nodded, not really caring about any of that as I ate. I was just making small talk, as I surveyed the conversing, mostly elderly attendees.

"Which brings me to you."

I raised a questioning brow.

"I was trying to find the right time to ask you, but I guess this is as good of a time as any."

I swallowed my food and asked, "Ask me what?"

"Will you be a bridesmaid?" she asked with a pleading tone and expression. "I feel like we've been becoming such good friends and I would love to have you in it with Race. I mean, he's gonna be walking with Aaliyah, since he's the best man, but I still want you both in it."

"I don't know Lisa. I've got so much going on that I don't know if I could dedicate the time it tak—"

"Hey Boo!" a nasally voice cooed before Lisa was engulfed in the swift embrace of another woman.

Beautiful dark orbs embedded in the cocoa brown, heart shaped face of a shapely bombshell, turned to greet me, along with a bright, wide smile. Song.

"*Greeer.* So nice to finally meet you." My eyes must've shown my thoughts, because she followed with, "I know we haven't met before, but I've heard *a lot* about you, and seen pictures. Green eyes, honey blonde hair. You're easy to spot."

"And you are?"

Her grin expanded arrogantly.

"Song. Race's ex-fiancée."

"Fiancée? I wasn't aware he was engaged before." I glanced at Lisa, who was watching us interact like a tennis match.

"We were together since we were kids. Girlfriend wouldn't adequately entail the type of relationship we had. After a certain age, girlfriend just sounds *soooo...* juvenile. You know?"

She tossed her long, black curly weaved locks over her shoulder, and placed a manicured hand to her plump bosom, flowing over the top of her royal blue dress. It was made of some type of winter grade bodycon material and fit her snug as a second skin.

It seemed inappropriate to wear a plunging neckline to a coming home party for an elderly woman. I *guest*-imated that she was maybe three inches taller than my 5'6 without heels, but in six-inch stilettos, her breasts were practically eye level. Modesty clearly wasn't her strong suit. I flagrantly scanned her from foot to head without even a hint of a smile on my face.

"You're a little different than I expected. I didn't expect you to sound so much like Whitley Gilbert. Doesn't she have that old southern bell sound just like her, Lees?"

Lisa smiled awkwardly. It wasn't the first time my voice had been compared to the bougie character from the old Cosby, college spinoff show, *A Different World.* Still, I felt like Song was trying to be insulting.

"*Soooo,* Greer. How long have you and Race been together now? A couple-few months?"

"It's been longer than that. In fact, I'm surprised to see you at a party for Granny, since you're not together anymore."

"Oh, I'm still family and always will be. No matter what my *current* relationship status is with Race. I'll always be welcome here. You probably don't know it, but Race and I have broken up before. It happens sometimes when a couple's been together for so long. I think it could be good for every couple to see what it's like without each other for a short while. Sow whatever wild oats they may still have lingering around. I'm sure you wish you and your husband had worked out the kinks before you walked down the aisle. Right?"

"Song! Oh my God," Lisa exclaimed in a hushed tone.

"*Whaaaat?* With all due respect, I'm sure I'm right. Aren't I?"

I envisioned myself pummeling that superior fucking expression on her face into a bloody pulp. She didn't come over to make nice. She came over to challenge me. Well, a challenge, she would get.

"Unfortunately, there's no shortage of morally corrupt sluts in Atlanta that freely sleep with taken men, whether they're married or not. I'm sure your cousin… what's her name again Lisa? Chealsea? I'm sure she would agree with me." I leisurely chewed a small pineapple slice without breaking eye contact with her.

Her visible display of supremacy waned. Her smile transformed into a sneer as she took one step closer.

"One mistake won't erase over a decade of love. *Sweetheart,*" she spat bitterly. "If you would've come up to the hospital to see Granny, I'm sure you would've seen just how strong our connection still is. I'm so glad I was able to be there for him in his time of need when you couldn't be."

I sighed, running the tip of my tongue over my gums in frustration. The burn of anger, heat my cheeks as we stared each other down like lionesses poised to attack. She wasn't the only one who could play dirty. And could bury her under my dirt.

"Sounds like a weak attempt to prey on him while he was vulnerable to me. I guess since trapping him with a baby didn't work, you're willing to go to any lengths to get him back, huh?" I cocked my head and squinted with feigned sympathy. "By the way, I'm sorry for your loss."

The color drained from Song's face and Lisa watched with her mouth agape before warning, "Y'all, this isn't the place for this conver—"

"No. It isn't. But this is where she chose to confront me about *my* man."

"He won't be *your* man for long, bitch."

"*Shhhhhh!* Everybody be quiet," Ron's wife Denise quieted the room before I could rebut. "They're pulling up to the curb. Everybody get in place."

Song's smarmy smile didn't leave her face as she stood between Lisa and I, turning her attention towards the front of the house. I ate the last morsel on the plate and briskly walked to toss it in a small trashcan by the kitchen door.

When I returned, I stood on the other side of Lisa, putting Song on her right, and me on her left. I knew if I was going to keep the pleasant disposition I intended to display, it would be harder if I had to do it next to Race's ex-tramp.

A few low murmurs were sprinkled throughout the now congested room, but it was mostly silent. The lights went out and someone said, "I hope she doesn't have a heart attack." Then was hushed by someone else.

Soon, the sound of keys were in the door and the light from the streetlamp streaked the hallway as it opened. Race's voice could be heard guiding Granny as he ushered her inside. We were more in the middle than towards the front, so I heard more than I saw. The next thing I knew, the lights flicked on, everybody yelled surprise, and all the attention was on the woman of the hour.

Race sat a pleasantly startled Granny down in a blue Hoveround, motorized wheelchair, as the crowd began to bustle.

"Now Horace, I done told you I didn't need no remote-control chair," Granny fussed through a huge smile, proving her complaint was only surface. "I can't believe you got all these folks out here fo' me. Boy, you somethin' else."

Granny playfully slapped Race's arm as he grinned wide and bent down to kiss her forehead. The worrisome cloud that hung over him while she was away dissipated before my eyes. She beamed as she began to recognize the faces of everyone who came to celebrate her.

"It's not remote-control Granny. You control it yourself, right here."

She squinted behind thick frames while Race showed her where the controls were with one hand, his other in the pocket of his charcoal-colored sweats.

Granny straightened her gray-haired wig as Geo appeared beside her to help her out of her coat, revealing a white sweater and jeans that practically swallowed her small frame. People began approaching then, hugging, and kissing her. Telling her how happy they were to see her home. She was moved by the outpouring of love, and as much as she tried to hide it, her delight was evident.

"Welcome home, Ms. Walker," I said bending to kiss her on the cheek when it was my turn.

"Chile, I done told you to call me Granny." She gave me a quick once over, glanced at Race, then back at me. "Well, you're lookin' a lot better than Horace said you was feelin'. I s'pose you ain't have the energy to come see me whilst you was tryin' to recover, huh?"

"No Ma'am. I just recently started being mobile again myself. I just know how to put on a good face, so I don't look like what I've been through."

"No, you sho'll don't. You must have a *strong* heart to fight off a bullet," she chuckled, along with others in earshot. "Horace say, he thought you was dead. I'm glad the good Lord chose to save yo' life, even though none of y'all chill'n these days see fit to worship in his house. I hope you give him all the glory for every breath you takin' right now. Your Daddy too."

"Yes Ma'am."

"From what I hear, y'all both need Jesus to mend y'all family. Shouldn't be no way and no how it got that bad 'tween parent and child. I'm not judging'. Lord knows my own daughter done did enough I could've shot her fo', and the law wouldn't have even given me a slap on the wrist. But that ain't the Christian way."

"Granny, come on now," Race diffidently chided.

"Horace, nah I know you ain't talkin' to *me* in that tone." She turned her frail frame sideways to address him. "You ain't never gon' be old enough to tell me what to do or what to say, long as God gives me the breath in my body to say it."

Someone turned up the old school R & B music already playing, an extra decibel, as if on cue to deescalate the scolding session.

"Granny. Everybody came here to welcome you home. I'm sure Greer doesn't want to talk about that in front of all these people."

"Well, all these people got a T.V. don't they? I ain't the onliest one in here knows what happened to the girl."

"You sure aren't," Song's nasally voice cosigned as she stood haughtily off to the side.

Granny looked back at me with a frown and her wrinkled lips twisted. I don't know what my mien showed, but it seemed to have quelled her abrasiveness.

"Greer, I'm happy to see you again. Healthy and healing, just like I am. I gets a little talkative about family sometimes cause I'm getting' old. You appreciate family when you're old. Just tryin' to give you some of my wisdom. I ain't embarrass you none, did I?"

"No Ma'am," I lied, wringing my hands through a forced grin.

"I'm so glad to see you're doing better and back home again. Excuse me, I'm gonna go to the ladies' room."

I avoided eye contact with Race, and all the other eyes I felt on me as I walked away. If all the guests didn't already know who I was from the news, they damn sure did now. I originally planned to stay for a couple, maybe three hours if everything went well. Now, Race would be lucky if I stayed past the next 45 minutes.

I knew the lay of the house from having Thanksgiving dinner with them and made my way towards the half bath with whatever poise I could manage. After relieving myself, washing and drying my hands, I stared at my reflection, comparing my features to Song's.

I didn't expect her to be here. Nor had Race disclosed that she was regularly visiting Granny at the hospital. I wondered what type of skimpy outfits she wore knowing he would be there and how close he let her get to him before spurning her advances.

Song's arrogance while speaking to me was having it's intended effect. I admit, I was intimidated. This haughty bitch and her antagonizing ways was trying to turn me into a serial killer.

Lisa was waiting for me when I opened the bathroom door. She leaned off the wall, a half full wine glass in hand.

"Hey. You okay?"

"Uh… yeah. Why?"

She shrugged. "Just felt like I needed to check on you."

I stood beside her, watching the people milling about on both ends of the hallway. For some reason, Song's annoying voice carried over everyone else's. Possibly because I was zeroed in on it, and not because she was actually that loud.

"I'm sorry for what happened back there."

"She's old. Old people say what they want."

"No. With Song." She sipped from her glass, watching my reaction over the rim.

I cut my eyes at her and leaned my head back on the wall.

"I didn't expect to see her here. Thanks for giving me the heads up."

"I wasn't sure if she was coming. The last time I talked to her, she said she might be working. It slipped my mind."

"Hmph. Slipped your mind. She's one disrespectful Trollip. That's for sure."

"She's just jealous. I haven't seen her jealous too many times before, but this is how she acts when she is."

"Jealous? I doubt that. She looks like she just walked off the cover of a magazine."

Her head jerked back, and she sucked her teeth dubiously.

"Yes, Song is beautiful. But Greer… have you seen yourself? *You're* gorgeous too. Gorgeous and the man she wants is in love with you and doesn't want squat to do with her. Listen, Song's my girl. You know that. We go too far back for me to cut her off over relationship problems that don't involve me or Geo.

But don't let her get in your head about her history with Race and being a part of the family. I mean, she is like a part of their family, but Granny would never let her use that to get between you and Race. Granny knows what she did, and she told Race to break up with her even before that happened.

Granny always said, 'Song's not the commitment type. One man will never be able to give her all the attention she needs.' And Song proved it to Race the hard way."

I nodded, brushing a strand of hair from my face just as the devil we spoke of approached.

"Babe, let me talk to you for a minute."

He placed a hand on the small of my back and gently lead me down the hall into a room at the end of it. I realized it was Carmen's room as he closed the door behind us. A surplus of tacky and cheap looking women's clothes were spread over the bed and hung on the backs of the closet and room door. They were too youthful to be Granny's, so they had to be hers.

"What happened with you and Song?"

Offended, I stepped away from his touch and raised a brow, folding my arms across my chest. "I beg your pardon?"

"She said some shit to Granny about you being feisty and telling her to stop coming to family gatherings."

"Are you kidding me?" I snickered. "She's a liar. I never said anything like that. You can ask Lisa. I was minding my business, talking to Lisa, and she sashayed her long-legged ass over to me, claiming she's *faaaaamily* and your breakup's only temporary." I mocked her nasal tone and bobbed my head satirically. "Why didn't you tell me she would be here when you invited me?"

"She said she wasn't coming."

"How often do you talk to her?"

"Greer?"

"What?"

"I don't talk to her."

"Well, Song begs to differ."

"Look, she texted me yesterday to send Granny her love because she was gonna be out of town working tonight. I never even replied to it because I didn't invite her in the first place. I figured she was just trying to get me to talk to her."

"Didn't you talk to her at the hospital?" My eyes rolled.

"*She* talked to *me* at the hospital. I wasn't there for her. I only saw her up there once. Greer, I don't want to have to keep defending myself about her every time her name comes up. I already told you where we stand. You either believe me or you don't. I've never given you any reason to distrust me."

"Race, *you* pulled me in here to talk about her. This was your idea. I didn't bring her up."

"You would have."

"Okay. But not here."

He placed both hands on the side of my folded arms and we stood silently for a beat.

"Race, I'm not gonna stay too much longer. I'm not really doing too good dealing with the pain with my decreased doses, and I'm tired. I only came because I told you I would and because I wanted to show up for your grandmother and for you.

Now that I've been made a spectacle, and Song's walking around here with my name in her mouth to a bunch of people I don't know, I really just want to go home."

Tension was evident on his face as he licked his lips and let out a slow breath.

"Alright. Can I come over when I leave here?"

I looked away. "Not tonight, Race. Tomorrow. Tomorrow night."

"Why not tonight?"

"We already talked about this. I just really need to be alone right now. I'll call you when I get there, and then I'm probably just gonna take a bath, and go to sleep."

"And that's better than taking a bath and sleeping, or not sleeping in the bed with me?"

I rolled my eyes playfully this time.

"It's not better. But it's needed."

"Aiight. If you say so. You gonna stay long enough for me to introduce my new woman to everybody and eat some cake? You don't have anything better to do at this exact moment, do you?"

A smile graced my lips, and I shook my head coyly. He was right. I didn't have to leave right *now*… to kill Angie later.

14

Greer

I stayed longer than I should have, but not long enough to outstay Song. Either way, I made sure our PDA's made her as uncomfortable as possible without being disrespectful to Granny. If I wasn't on a time crunch, I would have found a way to screw him and make sure I let her see how disheveled I looked before I left. Alas, time was not on my side.

When I got home, I changed into my cat burglar outfit, put in my contacts, darker foundation, affixed a wig, and slid into the dreaded too big sneakers I bought. Leaving, I crept out the backdoor, phone in hand, and waited until I was in the camera's blind spot to turn it, and the alarm on.

Then, I tucked the cell under the rolling garbage can for safe keeping at the back end of my home. I hated to leave it, but it was a necessary evil to leave anything traceable for the task at hand. My alibi, should I need one, would be that I was home all evening. My phone couldn't very well be traced on cellphone towers elsewhere when I was supposed to be at home, right?

One ten-minute walk later, I was unlocking Rolly and sliding behind the wheel, headed to Angie's backwoods abode across town. The evening traffic was light until the rain started coming down in sheets, making visibility troublesome in my old, windshield wiper challenged jalopy.

At first, I was pissed. I hadn't seen rain in the forecast for the evening, but when I thought about it, bad weather, was actually good. There would be less people on the streets, poor visibility and less of a chance anyone would be able to identify me or my car.

I drove in total silence, with only my plans to flawlessly execute the mission repeatedly playing in my mind. Because Angie's home was down a beaten path off a heavily tree lined, main country road, like most other homes in the area, there was no sidewalk for me to conspicuously park by.

I'd been to her home a few times before and it was lucky for me that my memory was good since I couldn't use GPS. About a quarter mile away from her place, I found a spot just off the shoulder where I could drive a short distance down between trees and not be easily seen by passersby. I hoped no overachieving patrol cop would happen by and see my car, or me trudging along in a hoody and a backpack in 40-degree weather and heavy rain.

It wasn't until I was drenched and cold, retrieving Angie's spare key from under a fake rock, that I started second guessing myself. Maybe I should come back to do it another day. Maybe the bad weather was a sign to call it off. But then again, I was already there… and already wet. This was going to be my best opportunity to get her, and not to get caught. It was now, or never.

I unlocked the door, put the key back where I found it, let myself in and turned on the lights. Dripping wet on the hardwood floor at the entrance, I steadied my breathing, basking in the heat, and processing my next move. I couldn't risk tracking water all through the house and alerting her from the door of an intruder. There only seemed to be one option. Strip.

I took everything off except my underwear and the latex gloves I wore under my winter ones and left them at the front door. Then I rummaged through her pantry, and under the kitchen sink until I found a stash of stored plastic bags. Every black person I've ever known has kept some after grocery shopping, and Angie was no different. I took two.

Backpack hanging from my left shoulder, I put my wet clothes in one bag and my shoes in the other. Finding her spare bedroom, I opened the French doors to the closet and dropped my backpack and bags on the floor inside it. Thankfully, the room was largely unused as anything more than a storage area for her things. It would be the perfect place to wait for her.

Digging in my backpack, I pulled out the baggie containing the powdered result of 10 crushed Ambien pills and headed to her kitchen. I compacted Michael's unused sleep medication the same way I suppressed the Cytotec I spiked Song's OJ with to cause her miscarriage. Knowing I'd have to mix it in an entire bottle, I needed more than a single dosage. I hoped 10 would suffice.

Traipsing back to the front of the house, I b-lined to the refrigerator and shook my head at its lack of content. There were more condiments, liquids, and Styrofoam containers with leftovers in them than anything of substance. I suppose with her working more than she was home, I should've expected that. At any rate, the half bottle of Bacardi Gold was my primary concern. It being less than full was even better for ensuring the ratio of meds that would hit her system.

I pulled a random cup from her dishwasher and poured a couple of ounces from the bottle in it. I left the cup on the bedroom's closet floor and went back to taint and shake up the Bacardi bottle before placing the empty baggy in my sports bra. Grabbing a handful of paper towels, I wiped up the water from the doorway and buried the wet wad beneath some paper plates in her trash can.

By 11:21 p.m. I'd scoped out the kill zone, confirmed I had everything I needed, and all that was left to do, was wait with the lights out, for my prey. She kept the spare room's door open, so I went back to the closet and sat on the floor opposite the cup and bags with the doors closed. I just prayed she didn't have mice, rats or roaches in her old log cabin styled residence. I was squeamish.

I nearly fell asleep waiting for the guest of honor to arrive. With my digital watch as the only electronic in my possession, I was bored as hell until I finally heard her enter the house at a little after midnight. Adrenaline fueled my anxiety as I listened to her movement around the house.

I didn't know what she was doing most of the time, but the beeping of the microwave and the blaring of the television for another 40 plus minutes gave me a clue. I hoped she was guzzling that Bacardi down as I suspected. I needed her to pass out the way she had the night I hit that reckless driver with her in the car. In its proper dosage, it took no more than an hour for the drugs to work and provided seven or eight hours of deep slumber to its taker. Though I intended to provide eternal sleep for Miss Angie Reardon.

Ten minutes after the house went silent, I tiptoed to her open bedroom door and peeked in at Sleeping Beauty. I could barely see her in the darkness, were it not for the moonlight illuminating her bed through the window. She lay on her left side in a knee length pajama shirt with a bonnet on her head and lightly snoring.

In the kitchen, only a quarter of the Bacardi was left in the bottle. Her empty glass and fork rested in the sink alone. I assumed she ate from one of the Styrofoam trays since there was no plate. Now that she was asleep, I could finally set up.

I brought my backpack out with everything I needed to thoroughly execute my mission. I clicked on the small table lamp in the living room which also dimly lit the adjacent dining room. I tossed the 20-foot rope with the noose already tied at one end, over one of the exposed wooden beams. I gave it about 5 feet in front of the large oak table so I could maneuver around it.

I estimated how high the noose had to be to hang her if she were standing on a chair, and how much rope would be needed to tie it to the leg of the table. Next, I placed a dining room chair under the rope and let the noose hang low. I stood back, surveyed the setup again, and smiled to myself. This was going to work.

I brought both 20-pound fitness belts out and adjusted them tightly around my waist. Removing the runner Michael and I used during our wedding ceremony, I went into Angie's room and unrolled it on the floor, parallel to her sleeping form. I needed the extra pounds and the runner to supplement the strength it would take for me to drag her into the dining room, without leaving abrasions and/or risking her waking.

I climbed up on the empty side of the bed, tossed the pillows from it onto the runner, then shoved Angie's blackmailing ass off. Aside from groaning, her only reaction to her "not yet dead weight" hitting the pillows on the runner, was to adjust her face to the side.

That part was easier than I expected. The hardest part came later. Lifting her up to sit in the chair in a position where she wouldn't keel over before I could hang her, was much harder. It took several minutes, but she never woke up. Once I caught my breath, I moved the pillows to the floor in front of the table, behind the chair she was propped up in. I wrapped the end of the rope loosely around one table leg, so I'd be able to use the leverage once Angie was suspended.

I had to move fast after that. Time waits for no one and I needed to get back home. I put the noose around her lolling head and slid the knot snuggly around her throat. Rope in hand, I stepped on the seat of another dining chair and stood on the heavy oak table facing Angie's back.

Gripping the highest part of the rope I could reach as tightly as possible, I leapt off. My bottom landed in a sitting position on the pillows; instantly yanking Angie's body up from the chair and hoisting her towards the rafters. I cried out involuntarily as my injuries, especially my shoulder, responded to my body jarring as I hit the floor.

Angie's dangling feet kicked the back of the chair as she rose, toppling it. My sleeping victim momentarily waking to claw the rope, sheer seconds before her neck snapped, and all motion ceased. That cracking sound was music to my ears, because if her neck didn't break, I would have had to hold on as she struggled for however long it took to strangle her.

My god she was heavy. Even with the full weight of my body and the additional pounds around my waist, I struggled to keep her up. Scooching back towards the table, I used one hand to pull the rope around the table leg while keeping a grip on the main end to keep her body up.

Miraculously, I managed to secure several knots around the leg to keep her corpse hovering at roughly the projected height necessary. All, without ripping my latex gloves. I wiped beads of sweat from my forehead with the back of my hand as I rounded Angie's hanging body to view her face.

Her dead eyes bulged with littered petechiae around the orbs. I expected that, but what surprised me, was the tongue protruding from her mouth. It was a strange, almost comical sight. I wish there was a way she could've seen my face and understood why she was being murdered that night. I wanted her to know it was me killing her. To regret betraying me before she took her last breath. But... she was dead. And *that* is what mattered.

I repacked the runner and weight belts, put the pillows back on her bed and retrieved the cup of Bacardi from the closet floor. In the kitchen, I poured the rest of the bottle down the sink and rinsed it out as thoroughly as possible without using dishwashing liquid. Then, slowly, and carefully, I poured the Bacardi from the cup back into the bottle.

I felt like traces of powdered Ambien, or Zolpidem if we use the actual brand name, in the liquor bottle of a suicide victim wouldn't logically jibe in this case. Like I said, I'm a crime show buff and I needed to cover all my bases. I also brought four loose Zolpidem pills to place in a paper towel in her nightstand for good measure.

I wasn't sure if the toxicology report would pick up the drug in her system or not. Especially if it took at least five days for her body to be discovered, but I didn't want to chance it. Though she'd be missing the prescription bottle, she was an NP. I'm sure the police would conclude that it wouldn't be hard for her to obtain them with or without a script.

I washed the glass and fork in the sink and left them in the dishrack to dry. I then retrieved Kendrick's funeral program from my backpack and brought it over to Angie's corpse to put fresh fingerprints on it. Once in her room, I left the semi crumpled paper on her bedside table while placing the pills in a top drawer.

Bingo! There was the bank envelope I gave her, still filled with cash. Oh yeah. That money was coming back to its rightful owner. If I wasn't afraid of the potential dust mites that might have gotten on the envelope, I would've kissed it up to God in thanks.

Since my clothes were still too wet to wear, I plucked a long sleeve shirt, socks, and leggings from her wardrobe as well. We weren't the same size, but her clothes fit well enough for me to wear them home.

It was gonna be a much colder walk back to my car than it was coming without my thermal gear and no coat, but thankfully, it wasn't raining anymore. At least I wouldn't be wet *and* cold. I dumped the contents of my backpack and the clothes I wore in a random apartment complex's dumpster during the drive and trekked from my car in too big shoes back home.

It was nearly three in the morning when I arrived at my back door, exhausted, freezing, and sniffling. I deactivated the cameras and alarm with my phone and reset them once inside. If the less than 60 second gap was ever questioned, I'd simply say I thought I heard a noise and deactivated it when I opened the door to check.

As tired as I was, I removed my disguise, disrobed, and showered as soon as I made it to the master bath. Being a germaphobe can be a bitch sometimes. I could not go to bed feeling sweaty and grimy from my earlier dirty deeds. I would find the time to get rid of Angie's "borrowed" clothes the next time I was out.

My body was screaming for an Oxycodone to relieve the awakened pain it seemed I was experiencing all over my body. Especially in my right shoulder. Hoisting live, then dead weight had surely taken its toll on my not yet 100% recovered physique. I surrendered to my aching muscles demands and slept like a log after taking the medication but awoke to an entirely different issue. God damn it, I was sick.

I had a killer migraine, I was developing a cough that made my chest hurt each time I did, and my nose was stuffy and runny. The sun assaulted my eyelids until I could no longer keep them shut. I awoke with an attitude at Mother Nature for her sunny disposition just before rushing to the bathroom to toss my cookies into the porcelain god I suspected I would be praying to all day.

I spent the rest of the morning juggling time between my bed, the kitchen, and the bathroom. I was too ill to entertain the phone calls from Shan and Nick. I was especially not entertaining *his* calls. He was threatening me in the last two messages and calling me a tease.

A tease? I didn't even know people actually still talked like that in the new millennium. I wasn't going to let his belligerent and insignificant ass irritate me when I was sick. I could only keep liquids down and the mere thought of eating solid food made me want to earl. Whatever bug was attacking me, it was working me over fast and hard.

I lay crumpled on my side in a fetal position with the television on as background noise to my pain when the phone rang. I recognized Race's personalized ringtone and reached for it on my nightstand with my eyes still closed.

"Hello."

"Hey Baby. What you doing?"

"Slowly dying I think."

"What? What are you talkin' about?"

"I'm sick as a dog," I said through coughs, opening my eyes to search for the box of tissue in the bed beside me. I plucked out two at a time and blew my nose into them, then tossed the tissue in the trash before dousing my hands with sanitizer. "I got some kind of bug."

"Aww damn. That fast? You seemed fine last night. It is flu season though. No telling who might have been sick at the party. Did you take anything for it?"

"No. I don't know what's safe to take while I'm still on my meds. I'm just keeping hydrated, staying sanitary and trying to sleep through it. The sleeping part is easy."

"Maybe you should call your doctor. I know it's Sunday, but y'all got an afterhours hotline, don't you?"

"That's for emergencies. I don't think a common cold, or the flu qualifies. Besides, there's probably nothing they can prescribe for me that won't clash with what I'm already on. I'll be fine. I have plenty of honey and ginger tea here already. If I'm not getting any better in three days, I'll call them or go to one of those in-pharmacy Ready-Clinics."

"You're friends with one of the NP's there aren't you? Maybe you should call her and ask for suggestions."

Unfortunately, Angie was too dead to be able to provide any good advice, but calling her was a good idea. I was calling at Race's suggestion if it ever came up in an interrogation, and my voicemail on her phone would indicate that I had no idea she was deceased.

"Yeah. I'll do that when we hang up."

I ran a hand through my hair and debated whether I was going to get up now, or later for my gazillionth trip to the bathroom. I was used to being my own nursemaid as I'd practically been doing it my whole life. My stepmonster was hardly sympathetic when I fell sick under her care, and at one point I was convinced she may have been causing it.

There was a time during my middle school years that I was chronically unwell. Mostly, during the summer no less, while she and my siblings remained mysteriously healthy. They were typical flu like symptoms that left me mucus filled, fatigued, and with persistent diarrhea. Stephanie refused to take me to the doctor because she said it cost too much just for them to send us home with over-the-counter treatments.

She blamed it on my so called "nasty" and unclean habits, but I didn't see where I was any less cleanly than she or the other three kids. Daddy was on the road driving most of the time, so he was rarely home to witness or override her spiteful decisions regarding my care.

To prevent my passing on my illness, so she claimed, I was frequently quarantined alone in the musty and dusty basement. I didn't see how restricting me to the dirtiest part of the house made sense, but of course, my opinion didn't matter. I was provided with a twin bed to sleep on, a radio and occasionally books for entertainment.

School was out in some of the months I was on again, off again sick. So, I had nowhere to be that my presence would be missed. Stephanie didn't lift a finger to comfort me, but she consistently took my temperature and kept me hydrated with water and various types of soup. At one point during a stint of illness, I drew my own conclusion that the abundance of liquids she fed me with hardly any solid food, was contributing to my terrible bouts of diarrhea.

I decided on my own to flush the soups and only snack off the crackers she brought down with them. I barely had an appetite anyway and seeing as I was often lethargic, it didn't take much to fill my hunger before I would drift off to sleep.

After two days of living off crackers and water, to my surprise, I found myself gradually feeling better. That's when I began to suspect stepmommy dearest of being the *real* agent of my mysteriously recurring illnesses.

She was the home remedy guru of the house and if anybody would've known how to slowly poison me, it would have been her.

I wholeheartedly believe she was trying to kill me, and that's when I stopped eating and drinking anything Stephanie made that was specifically or separately made for me. But just in case I *was* somehow at fault for my own ailments, I became extremely cautious of anything that could potentially make me sick.

I think that's how my germaphobia developed. It became second nature for me to be distrustful of people making any food or beverages specifically for me outside of my eyesight. I started keeping Clorox wipes in my bag and avoided or DE sanitized anything I deemed a potential threat to my health.

I simply learned to unapologetically rely on myself to keep my environment safe and clean. Noticing how most people aren't half as cautious as I am, is how I've been able to come up with the devious things I've had to do to some of *their* food and drinks.

However, my conscience worried that this sudden illness I was suffering may have been some form of instant Karma for accelerating Angie's inevitable demise to hell.

"Shit, I still have three more clients to do. You need me to reschedule them and come play doctor?"

"No," I tittered. "The last thing I want to do is get you sick too."

He shocked me by abruptly ending the call. Before I could grasp what happened, he was calling me back on facetime. I hesitated before answering. Not at all thrilled to be seen in my current condition.

"What are you doing?" I answered in a peeved tone.

"Trying to make sure you're really sick and not trying to dodge me."

I could see the inside of his office in the tattoo shop in the background. He was wearing a blue baseball cap with the bill turned to the back and a blue jersey I could only see the top of.

"Are you serious?"

"Hell yeah I'm serious. You do look pretty fucked up though."

"Really?" I scoffed through a partial laugh. "Could you be any ruder? That was not necessary to say out loud."

"My bad," he apologized. His pearly whites drawn into a smile. "I'm just sayin' seein' is believin'. From what I see, I believe you."

"You're such a jerk."

I heard someone knock on his office door and yell out that his client was there.

"Aiight, I gotta go. I'll call you when I get out of here. I may come by anyway and check up on you. Bring you some soup or something. I know your hardheaded ass won't eat if I leave it up to you."

I pretended to be offended and blew out an aggravated breath.

"Goodbye, Race."

"Ha! You love me?"

"Yes." I answered begrudgingly.

"I love you too." He blew me a kiss and hung up.

As terrible as I felt inside and out, his love for me made me feel a little bit better. After all, everything I was doing was for the betterment of us. For love.

15

Greer

December 25th 2015

"Merry Christmas."

"Daddy?"

My hand holding the liquid eyeliner brush froze midair as I gazed down at my cell on the bathroom counter. The name and number displayed on the screen was for my Aunt Carrie. *This,* wasn't Aunt Carrie.

"Baby Girl, how are you?" he asked tentatively. "I uh… I know ya' ain't expect it to be me on this here phone. I ain't know if ya' would answer a call from mine. Seein' as I'm not s'posed to be callin' ya' anyhow. Carrie let me use hers."

"Why *are* you calling?" My voice cracked reticently. My heart beating like a bass drum in anticipation of his response. Was this real?

"Whateva' happened, you're still my daughter. I know you don't believe it no mo', but I *do* love ya'. I never meant fo' none of this to happen. I made mistakes, but I tried to make up fo' them. Maybe I ain't do so great sometimes, but it's not fo' lack of tryin'. I don't want thangs to be this way tween us. We always been close. I want us to fix it Baby Girl. Let's talk. Face to face."

Stupidly, despite what he's done. Despite the hatred I've been nurturing daily for the man on the other end of the phone, I was somewhat elated, to hear from him. Almost mirthful with the knowledge that he still loved me and cared enough to say so. Even now. Still, I tamped down those emotions in exchange for what he deserved. Indifference.

"You put a restraining order out on me. Have you forgotten that? I'm not *allowed* to talk to you, face to face."

"I ain't the one who wanted the restrainin' order, Baby Girl. Prosecutor said that was automatic, 'cause, it was tween family. I ain't want this to go no fu'ther than where it was. It's been eatin' me up since it happened. It already went too far."

"Well, seeing as you almost killed me, I'd have to agree with you. Daddy."

He sighed. "We got a lot to talk about. I ain't comf'table talkin' 'bout it on the phone. This too big fo' a phone talk. Thought maybe you'd wanna come ova' and see how we can fix it."

"I don't think so. I have no desire to be arrested for trespassing or violating the restraining order. Especially on Christmas Day. What is this, Daddy? Why're you calling me after all this time to talk? Did Debbie put you up to this?"

He balked at the suggestion.

"Since when ya' know me to listen to Debbie?"

"I learned a lot about you that I didn't know before."

"Alright, Sassy Mouth. Well, I'm already violatin' that order right nah. Call came from me. Didn't it? I'm not tryin' to set ya' up fo' the po'lice if that's what ya' thankin'. We can meet somewhere else if ya' want. I can travel. Yo' house?"

I ran both palms across the edge of the countertop as I stared at my own befuddled reflection in the mirror, pondering his offer. Truth is, it would be easier to exact my revenge if I got back in his good graces, regardless of his motives. I needn't look a gift horse in the mouth.

"When are you suggesting this? Today?"

"No. Not today, but soon. As soon as possible. Befo' the new year. You back to work?"

"Not yet."

"Alright then. What about Monday or Tuesday? I can come by any-time work fo' you. Seein' as I'm retired, I always got a lot of time on my hands to do wit' what I want."

I was hesitant. Something about this was just too… *too* easy. I know this was my father I was talking to, but I didn't trust him. Not anymore.

"Just you?"

"Jus' me."

I nodded as if he could see me. "Okay. After one or two o'clock Monday, works for me."

"After one it is. Nah, you wanna talk to yo' Aunt fo' real, or you done?"

"Might as well put her on if she's actually there."

I heard the phone shuffle and then she came on.

"Hey there. Now before you get into me, don't be mad. I love you both, and you know how I feel about family. You two have always been the closest out of Chuck and all the kids. Ya'll not talkin' isn't right.

He ain't been right since that night, and I'm thinkin' you haven't been either. Stubborn as he is, I got him to call before Debbie and the kids come. What better day to make peace than on Christ's birthday?"

Of all my relatives, Aunt Carrie was the only one who always ac-knowledged me with respect and at least attempted to show me some compassion. At 50 years old, she was still traveling the circuit as a backup singer for an R&B group that had several hits in the 80's. She lived in Atlanta but was only in town maybe four times a year, not in-cluding whichever holiday's she chose to come back for.

Just like my Daddy, she lived her life primarily on the road. But *unlike* her older brother, she never married, or had any children of her own. Though she talked like she was interested in men, I've never known her to be romantically involved with one. Something my judg-mental stepmother speculated about in a damning way, all while she was alive.

It was no wonder Aunt Carrie claimed she couldn't make it back to town for her funeral. If it weren't for my propensity to want to be there for my father, I wouldn't have shown my face at her homegoing either.

I've faked a lot of emotions throughout the years, but I refused to waste tears on that woman that day. They're lucky I didn't throw a party.

"I'm not mad Aunt Carrie. Just surprised. Merry Christmas."

"What are your plans for the day?"

"I'm getting dressed now to spend it with my boyfriend's family."

"Okay. Good. I know you never cared much for Christmas, but I still hate the idea of anybody spending it alone. I'm glad you and your boyfriend are doing well. I'm gonna have to meet him one day. I leave out tomorrow so maybe sometime in the spring when I'll be back in Atlanta next."

"You will."

"How have you been recovering?"

"I'm doing good. Getting over a bad cold right now, but I'm otherwise peachy," I told her while beginning to apply my makeup again.

"Excellent. I hope we'll talk again soon. I'm over here cooking the ham, mac and cheese, yams and collards for your daddy. Apparently, Debbie was too busy to make anything to bring, but she's planning on bringing her whole family over to eat anyway."

"Hmph. Busy doing what?"

Aunt Carrie chuckled.

"Now, you know I don't like to talk about you girls to each other. I'm just going to take her at her word and enjoy the sweet potato pie Will promised to pick up from Publix. Merry Christmas, Doll face!"

"Merry Christmas," I simpered, ending the call.

When Race let himself in the house 30 minutes later, I was near ready to go. My hair was parted down the middle with single flat twists on each side that connected into a loose ponytail in the back. A rhinestone leaf shaped clip strategically placed in each braid accentuated my look.

I wore a red cashmere, off the shoulder top with red jeans, diamond studs in my ears and a diamond infinity pendant necklace around my throat. I thought I looked casually pretty for a home holiday party, I hoped if Song showed up, I would at least rival her.

"Pretty," Race said from the bedroom threshold.

"Thank you."

"I'm surprised you're not wearing pink."

"I figured, it being Christmas and all, red would be more festive. I keep telling you and your brother, I don't wear pink, all the time," I answered while putting on my chocolate Coach riding boots.

"Well, now we almost match," he swept a hand over his red, pullover, three button Henley with a standing collar and the red sweats with black stripes down the side. "Are we that couple who dresses alike now?"

"Ha! Not on purpose."

"It's cool. I don't mind being corny with you," he approached, towering over me as I stood. "Merry Christmas."

I stared down at the long gold jewelry box and beamed. "I thought we were going to wait until we got to Granny's to exchange gifts?"

"I never said that. I want you to open yours now."

I took the box from him and found a beautiful, white gold, diamond tennis bracelet inside. I covered the grin on my face with my palm and squealed.

"I take it you like it," he said kissing my forehead and removing it from the box to put on me.

"I love it. Thank you," I kissed his lips and held it up to admire it on my wrist. "Lovely. Okay, so let me give you yours."

I grabbed my purse from the dresser and plucked the red envelope Christmas card from it. "Merry Christmas."

He cut me a sly look and used his index finger to rip it open. Sliding the card out, he opened it, removing the folded piece of paper inside, and reading the inscription. My mushy message earned me a smile as he unfolded the paper and the corners of his mouth expanded.

"Venice?"

"I've always wanted to travel. I've never been to Italy before. I figured… we could go together. Valentine's week next year. I'm hoping this is enough notice for you to take off."

"Hell yeah," his lips smashed against mine and we tongue danced until I broke for air.

"Babe, we need to go."

"I know."

"*Sooooo*, is it going to just be family there, or are other people invited too?"

His face tightened, knowing I was referring to Song.

"Me, Geo, Lisa, Ron and his family, Granny, and us."

"Are you sure?" My brow arched.

"I'm sure we're all that's supposed to be there."

"Has she come with you to Christmas at Granny's before?"

He tilted his head back annoyedly.

"Yes, Greer."

"So, she may be so inclined to invite herself to this one as well? You know; since she's still like family and all."

"Babe."

I pursed my lips at the admonishment in his tone but chose to drop it. I didn't want Song to be the reason for an argument between us, but it was hard to repress my jealousy now that she'd blatantly disrespected me. For the sake of keeping the peace, I inserted a smile on my face and walked around him towards the door.

"I'm ready to go when you are," I called behind myself.

We eventually listened to songs on his iPod playlist in the car, since I made a spectacle out of myself by huffing and puffing every time a Christmas song came on. We fell into an easy conversation that segued into my informing him of my call from Daddy. To my surprise, he expressed his reservations about it immediately.

"You don't shoot your child twice and then call for a visit like everything is everything. What about him murdering your mom and trying to kill you as a kid? What about him claiming you killed your ex?"

"We didn't talk about that. I guess it'll be discussed when I see him."

Race shot me a skeptical look from his peripheral and tightened his grip on the steering wheel.

"What?" I queried frowning.

"Nothing. You're gonna do what you're gonna do regardless of what I say."

"What do you have to say? You *don't* want me to make up with my father?"

"Greer, the man shot you. *And* you think he killed your mother. What did I miss? Why would you want to make up with him?"

"For the same reason you keep making up with Carmen after everything she's done to you. Because he's my father."

"Carmen never tried to kill me."

"Not explicitly."

He shot me a look that dropped the temperature in the car an extra degree, then shook his head with a smirk that was anything but pleasant.

"Do what you want to do, Greer. That's what you do anyway right? You don't listen to my advice. You don't wanna share your troubling thoughts and feelings with me, but you claim you love me. What am I to you really? Just a seat filler for Michael?"

My heart sank along with my eyes. I shouldn't have lashed out at him like that, but I felt attacked. Yes, Daddy was wrong. There was no question about that, but he was still my father. Of course, my kneejerk response was to defend him when someone else was lambasting him, the same way Race did for Carmen.

"Don't be ridiculous."

"Don't be ridiculous? This from the woman who is constantly questioning my loyalty behind an ex I've *repeatedly* told you I'm 100% over? She cheated on me, got pregnant with a child that could've been mine or the other guys, and probably kidnapped and gave away my cat for spite.

What the hell makes you think her simple presence is gonna miraculously make me overlook all that shit and want to get back with her? Huh? Cause you can't seem to let it go, and I'm sick of being questioned about it.

That, on top of me witnessing you get shot and you cherry picking when you want to see me... yo," fury burned behind his orbs as he continually glanced between me and the road. "Maybe we need a break. Cause I'm definitely starting to feel like I might need a break."

My heart plummeted into my shoes. I'd gone too far. Said too much. But I couldn't lose him now. We were building a love that was supposed to develop into an eternity together. One I'd kill to see to fruition.

We were coming up on the final stretch before we reached his grandmother's home. I stared at his profile, wordlessly choking back tears while he stoically peered straight ahead. I didn't know what to say to reel him back in, but whether he knew it or not, we were going to be together.

"Race," I croaked. "I'm sorry. Please don't break up with me for being flawed. I'm intimidated by her. She's so beautiful, and she's already experienced your love on a level I have yet to reach. The one time I met her, she threw it right in my face. Let me know point, blank, period, that she was not going to give up on getting you back.

"I haven't dated a lot of men. I don't have a lot of experience with love. I told you that before you, there were only two men who have ever had my heart. My daddy and Michael. Now, one is dead, and I'm estranged from the other. If we don't find a way to make up, all my family ties will essentially be severed. Daddy's always been the glue between my siblings and I.

"I've just been surrounded by so much loss these past two years, Race. I'm doing what I can to... *be* normal. *Act* normal. I know I've got a lot of baggage and I know you're putting up with a lot more from me than I have to put up with from you. I'm seeing a therapist. I don't know what else to do to better myself without losing you in the process.

"On top of everything else, it's Christmas time. Everybody's festive and happy. Spending time with their families and sharing joyous memories that I have had few and far between. I know I've been moody. I'm not just fighting depression over all that. I'm also still in pain after being shot and battling anxiety about these charges against me.

"I could already go to jail for what happened between me and Daddy, and behind the scenes, my stepsister is out there campaigning with the woman who killed my husband to pin it all on me. If you were me, you might not be the most secure, confident, person to be around all the time either."

Tears drenched my face and I swiped at them with the back of my hand. At his last glance, Race's angry expression had softened. He didn't respond to my heartfelt monologue, however.

We drove the last mile or so to Granny's in silence. Me, looking into my compact and dabbing at my face with a powder pad to correct the light coat of makeup I took such care earlier to perfect. He, laser focused straight ahead.

He parked in the closest empty space to Granny's house he could find and killed the engine. The temperature was in the low 50's, so I wore my black wool coat with no gloves. As soon as I placed my right hand on the door handle to get out, he placed a hand on my left.

"I don't want to fight," he said earnestly. "We're both dealing with family and personal situations right now that are making us a little temperamental. I snapped out on Geo at the shop yesterday for doing something I forgot I asked him to do for me. We just gotta do better."

"So, am I still your girl?" I asked coyly.

He laughed, nodded, and pecked me on the lips, grabbing the big bag of wrapped gifts from the backseat and opening the driver's side door.

Stevie Wonder's "Some Day At Christmas" was playing full blast when we entered the house. It smelled of pine, good food and cinnamon from the door. Decorations still adorned everything as it was when we welcomed Granny home from the hospital, except the tree was riper with gifts.

Faces lit up at our arrival, apparently, they were waiting on us to eat. Everyone greeted us in unison, but Granny had to be extra.

"Bout time!" Granny yelled from her Hoveround as Race bent to kiss her cheek.

"Sorry Granny. I had stuff to do first."

"Boy, gon'. You know what time we likes to eat 'round here and you bout 30 minutes off. I'm old. Every second I'm breathin' could be my last, and you mayhap lost me some time bein' hungry."

"For real Granny?" Geo chimed in chuckling. "You 'bout to die early if you don't get a taste of them yams ASAP, huh?"

"Might could be. Might could be," she confirmed motoring over to the table.

"You gonna sit in a dining room chair or you want to eat from that thing?" Ron asked with his middle child in his arms this time.

"What's her name again? I don't know why I can't remember their names?" I asked when Race stood beside me.

"Who? Ron's daughter?"

"Yes."

"Joy."

"She's cute."

"She is, but she's a terror," he said closer to my ear. "You must not remember her throwing a tantrum at the table Thanksgiving either."

I shook my head. Kids were cute to look at, but I was good at blocking them out when I needed to also. They usually liked me, and I liked them back. From a far.

Granny fussed the whole time Geo helped her into the chair at the head of the table, while Ron struggled to keep Joy's wriggling body in his arms. She bent over backwards, flailed her arms, kicked, and screamed, trying to get down.

"Denise," Ron called frustratedly.

"What do you want me to do?" She answered equally perturbed as she sat in a recliner with a towel over her shoulder and a breastfeeding Malia beneath it.

He huffed and she rolled her eyes.

"Bring Granny's baby over here to me," Granny insisted, with outstretched arms.

Ron happily passed the child to her as Lisa, gave me a look to follow her, and ducked into the kitchen. I noticed plates, silverware, napkins, and glasses were already on the table, so the food is all that was missing.

"Babe, I'm gonna go help Lisa set the food out."

Race nodded, planting another kiss on me before I departed.

"Need some help?"

"Yep," Lisa answered partially pivoting towards me.

"What's up?"

"Girl…" she started, pursing her lips, and shaking her head while removing the foil from the mac and cheese. "I am pulling my hair out by the roots. Me and Geo spent Christmas eve with my parents since we were going to be spending Christmas over here. Why did he and my father get into it over his dreads?"

"Get into it how?"

"My dad thinks he should cut them off before the wedding, so he won't look "so hood" in his words, on my big day. Why'd he go and say that," she stated handing me a bowl of greens. "They got into it right there at the dinner table. Me and my mom tried to shut it down. I'm glad my sisters weren't there. I don't know what would have happened if everybody got into it.

Once my dad started threatening not to pay for the reception if Geo was going to show up looking like a "thug", it all went straight to hell from there. Geo pushed away from the table, they both started cussing…" she sighed. "It just got totally out of hand.

I told my father I didn't need him to cut his dreads, and since it was my wedding too, it should only matter what Geo and I wanted. Then my mom got mad with him, saying that what they wanted should matter too since they were paying… Girl, we left out before dessert. Now, shit is hot between me and him, and me and my parents because he doesn't think I defended him enough. We didn't even come here in the same car."

"Oh wow," I said wide-eyed, following her out to put the dishes we carried on the table.

We stopped talking in the dining room but picked back up in the kitchen.

"Is this the first time your dad brought Geo's hair up?"

"No," she rolled her eyes. "But I never cared. So what if he doesn't like his dreads. I do, and they don' have anything to do with anything. My dad is old school though. He equates dreads with lawlessness, despite knowing Geo is a tattoo artist who is a partner in Tat Life and not a drug dealer.

They've butt heads before, but never to this level. Geo has never cussed him out before either."

We made 2 more trips to bring trays of food out before she leaned up against the counter with a sigh on what would be our last trip out.

I stood beside her and clasped her hand in mine.

"Y'all will work it out. Most couples fight over something stupid during wedding planning. He'll get past it."

Her sad eyes turned to me; tears threatening to brim.

"I can't afford $30K on my own right now out of pocket with everything else my money is tied up in. The only reason I was even having it at the Ritz Carlton is because they said they'd pay for it as a wedding gift."

"How many damn people are you inviting?"

"Three hundred."

"Thirty thousand just for the reception though? Whew! Yeah, that's pretty steep. Maybe Geo wi—" she was already shaking her head and holding a hand up to cut me off.

"Geo doesn't know how much it costs. He never would have agreed with me spending that much on a party for one night. He's made that abundantly clear. He was ranting and raving about it costing too much already when I told him it was $10K."

"You did what?" I snickered involuntarily at her foolishness and she shot me a look.

"I'm sorry. I'm not laughing at you. I'm just surprised you would lie to him about the cost. Don't you think he's gonna eventually find out, whether you tell him or not?"

"Not if he's not paying for it."

"Maybe you can downsize the ballroom or invite less people. I assume the bulk of that money is the catering?"

"Yeah, it is. Still, I can't believe my father is being so pigheaded about something so stupid on *my* wedding day. He's been uptight ever since he found out we were engaged because Geo didn't ask him for permission to marry me. He feels disrespected, and I guess this is his way of getting back at him.”

“What does your mom have to say about it?”

“What the hell is you gals in there doin’?” Granny yelled. “We in here waiting on y’all to bring out the rice, rolls and sweet tea so we can bless the food and eat, meanwhile y’all in there heein’ and hawin’.”

Lisa and I looked shamefaced at each other and grinned as she grabbed the sweet tea and rolls, while I picked up the huge bowl of rice.

“We’re comin’” Lisa replied as we filed out of the kitchen hurriedly.

We both sat in the empty seats next to our men avoiding Granny’s scolding gaze. Ron Jr. had also emerged from wherever he was to join us at the table. Granny said a longwinded grace, and everyone responded in a resounding “Amen” before digging into whatever bowl, tray or pan was closest.

My fork only met my mouth twice before the doorbell rang. Everyone looked at each other quizzically, and I instantly tensed, anticipating the unwelcomed arrival of Race’s ex. Maybe he was thinking the same thing as he pushed his chair away from the table and went to answer it.

I had the perfect view of the front door from my seat at the table, watching with an underlying disdain brewing for Song’s arrival as he opened it.

“Hey Son! Merry Christmas!” Carmen bellowed, practically tripping over the threshold in a long, gray, faux fur coat as she stretched her rail thin arms out in greeting.

Lord help us.

16

Greer

"Hey there Young Buck," a scruffy older man wearing a black skull-cap over long salt and pepper dreads, slid by Race with a snaggle tooth greeting.

Race's jaw was as tight as a vice grip as he slammed the door behind them and followed the man and Carmen into the dining room.

Carmen looked high as Halle Berry playing a crackhead in the movie "Jungle Fever"; except not as pretty. Her dark brown eyes looked hollow, lifeless, and unfocused, as she tried to fake the joy those tiny pupils were clearly devoid of. I'm sure no one was fooled.

She stopped by Granny, at the opposite end of the table from me, but the rankness that wafted off the two of them assaulted my nose from a distance. I opted to only breathe through my mouth, which meant I would not be able to eat and breathe at the same time in their presence. God damn surprise visits.

Upon closer look, her coat was patchy and matted with stains I dared not imagine the origin of. I cringed at the thought of what kind of germs she was carrying on her person. The coat was buttoned up, so I couldn't tell what she wore beneath it, but I doubted she was warm given how she danced from one dingy sneakered foot to the other and rubbed her hands together.

"Merry Christmas Momma," Carmen bent down to kiss Granny on the cheek but was met with an open palm.

"Chile, if you don't get yo' stealin' self on back from me, Imma' bust you in the head with this plate. Don't you come showin' yo' triflin' face up here on Christ's birthday, after you done stole my good silverware, and all the jewelry I had left from the last time you thieved from me."

Carmen tongued the inside of her cheek and ran an agitated hand through her thinning ponytail.

"C'mon Momma. It's the holidays! We supposed to be celebratin' family."

"Family my black ass. Family don't steal from family."

Race remained behind Carmen's companion, chin up, broad arms folded, and a contemptuous look etched in his countenance. Geo hadn't moved from his chair beside Lisa, but he and Race exchanged looks that let me know the both of them were ready to pounce if necessary.

"What you talkin' bout? Why you keep sayin' I stole from you? They at the pawn shop, Momma. You could get 'em back. Ain't like I sold 'em on the street. Besides, you never even use that silverware. Look here," she picked up a fork by Granny's plate and showed it to her. "You got silverware right here. Bam! Everybody can still eat. Right? And you don't wear that jewelry anyway. You wasn't gone do nothin' but leave it to me in your will. It was mine."

Granny shook her head dubiously and looked up to the heavens.

"Carmen, I'm not 'bout to sit here and argue wit' you. I gave you everything I had and that wasn't enough. I ain't got nothin' else for you to steal."

"And who is this nigga?" Geo barked. "This ain't even the same dude you was fuckin' wit' when you robbed Granny,"

"My kids are at the table George," Ron scolded, receiving a lethal look in return.

"Man shut up."

"I'm just saying to watch the profanity around my kids."

I'd never heard anyone call Geo, George before. Though I was aware that was his actual name. I assumed, like Race, that they both hated their hideous birth monikers, and that was why no one used them.

Geo hissed and turned back to the stranger.

"The fuck's your name, Bruh?"

"Alright now boy. Stop all that cussin'," Granny chastised.

"Name's Gene," the man spoke up in what I guessed was supposed to be an intimidating voice, but that didn't match his nervous demeanor.

He didn't look much better off than Carmen to me. He wore a blue, black, and green windbreaker over big jeans and surprisingly clean Jordan's. He was close enough for me to see his dirty fingernails however, and I silently prayed, if Granny was going to allow them to eat with us, that she'd make them wash their hands first.

Ron let out a deep sigh and massaged the new furrows creasing his forehead as his wife continued eating, disinterestedly watching the show.

"You ain't got to talk disrespectful to him. I ain't even been home two minutes and you already bad mouthin' me and talkin' crazy to my man. Y'all don't even know him yet," Carmen protested.

"Home? This ain't your home no' mo'. Not wit' me havin' to lock up everything I own from ya'. I'm getting' too old to keep tryin' to make you do right. Worryin' bout you prol'ly half of why I almost done died."

"What you talkin' about almost done died?"

"Granny was in the hospital," Ron Jr. spoke unexpectedly.

All eyes were on him before Carmen responded.

"For what? What happened Momma?"

"Don't worry 'bout what happened. Just know I almost died and instead of you bein' here to see me through, you was in them streets pawnin' my goods and sellin' your goodies to buy smack.

I done washed my hands this time," Granny threw her palms up in surrender. "You can get whatever belongs to you in that room there, but then you gots-ta go. I talked it over with the Lord and he say I been holdin' your hand long enough fo' you to be better, but ya' ain't. And I ain't got the energy no'mo.'"

"I ain't even know you was sick," she said dramatically. "How you gonna punish me for goin' to live my own life cause I ain't know you was sick? Then, you don't even wanna tell me what was wrong? I just needed a vacation. I just needed a break is all.

Y'all sittin' here judgin' me and sayin' I'm back on drugs, but I ain't. I'm just livin' my life for once without y'all on my back."

"For once?" Geo spat. "What, you think we're stupid? You think we can't see or *smell* you and this mu'fucka you strolled up in here wit'? You forget I used to sell? I know that nasty, chemical, stench of black tar heroin when I smell it. And you look high as shit. You ain't *foolin'* nobody.

I don't even know why me and Race keep tryin' to save you. You don't want to be saved. What you and this nigga come here for? Money?" He sounded tough, but the pained look on his face was deeper than anger. Lisa placed a sympathetic hand on Geo's shoulder, attempting to calm the gasket he was preparing to blow.

"Hey! I'm still yo' momma, Geo. You ain't gotta be so nasty to me. It's Christmas. I thought you'd be happy to see me since I keep hearing how y'all lookin' for me. What you was lookin' for me for if you didn't want me to come home? Why I gotta want somethin'? Ain't I still family? I came to break bread wit' my family and celebrate like everybody else. Y'all all got y'all people here, so I brought mine. Why y'all bein' so rude to my new man?

Lemme tell y'all somethin'. Gene's been takin' care of me. *Damn* good care of me. And he don't deserve y'all comin' at him sideways and I don't deserve y'all accusin' me of bein' back on drugs. Do I look like I'm back on drugs?" She splayed her arms out and spun around like Wonder Woman about to change from Diana Prince. "Huh? Huh? I look *goooood.*"

"C'mon baby. Let's go. I told you we shouldn't have come here. You ain't got to prove nothin' to these people. They ain't no better than us and I ain't about to be tap dancin' for none of them before I end up havin' to lay one of these fools down."

Race snickered sinisterly. He hadn't said a word since they entered the house, but he stood beside Gene like a waiting bouncer in VIP.

"What you say, Bruh?" Geo questioned, standing from the table. "Who *you* gonna lay down?"

"You! If I have to!" Gene yelled boldly. "I ain't scared of y'all young niggas. You better get 'em Car! You better get yo' damn jits fo' I bust a cap in 'em," he threatened.

"What?" Race finally spoke, unfolding his arms and coming chest to chest with him.

"You better back up Young Buck," Gene stepped back. "I don't wanna have to blast on one of yo—", a hand moved towards his waistband but didn't get a chance to lift it before Race fed him a knuckle sandwich, with extra knuckle.

Before I knew it, chairs were toppling, and Geo and Race were pounding Carmen's boyfriend in unison. Ron grabbed his oldest daughter from her highchair and Ron Jr. by his side. Denise darted to their baby lying asleep on the couch across the room as her husband verbally tried to defuse the situation.

Lisa was flustered and frantic, yelling for them to stop while dodging the brawl. She was smart enough not to physically try to break it up, but she pranced around them like she was going to.

Carmen's skinny body was slung from side to side as she struggled to pull one son off Gene, then the other. The whole thing was amusing to me as he caught a beatdown while The Jackson 5's "Give Love on Christmas Day" played through the speakers like theme music.

I don't know what kind of weapon Gene supposedly had in his waistband, if any, but he wouldn't be using it on the Bank's boys.

Caught up watching the melee, it was a long while before I noticed Granny watching *me*, from my peripheral. I didn't look her way, but the smile I didn't intend to wear, slowly faded as I realized my inner thoughts were revealing themselves outwardly. Her stare was expressionless. She studied me with both elbows on the table. Her hands steepled beneath her chin the way Race often did. It felt like she was looking at the *real* me. The me I didn't want anyone to see, unabridged.

Ron never stopped trying to convince the men to stop fighting from behind the table, but it was Granny's words, despite her eyes still being glued to mine, that broke it up.

"Alright! That's enough! Y'all stop this god damn fightin' in my house, fo' you break somethin'!"

Geo and Race backed off, allowing Carmen to fall onto the curled-up heap of a man she came with. Her light complexion was red with fury as she lay across Gene gathering the top of her coat in her grip. I could see where two buttons, or whatever fastened it previously, were now missing.

"Y'all ain't have to do this!" She screamed, waving her free hand at Geo and Race. "We ain't come here for this shit! Momma you know this wrong!"

Both men huffed and puffed, pacing around like caged lions as Denise pat her still sleeping baby's back on the couch and the child in Ron's arms chose that moment to cry.

"Is he still breathin'?" Granny asked pitilessly.

"Do you care? Do you care if they killed him Momma?" Carmen screamed, flipping over, and trying to move Gene's hands from covering his head.

It was weird. On top of being an obvious addict like his bitchass girlfriend, he was also a sniveling coward. No matter how much Carmen pulled on him, he kept resisting, refusing to rise from his huddle on the floor.

"C'mon Baby. Get up. We can go. We can go. Just get up."

"Get your punk ass up dude," Geo cursed when Carmen's begging didn't work.

"Well is he dead? What's he doin'?" Granny asked leaning for a better view.

I wasn't grinning anymore, and my stomach was livid that these two druggies had come in to interrupt dinner. I tilted my head in scrutiny of the man to see if there was an understandable reason why he wasn't getting up, but I suppose Race got tired of waiting.

The sound of a cocking gun drew my and everyone else's attention next.

"Get the fuck up and get out, or lay down and stay down," Race ordered.

Gene stumbled to his feet like the floor was on fire, and I saw then, the urine stain on the carpet.

"Carmen! Carmen! Get yo' jit. Get yo' jit," Gene begged through blood-stained and swollen lips.

He had a knot in the middle of his head and various cuts on his face that were beginning to swell.

I held back my smirk. Pussy.

"Race! Race! No! No!" Carmen's hands wiped and pushed at the gun as he held her off.

"I'm not gonna shoot the bastard. I'm just sick of him playin' possum. I knew he'd get up when he heard the steel."

"Car, you gon' let your jits beat on me like that? Huh? You gon' let them ke—"

"You want her to protect you? Where's the piece you were threatening to pull on us? What was in your waist?" Geo snapped.

"I ain't got no god damn gun! I ain't say I had a gun!"

"He don't have a gun! Y'all ain't have no right puttin' your hands on him like that!" Carmen cosigned, still grabbing at Race's arm.

"What were you gonna blast us with then?" Race shoved Carmen again. "Stop grabbing my arm before I accidentally shoot this nigga."

"Put the damn gun away, Horace!" Granny demanded starting to stand from her chair.

"What are you doin'? What you getting' up for? Sit down, Granny," Geo rushed to help her.

"All y'all actin' a fool on Christ's birthday cause don't none of y'all 'cept Ron and Denise respect the lord enough to go to church. Heathens and whores and addicts. Every one of y'all needs to find Jesus."

"I go to church Granny," Ron Jr. chimed in.

"I know you do baby," she replied less gratingly.

"Momma, you gonna let them do me like this? Do my man, a guest in your house, like this?"

"Chile please," Granny said now leaning on Geo. "If you came back because you wanna get some help and get clean again, then you can stay. Otherwise, I need you and yo' armadillo fightin' friend to go. I can't do this no mo'. Your boys can't do this no mo' neither."

Armadillo fightin'? I wanted to laugh out loud. He did kind of curl up like one of them as soon as the beatdown ensued. I felt like an awkward spectator in the crowd. I knew I was supposed to be doing something. Reacting in some way like Lisa or Denise were, but I was drawing a blank.

I hadn't eaten since early afternoon and my mind was only on two things. Eating dinner and getting these garbage-smelling smack addicts away from me so I could breathe through my nose again.

"Well, we wasn't expectin' to be put out as soon as we got here. Can you at least give me twenty dollars for a Uber or something?" Carmen asked with one arm intertwined with one of Gene's as he pouted.

"Uber doesn't take cash," Ron declaimed, comforting a now quieted Malia.

Carmen cut her eyes at him.

"I *meant* a cab. I just said Uber."

"How was you gonna get home if you stayed longer? Was Old Gene gonna call a magic carpet?" Geo taunted.

"I got some friends who was gonna come drive us, but it's too early to call them. They wouldn't be ready yet."

"Oh, you got a phone? Cause you didn't answer none of our calls."

"*Yyyyeah,*" she said swiveling her bird thin neck with an attitude. "I got a new phone wit' a new number."

"Umph," Geo nodded, folding his lips in.

They went back and forth over her having a phone, where she was supposed to be taking a cab to, how she knew it would cost twenty dollars, blah blah blah. I honestly stopped listening after I tasted a forkful of the mac & cheese. I knew Granny made it because it was just as delicious at Thanksgiving.

I'd only intended to eat a few bites, but a few bites turned into several.

"I guess you were really hungry, huh?" Ron questioned with a cocked brow.

When I looked up from my plate, noticing he was talking to me, I felt my cheeks flush red. Everyone was back standing or sitting at the table again, sans Carmen and Gene.

"Uh," I looked at each of them, embarrassed. "I'm sorry. I haven't eaten all day."

"It's okay. Gon' and eat," Granny curled her lip perfunctorily. "We all wish we was eatin' 'stead of messin' with Carmen and that devil man she brought to my house."

That's when I realized, the two of them were gone and Race was standing beside my chair. A tempered storm apparent in his eyes, I hoped my choosing dinner over involving myself in the drama with his mother didn't contribute to his upset.

"You okay?" I asked.

"Yeah. You ready to go?"

"Go?"

"Leave," he said agitatedly. "You can make a to go plate."

"Horace," Granny sighed his name disappointedly. "You don't need to leave. She's gone now. We're all here to have Christmas together."

"I know Granny, but I'm not in the mood anymore and I don't want to bring down anybody else's Christmas."

Geo kissed his teeth while turning the chair he previously sat in upright and sitting in it.

"Race, man don't even let them get to you. We whipped that nigga's ass and Carmen went where she wants to be. We can't keep tryin' to make her do what she don't want to do. She loves that smack and them streets more than us. I ain't even gon' sweat it no'mo."

To me, Race and Geo didn't usually sound so… country. But once they were around their grandmother, their country boys in them came out full throttle.

"Nah. We gonna head out. Make us a couple of plates to go babe," he ordered. Solidifying that his wishes were not to be deterred.

"What about your Christmas gifts Uncle Race?" Ron Jr. asked.

"I'll open them later, little man. You can still open the ones I got for you whether I'm here or not. I'm sure your dad is gonna record it so I can watch later."

Satisfied with that answer, Ron Jr. nodded and smiled as I got up to get Styrofoam trays from the kitchen. Lisa came with me and took one of the trays from my hand to help.

"I wish you'd stay," Granny repeated.

Race rounded the table to her and bent down to kiss her on her forehead as he often did.

"I'll come back by tomorrow. Somethin' else might happen if we stay, and I don't want to mess Christmas up for everybody more than it already is."

He shot Ron a nasty look and Ron averted his eyes to Denise, who was holding her sleeping daughter over her lap while eating.

"Bruh, I'm tellin' you. Brush it off. I got your back. You can't take nothin' pussy ass Ron has to say about you seriously," Geo spat with a half chuckle.

I looked at Lisa perplexed. What had I missed? What had Ron done?

"I swear, you act like you don't have any home training. I hope you grow up before you and Lisa have kids," Ron rebut.

Geo's smirk disappeared.

"Yo. Don't make me smack you in front of your wife."

"George!" Granny scolded.

"See. This is why I'm leaving." Race confirmed as Lisa and I continued filling the trays and Geo and Ron shot daggers at one another.

We said our goodbye's, taking our food and a few gifts for us that Granny insisted we bring home. The instant we hit the inside of the car, his mouth was running. Race is usually very even tempered, so seeing that angry side of him when he and Geo fought Gene, and this heated version of him in the car was good. I wanted to know all of my man.

Apparently, while I was consumed with eating, Race had given Carmen and her man the Jackson they were cadging for, simply to expedite their exit. Ron and Geo protested, but once the money was in Carmen's hand, she and Gene made no haste.

Ron lambasted Race for enabling Carmen again, which lead to an ugly exchange that Denise and Granny diffused.

"But why *did* you give her the money?" I asked abashed.

He grit his teeth, gripped the steering wheel harder, making the bruised and bloody flesh on his knuckles stretch.

"Oh, Babe… your knuckles."

"They're fine."

I stared at his profile a moment longer before clearing my throat and leaning back in my seat. I wasn't going to push him to talk if he didn't want to. Hell, I didn't actually want to talk either. *I* wanted to eat. However, after minutes of dead silence, he decided to answer.

"I just wanted them to leave." He looked between me and the road, and when I said nothing, he continued. "If all it was gonna take to make them leave was twenty dollars, I was gonna give it to them. I've been through this too many times with her before Greer. Like Granny and Geo said, I'm sick of trying to help her when she doesn't want to be helped.

I know they're gonna take the money and get high, but they're gonna get high whether they get it from me or somewhere else. She didn't come home for dinner. Not *just* for dinner anyway. She came to try to scam us out of some money and probably to see what Christmas gifts they could steal.

We could've threw them out, but I didn't want to have them out there making a scene in front of Granny's house or scaring the kids more than they already were. Granny puts on a brave face, but it hurts her to see Carmen like that too."

"Okay. I can understand that. But why not stay then?"

He shook his head. "Ron wasn't gonna let it go. I know my brother. Once he gets on his high horse, he can't come down until you bring him down; and there was enough fighting and arguing in that house already for the night.

I just needed to get away from him. From all of them really. Granny too. They always want me to be the one to fix everything, but then they want to pick apart and criticize how I do it. It stopped feeling like Christmas the minute she brought that guy in the house with her.

We've gotten her back clean before, but she never brought anybody to Granny's while she was high. While they were both high. She's gone Greer. I looked into her eyes… and it was empty. She wasn't in there anymore. Them drugs got her for good this time, and I can't help her."

My heart broke for him. I sort of understood how he felt. Not about Carmen specifically, because she was a worthless piece of shit who deserved to be cut loose. But as a son loving his mom, I understood the struggle. I was stuck between decisions myself. With my dad. Was I going to forgive and forget with him? Or give him what *he* deserved?

"Let me clean your hands up for you. You ripped your knuckles up pretty bad," I told Race as we ascended the stairs at my house after leaving the food in the kitchen.

He looked down at the bruised flesh where blood was drying around the joints and flexed his fingers back and forth with a pained mien.

I flicked the light on in the master bathroom and gestured for him to sit on the closed toilet seat as I opened the medicine cabinet. I grasped a bottle of Witch-hazel and gauze in one hand and a tube of Neosporin in the other.

"What were you thinkin' tonight?"

"What do you mean?" I asked squatting on the edge of the tub to begin tending to my patient.

"You ain't move, you ain't say nothin'… you ain't flinch. You just ate, with your greedy self," he smirked. "But before that?"

I rolled my lips around and inhaled, contemplating my response.

"I don't know. I didn't know what to do. That's your mother. It wasn't my place to get in the middle of a family spat. If I said the wrong thing, I could've had your whole family down my throat. I didn't want to risk it. I didn't want to risk making *you* angry with me.

"However you decided to handle it, I had your back. There wasn't anything for me to say or do until you said so. Kind of turned me on. Watching you show Gene what you're made of."

I smiled coyly and he licked his lips, bringing both hands to my cheeks before I finished putting Neosporin on them. His lips were on mine and his tongue in my mouth before I could question what was happening. When the kiss broke, we both grinned.

"Bedtime?"

"Bedtime," he confirmed knowing damn good and well neither one of us planned to sleep.

We stood and I moved to replace the Witch-hazel and Neosporin in the cabinet.

"Wait," he reached in the cabinet, picking up one of my color contact lens boxes. "You wear contacts?"

"S-Sometimes."

"Color contacts?" he continued inspecting the box.

"Can you get out of my business?" I teased, snatching the box from him, and placing it in the medicine cabinet, closing the door behind it.

He frowned. "What you got color contacts for though?"

"If I tell you, I'll have to kill you," I laughed.

But I wasn't kidding.

17

Greer

December 28th 2015

I threw the clothes I wore home from Angie's in a garbage can at a gas station on my way to Perimeter Mall. They'd been in my possession way longer than I intended because I got sick and hadn't been out alone much until now. It was a beautiful, sunny but brisk day, and what I did intend to do, was take advantage of it.

I was supposed to see Daddy later and I wanted to give him some gifts to give to Tamia and Willow, for me; even though Christmas was over. I missed my nieces. Well, I missed Tamia. Willow was too young for me to have bonded with her, but Tamia reminded me so much of myself.

I hoped Debbie wasn't stamping out the light in her oldest daughter the way she and Stephanie had done me growing up. I settled on a pink, lace covered diary and a pair of gold heart studs for Tamia, and a plush, speak and learn teddy bear for Willow. A few hours later, I was exiting the mall with an added couple of outfits for myself and a burner phone from an electronics store.

It was killing me not to have the use of my phone at Angie's when I wanted it and not to be able to use GPS if I needed it. A burner phone was the perfect alternative asset for me while I completed my remaining tasks.

"Greer?"

I turned around as I pushed through the doors to exit and saw no one, so I kept going. Just as the door closed behind me, my name was called again. I pivoted to see Ms. Nina, in black pants and low heels under a dark green coat that reached her knees. Her gray hair was hidden under a knitted black visor style beanie, leaving only her sideburns exposed.

Her eyes narrowed as she closed the distance between us. Not at all the pleasant greeting I would've expected. Her purse and two shopping bags on one arm, her matte brown lips pressed into a slit.

"I thought that was you."

"Ms. Nina. Hey."

"I see you're looking in good health," she surmised looking me up and down.

"I'm doing as well as can be expected I suppose. I assume you've been well. It's been a while since we've spoken or seen each other. How was your Christmas?"

"Lonely, without my son. I miss him. Very much."

"Me too."

"I doubt it."

"Ms. Nina! Why would say such a thing?" I asked appalled. "I will always grieve Michael's death."

"Murder. Michael's *murder.*"

"Yes. I know how he died. Why are you so angry with me? I thought you and I were starting to build a bond."

"You know, I never realized what a good actress you were before. You definitely missed your calling."

"I beg your pardon? Are you *trying* to hurt my feelings?"

She scoffed. "Hurt your feelings? Oh, I doubt that. I'm not as ignorant to the type of person you and your father are as I was before. At least one good thing came out of my relationship with your father. If we hadn't started dating, I would never have gotten to know Debbie better." She took a step closer. Our faces, inches apart. "My eyes are wide open to both of you now. And *you're* not going to get away with killing my son, either."

Astonished, I jerked my head back, clutching my invisible pearls. "What on earth are you talking about? Are we in the Twilight Zone? I should've known Debbie had something to do with this. It's always *Debbie*. Ms. Nina. You know my sister and I have always had a volatile relationship. She hates me. She'll say anything to make everyone else hate me too.

I've heard about her supposed "assistance" in Marlene's upcoming appeal hearing. I had no idea she dragged you into it too. Her attorney must really be desperate. There's absolutely *no* truth to her allegations. None whatsoever. Why are you even entertaining her foolishness?"

"I visited Marlene in jail, Greer and we talked for a *very* long time. There was no reason for her to kill my son. She didn't want him to leave you for her and she wasn't leaving her situation for Michael.

Listening to her testimony in court didn't provide an inkling of the insight I gained through actually talking to her. Tell me this. *Did* you know Michael was having an affair before the day he was murdered?"

I rolled my eyes and huffed out a warm breath that quickly vaporized in the cold air.

"Why does that matter, now?"

"Because you've lied to me. And because it's a motive. You told me you had no idea he was cheating until afterwards. Debbie says you had some type of surveillance set up in your house. She also said you claimed you told the police about it, but Marlene's attorney says there is no mention of you recording them together."

"Yes. I knew he cheated. Okay? When I found out, I confronted him about it, and he was supposed to have ended it. I didn't tell you because I was embarrassed. That was my personal marital business. How awkward would it be to have to discuss your husband's infidelity with his mother? Plus, for all I knew, you already knew. You haven't always liked me. It would've been even more embarrassing to find out you knew and were indifferent about it."

"Don't be ridiculous. I never would've approved of him having an affair, regardless of how I felt about *you*. You know the history between Michael's father and I."

I shrugged, glancing at a few nosey shoppers trying to eavesdrop as they passed.

"Yes, I do know about your history with him. But I couldn't be sure what you would do at the time. Besides, I was taught to keep what happens in my marriage, *inside* my marriage. I would never have told Debbie anything. Then or now. Of course, I didn't tell the police I set up surveillance in my house on Michael. Because I didn't.

Debbie found out I had Stephanie's old phone and lost her mind over it. There's no telling what she did with it once she got it back to try and incriminate me. Whether I knew about his affair or not, let's not forget, I had an alibi. It would've been impossible for me to murder Michael at the same time I was 35 miles away helping my father recuperate from cancer treatments."

"Says *you* and Chuck. Before you shot him, or maybe even now, I believe he would've done anything for you. Why wouldn't one murderer cover for the other?" She addressed me with scorn.

My surprised silence was genuine. Had she called us both murderers?

"Don't look so shocked. I believe Chuck killed your mother exactly as you said it happened. Or rather, as Shawn said it happened. Despite how skilled of a liar the two of you must be, I read some of the pages of that diary myself, and I know the difference between real and fiction. That wasn't a made-up story."

"So, you have it."

She frowned. "Have what?"

"The diary."

"No ma'am, I do not. I left it right where I found it in your room. I wasn't going to help him hide that book once I realized he only wanted it because it was true. I haven't seen *it*, or him since."

"Daddy asked you to hide it for him?"

"No. He just asked me to get it since I had my own key. I'm sure he planned to destroy it, and if you don't have it, he probably *did* destroy it. Not that it was necessary. They already got the wrong person in Michael's case. They certainly won't be anxious to open up a closed one from over 20 years ago. Especially when the author says its pure fiction. I suppose Shawn's wrapped around his finger too."

"I'm confused. You read the diary and you believe me about Daddy, yet you're standing here accusing me of murdering Michael. Why?"

"Because you did it. She looked me straight in my eyes and answered every question I asked without flinching. Not once. I'm going to pay to have a lie detector test administered to her on Saturday to help with her appeal."

"Why waste your time and money on that? Maybe you're not aware, but those aren't admissible in court, Ms. Nina. I'm sure a good liar can be very convincing."

"You would know, wouldn't you?"

"No. I wouldn't know. I've never lied to you."

She disregarded my response with an eye roll. "I bet you've been lying to me since the day we met. I never bought in to this… this… goody two shoes act you've been trying to sell. You had my Michael fooled because it all came wrapped up in a pretty little southern bell package; but not me.

I knew you were hiding a mean streak under there somewhere. Just know, I'm not going to let you get away with killing my son. I don't care if he cheated on you. That's not punishable by death. You're not the only one who knows how to watch somebody when they don't think anybody's watching, either. And *you* my dear, have been slipping."

My heart palpitated so hard it could've jumped out of my chest and run into traffic. Was she watching me?

"What is that supposed to mean? What could you possibly be watching me for? He's been dead almost two years now. What do you think is going to happen? Am I supposed to go visit his grave and suddenly confess?"

She shrugged just as I had earlier. "Or maybe you'll visit Kendrick's grave and confess instead. That *is* the name of the boy you were having an affair with at work, isn't it?"

"*Kendrick?* I don't know why his name is even being brought up. I didn't start seeing him until long after Michael passed away. Your son, was the cheater. Not me," I jabbed the air with my index finger for emphasis. "So what exactly are you insinuating?"

"Nothing I'm willing to share with *you*, yet. You forget, I'm retired, with lots of money and nothing but time on my hands to follow up on you. You'll know what I've got on you soon enough. And if you don't go to jail for killing my Michael, you'll go to jail for something else. Sort of like how the white folks did OJ."

"You're starting to sound like you may be a stalker. Am I going to need a restraining order against you? You better not be following me or watching my house."

"And if I am? What are you gonna do about it? Kill me? I'm not afraid of you."

She grinned ominously, shaking her head while reaching into her handbag. I took a step back, not sure what she was about to pull out. That seemed to amuse her further.

"Believe me darling. If I was going to shoot you, it wouldn't be in broad daylight. Anyway, that reminds me. I don't need this anymore since you changed the locks and installed your little security system." She opened her palm to reveal a key that I'm sure used to unlock the doors to my house. When I didn't take it, she tilted her hand and let it fall to the ground.

"How do *you* know I have a new security system?"

"Wouldn't *you* like to know?" She shoulder-checked me and tried to strut off, but I grabbed her wrist.

"I'm not playing with you Ms. Nina. You better not be following me or recording me, or whatever it is you think you're doing. If you don't want to be in my life anymore, then fine. If you want to believe my psycho sister and the trifling side-whore who murdered your son over me, I can't do anything about that. But if you know what's good for you, you'll leave me alone."

"There she is," she taunted. "This is the real you talking to me now. Or what, Greer?" She snatched out of my grip. "What will you do if I don't stop..." she lowered her tone in a sardonic whisper. "*Whatever* I'm doing? Huh?"

I was too livid at the thought of her following me, or maybe even paying someone like a P.I., to reply. With one last nasty glance in my direction, she walked away towards the covered parking deck.

I stood another 30 seconds in the same place. Face red with trepidation as my tongue swept across the top of my gums in thought. She was probably just trying to get under my skin. Maybe she'd found out about the locks and the system by attempting to let herself in while I was out.

To my knowledge, Ms. Nina was far from tech savvy. She barely knew how to work the DVR on the cable box. But... why had she brought up Kendrick? So many questions ran through my head as I walked to my car. How exactly was she watching me? Was she tailing me? Taping me? How long had she been doing it? More importantly, who else knew?

One thing was for certain. I was going to find out.

Daddy's cherry red Buick Roadmaster pulled up behind me in my driveway before I turned the ignition off. It wasn't even one o'clock yet. He was early. I grabbed my purse and bags from the passenger's side and got out at the same time he did.

"You're early," I called behind myself, walking to the door.

"I thought traffic would be worse than it was. I ain't been out drivin' this time of day in a good while."

I opened the door and disarmed the alarm as daddy followed.

"When'd you get that?"

"After I got out of the hospital, somebody broke in."

"You wasn't home was you?"

"Yeah, but I got out of the house before he could get to me or steal anything. He broke in through the basement door. No big deal. Crime has gone up around here lately It was time for me to get one."

"Ain't you s'posed to be movin'?"

"I will be, but while I'm still here, I'd like to feel safe, or at least comfortable in my own home. Especially since I don't have my gun anymore."

"Welp. I can understand that."

His green eyes read concern as he began to take his coat off, but then I thought about my conversation with Ms. Nina. What if she had my place bugged or video cameras I didn't know about somewhere in the house?

I would think the alarm company would've said something while installing the security system had they found anything. But maybe they hadn't, or just didn't think to ask. Given the anticipated nature of the conversation we were about to have, I couldn't afford any sneaky eyes or ears to be in it.

"On second thought, Daddy. Let's go out and grab something to eat. I'm kind of hungry already and I didn't cook anything."

"I don't thank what we got to say should be discussed in public."

"We can order food to go and talk in the car."

He eyed me dubiously. "What's wrong wit' talkin' here?"

"Daddy, there's still a restraining order in place. We're not supposed to *be* together, let alone, be seen together. People have been popping up at my house left and right uninvited. I just think it's too risky.

"My Yukon is big with a lot of leg room. I think we can talk comfortably in it. Let me just drop these bags off in my room and we can go. The doors are unlocked."

He shrugged his coat back on without another word and went back outside as I ascended the stairs. His gray curly hair was slicked down on his head the same way Smokey Robinson often wore it. He took his slight resemblance to the popular Motown singer as a compliment and milked the comparison often.

Minutes later, we were headed to a little café Daddy and I like on the outskirts of the neighborhood. We rode in silence, sans conversation about what we might order. I hadn't gone this long without seeing my father since he stopped driving trucks more than six years ago.

He seemed to have aged more, although the mature good looks that turned the heads of younger and older women when we were out, were still intact. His red and black flannel shirt was tucked into the waist of his belted jeans with a single gold chain around his neck and diamond studs in his ears.

Charles "Chuck" Foster. Was I still gonna have to kill him?

We placed our orders at Bijou Bistro and went to wait in the car for the 15 to 20 minutes they advised it would take our food to be ready.

In the meantime, I let the car run so we could use the heat and took my coat off to get comfortable.

"So. What did you want to talk about?"

His brows furrowed and he rubbed the stubble on his chin in thought, gazing out the windshield instead of at me.

"I s'pose it's mo' than one thang we need to hash out, but first thangs first. I'm sorry, Baby Girl. I know it don't mean a lot to ya' right nah, but I mean it from my heart.

It prolly' don't make sense that I'm sayin' I love ya' when I shot ya', but I thought you was gon' kill me. You was drunk, and angry and holdin' a gun. After I admitted what I done to yo' momma, y-y-you got even worse. I ain't want to die. I panicked and got my gun.

I guess I shoulda' took my punishment like a man, even iffin' you *was* gonna shoot me," he looked into my face then. Remorse clear and evident. "I know I woulda' deserved it fo' what I done to you. You was a innocent chile' and I was selfish.

I know that's why you was hurt so bad. Me and you bein' so close, then you find out what evil I did to you as a baby. I know that. But... I did what I did. You might not believe me, but I'm glad you survived back then, and I'm glad you still here right now."

"You know what's ironic?"

"What?"

"The day you shot me, was Momma's birthday. I saw it on her driver's license from the box of her things you gave me. Irina Amanar. DOB, November 30th 1959," I watched my twiddling thumbs and sighed.

Daddy grunted. "Welp, I cain't say I knew that. Not sure I ever knew it to memory. Don't thank she celebrated it round me befo'. I also wanna say, I ain't come see ya' in the hospital, cause at first I was mad, and then it was too late. What wit' the restrainin' order and such. You been recoverin' good?"

"Yeah. I have. What about you? How's your side?"

"*Aaaaa,* I'm old. Seems like everything hurts even when it ain't been hurt befo'," he chuckled. "I'm fine far as the bullet wound goes. Went right through."

"Good. I figured as much. I wasn't aiming to kill you."

"I know. I s'pose this what they call, *ironic.* Tween me and you. After all that murder T.V. we watched together, "Snapped", "Wives With Knives", "Deadly Women" and such; I reckon you and me neva' thought we'd be just like one of them people tryin' to kill family, did we?"

"I know I didn't. Can I ask you something?"

"Sure"

"Do you have the diary?"

He looked confused. "No. I ain't been to yo' house to take it."

"Did you send anybody to get it?"

He tilted his head annoyedly. "I just told ya' I don't have it. If you don't, I don't know who does." He paused a beat. "I asked Nina to get it fo' me the day after, but she said she couldn't find it. Ain't had no words fo' me since. Maybe she took it."

I pretended to think about what he said, knowing Ms. Nina had already denied possession of the book.

"Greer, you wasn't neva' meant to know 'bout what I did. Thang is, I ain't know Shawn knew till you showed up talkin' 'bout that diary." He neva' said nothin' 'bout it."

"Did Stephanie know?"

"*Nooo.* No. No," he shook his head emphatically. "I neva' told a soul. Was gonna take it to my final dirt nap. I ain't proud of it. But I tried to make up fo' what you loss by raisin' you. I know that didn't turn out perfect eitha'. What wit' Steph bein' mad all the time an holdin' me an yo' momma's business against ya'. I always loved ya' though, Greer. Even though I did what I did. I still loved ya' and I just learned to love ya' mo' as you got growed up."

I felt the salt building in my eyes, preparing to trickle tears.

"I hear you, but… how do you try to kill somebody you love?"

He rolled his tongue around the inside of his cheek before answering.

"You loved Michael, didn't ya?" I parted my lips to protest, but he held a hand up to silence me. "Don't even botha' denyin' it eitha'. I know you did it. And I don't care. I know'd why you did it, and I bet if Steph had the gumption to, all them years ago, she woulda' done me the same.

Irina was a good woman, but she wasn't no innocent. No mo' innocent than that gal you put in jail, or the husband you put in the dirt. You and me both gonna have to answer to God fo' the wrongs we did here on earth. Me sooner than you, I'm sure. But while we're here, I'm hopin' you can fo'give me for my part."

I wished I could site the flaw in his logic, but he was right. He only knew about Michael and Marlene. He didn't even know about the retribution I sought against Song and her unborn child. Let alone everybody on the list. I suppose my audacity was as great as Daddy's.

In Stephanie's position, I might have done worse to clean the slate for my family. Erase the bastard proof of my husband's insolence to our marriage. Daddy had simply tried to clean up his mess on his own. I guess Ms. Nina was right after all. Like father, like daughter.

"I do. I do forgive you."

"Thank ya. Knowin' you fo'give me makes what I'm 'bout to say a little bit easier."

"What?" I asked worriedly.

He took a deep breath and ran both hands up and down the legs of his jeans before turning back to look at me.

"I'm sick again."

"Sick? Sick how?"

"When they was treatin' me in the hospital fo' my gunshot wounds, they took some x-rays. Long story short. I had to have mo' tests run after that. Doctor say they found some golf ball sized tumors on my liver. When all that testin' came back later, they told me I got stage four liver cancer."

I covered my mouth, involuntarily weeping in response. Funny how just days ago I was wishing death on the man, and now I was sobbing at the news that he would be dying soon by someone else's hand. God's.

"There, there nah, Baby Girl," Daddy comforted me with a pat on my leg. "I done beat the devil enough times, and now it's time to let God's will be done. I ain't 'bout to go through no mo' chemo or none of that otha' stuff to drag it out. I'mmo just enjoy whateva' life I got left till I ain't got it no mo'."

"H-how long do you have?"

"*Aaaaa*, don't you worry 'bout that. Long enough. That's how much time I got." He smiled.

"Does everybody else know?"

"Everybody that matters knows."

"Do they know you're wanting to let *me* back in?"

He nodded.

"Yeah. I told 'em I was gonna drop the restrainin' order and tell the judge I ain't wanna press no charges against ya' in court next week."

"And what did they have to say?"

"It don't matter what they said. I'm gonna do what I wanna do. They don't live fo' me and if I'm honest, you and me share somethin' I don't share wit' nobody else. And I ain't talkin' 'bout killin'," he quipped.

As crass a joke as it was, I smirked, then laughed between my tears. I glanced down at my watch and saw that it was a little past the time the restaurant said our food would be ready.

"I'm gonna go in and get our food," I told him, putting my coat back on. "I changed my mind. If somebody sees us, then… they just do. I don't care. Let's take the food back to the house and eat it. We can watch one of our shows on the ID Network and talk; like we used to. I miss doing that with you. I miss you."

"I miss you too, Baby Girl."

I really did miss my daddy. Hearing that the cancer was back, in his liver and not his prostate this time, was jarring. Stage four was the last stage before death. Life was too short. Which made the need for me to swipe the key to his eldest daughter's home off his key ring even more urgent. I always knew I was gonna outlive Daddy, but I needed to make sure we were *both* gonna outlive *Debbie*.

18

Greer

December 30th 2015

"Suicide? Oh my God."

Dr. Lancaster shook her head with pity. "I was surprised too."

"Wh-I-She..." I feigned speechlessness. "I don't even know what to say. Did she leave a note?"

"Not that I know of. There's talk that she did it because the police were getting onto her about Kendrick's death."

"Getting onto her? She killed Kendrick?"

"I have no idea. The rumor mill is buzzing with a lot of speculation. I just know I will be all too happy when the sight of a police officer in here won't mean another one of my employees is dead.

"I know you'll be back in two weeks but Dr. Shewmer and I have already set up some interviews for a new NP. We can't afford to be down another employee for too long since Angie was seeing a lot of follow patients for Dr. Shewmer, Preston, and I while we're doing hospital rounds."

"Of course. I understand."

"On another note, you're progressing quite well. The mobility in your right arm is healing surprisingly fast. Have you been incorporating the exercises I suggested?"

"Yes. Mostly yoga and cardio, but I've also done some weightlifting." About 150 pounds of *dead* weight to be exact.

"Good. Good. And how are you holding up on the lower dosages? Has your level of pain and frequency decreased?"

"I think I'm handling it okay. I do feel nauseous at times though."

"That can happen sometimes while your body is readjusting."

"I will say that the more I'm weening off them, the less I feel like I need them. I still have some instances of pain, but it's considerably less than when I was discharged, and I feel stronger."

"That's what we want. Do you have any questions for me?"

"Nope."

"Alright then, you can get dressed. Make an appointment to see me in another two weeks. I know you'll be swamped, just getting back to work and everything, but work it in my schedule for a time when you think your workload will be lighter."

"I will."

"Take care," she said with a smile and polite nod, leaving me in the exam room alone to change.

I was cheesing harder than a Cheshire cat snagging a mouse at the news of Angie's suicide. My plan had worked. I only hoped Kendrick's case would be in my rearview mirror soon as well. I was going to take the fact that I hadn't heard anything else from Detective Herrera as a good sign.

Ms. Nina's mention of Kendrick's name made me nervous. There's no way she could've known what I'd done to him. I certainly hadn't talked about it in an incriminating way to anyone. But what if she saw Detective Herrera come to my home through whatever means she was surveilling me? What if she somehow *heard* what was said? The speculation was going to drive me insane.

I didn't tell Daddy about my run in with Ms. Nina at the mall. According to him and her both, they were no longer involved. I didn't want to give him any reason to reach out.

I waited until he went to the bathroom to rummage through his coat pocket and snag the key to Debbie's off the ring. He had a bunch of keys on it and I doubted he'd even notice it was gone. He rarely had to use it in all the years it was in his possession.

Nine out of ten times Will and Debbie brought the kids over to his house. Their family had never been on a vacation or gone anywhere for Daddy to need to watch their place either.

I wouldn't have to swipe a key to get into Ms. Nina's place. Michael had a spare key to her house that was in a box in the basement with many other things belonging to him. Unless she'd changed the locks, I would have no problem getting in.

Still, Ms. Nina had me paranoid. I googled ways to search your place for hidden surveillance and was up all night doing an amateur sweep. I searched every nook and cranny inside and outside but didn't find anything. I knew she would be going to bible study tonight like she did every Wednesday, and though it wasn't in my original plans to do so, I was going to make room to pay her home a visit.

After my doctor's appointment, I had to meet with Sylvia Brass at her office to discuss my case and upcoming pretrial. She had good news and bad news for me when I arrived. She gave me the good news first.

Mr. Adamson, the Prosecutor, was an ass but didn't want to waste a lot of time and money on me with a highly publicized serial killer case now in his lap. Eleven elementary school teachers were kidnapped, raped, and buried alive on a 50-acre farm in Cobb County. One miraculously survived. Two of the three assailants were apprehended last night.

The manhunt was on for the third and the pressure to indict and prosecute these men was already soaring. According to Sylvia, Adamson was trying to get as much menial stuff off his plate as possible so he could devote his time to ensuring the case was ironclad.

Also, even though neither side had the diary, both party's assertion that it existed supported my state of mind. Daddy had also done what he said he would and contacted both attorneys to let them know he did not want to press charges. He also made a statement saying that although he was afraid for his life, he realized in hindsight that I wasn't aiming to kill him when he was shot.

I was not required to show up for the pretrial hearing since it was primarily for attorneys to hash out everything to avoid trial altogether, but I could if I wanted to.

I felt like the fact that my presence wasn't required was a good thing. That meant nobody was trying to lock me up afterwards. I anticipated going anyway. I like to know exactly what's going on firsthand when I'm involved. Especially where my freedom is concerned.

The bad news was that my blood alcohol level on the night was too high for the courts to ignore. I couldn't argue that anyone else was driving and part of my defense was that I was inebriated and not in complete control of my faculties.

The fact that I hadn't been pulled over in my vehicle was a nonfactor since they only had to show that I had broken the law either way.

Sylvia said she would argue for the lowest amount but was sure I would have to pay fines upwards of one to two thousand dollars. I could possibly be put on probation for at least 30 days, and/or get 20 to 40 hours community service. There was also a possibility my license would have restrictions for a limited time, like driving to and from work, depending on the judge's propensity for leniency.

I wasn't thrilled, but it wasn't the worst that could be done to me I suppose. I asked Sylvia if Debbie's slander campaign to help Marlene during her appeal could hurt me in this case, and she assured me it wouldn't. Even if Debbie showed up to the pretrial hearing to trash me, her words would likely hold less weight than Daddy's.

I didn't bring up Kendrick's case to Sylvia because I figured if no detectives had been to see her and she didn't discover any reason to in her findings, I was good. Overall, as long as I wasn't going to have to go to jail, I thought I would be able to cope with the ultimate consequences.

I left there feeling somewhat optimistic. Now that I'd come to terms with what Daddy did, I only had a couple more tasks to complete before I started back to work and hopefully, back to normalcy.

I chatted with Shan briefly while I drove, updating her on what my attorney said and cackling about our plans for New Years. She and Jahari were flying to Atlanta in the morning to celebrate the coming new year and Bri's birthday.

Of course, I hadn't spoken to Bri's obnoxious ass or any of Shan's other sorors since the time we drank together at SIX FEET UNDER and Bri got sick. With a little help from my Visine bottle.

Anyway, Bri invited Shan and Jahari, and by extension, Race and I were also invited. I was looking forward to spending time with my bestie and my man together. They hadn't had a lot of time to get to know each other and he and Jahari could bond too. I also had a killer bodycon sequin; gold scoop neck dress I was dying to wear.

Shan and I talked until I arrived at my destination and unfortunately, she hadn't uttered a word about Wendy. The responders to my Craig's List ad had proven disappointing thus far, but I was hoping one of the cowards had done something and simply hadn't updated me yet. I guess the whore home wrecker was still living her best trifling life. Que sera sera.

"Hey Rodger, is Will around?" I asked entering the garage area with a big shopping bag on my wrist when I spotted someone *other* than Will behind the counter through the store window.

His back was to me, and I assume I startled him as he nearly choked on the bottle of Vitamin Water he was guzzling like the slob he was.

"G-Greer. *Heeey,*" he wiped his mouth with the back of his greasy hand and smiled. "Uh… yeah I think so. Let me buzz him for you." He threw the unfinished bottle in the trash and walked over to a phone on the intake desk. "Hey… Greer's out here for you… I don't know… Okay."

I looked around impatiently. Anxious to get away from Rodger's leering eyes. All I wanted to do was drop off the girl's gifts and complete my mission. Inconspicuously sticking one of the trackers under Will's car.

"He's in a meeting with somebody in his office right now. He'll be out as soon as possible."

"Thanks." I sat in a chair posted up against the wall near the entrance from the garage to the storefront.

"You look nice."

"Thanks," I answered looking down at my phone and hoping he'd go away.

"You wear pink a lot, huh? You're favorite color?"

"Umm hmm."

"Looks good on you. Brings out your eyes."

I sighed quietly and continued scrolling my phone. He leaned against the podium style intake desk in a manner I assumed was supposed to make him look cool. Epic fail.

He cleared his throat and adjusted his glasses. "So, Greer, I was wondering if you wanted to go out with me sometime. You know, to a movie or dinner. Dinner and a movie."

I cut my eyes towards him and displayed a curt smile. "No thank you."

"It doesn't have to be a movie. It can be somewhere else. Or we can just have a quick cup of coffee and get to know each other a little better. Just me and you. I know you like Starbucks. There's a Starb—"

"I have a boyfriend Rodger. But thanks."

"Well you ain't married yet," he chuckled, leaning up from the podium and shoving his greasy hands in the pockets of his coveralls. "You're single till you're married. Heard that one before?"

There were four other mechanics working on cars that I could see, and two of them were nosily eying our interaction and snickering.

I hoped my lack of response and impatient glance at my watch would be answer enough to make him get the hint and get lost. No dice.

"What day is good for you? You should give me a chance. We actually might have a lot in common."

"Rodger. I said no. I'm not interested. Now, I'd just like to wait for Will if you don't mind." I was stern and unsmiling. The last thing I had time for today was beating off Rodger's overbearing advances.

"Eh Rodg, let that lady wait in peace man," one of the men teased.

Rodger glared dejectedly between us and snapped his jaws shut with an audible click. His upper lip twitching with embarrassment. I averted my attention back to my phone and saw him stalk off towards the parking lot like an insolent child.

The door from the storefront swung open and Will came in looking perplexed. When his eyes landed on me, his countenance intensified.

"Greer," he nodded.

I stood, straightening the pocketbook on my shoulder, and holding the shopping bag out to him. "Hey. I know you asked me not to come back by here anymore, but I bought these Christmas gifts for the girls. I was hoping you would give them to them for me since I know Debbie would never allow me to bring them by the house."

He warily accepted the bag. "Debbie's not gonna like this."

"Maybe not, but those are my nieces Will. I can't make her let me see them, and I understand that she's your wife, and you have to take her side. I still want to at least show them that I love them.

"Debbie can't be that heartless to deprive two innocent little kids, her daughters, of Christmas gifts. Can she?" I grinned bashfully.

"I don't know Greer. You know my wife don't care about none of that. Especially when it comes to you," he said looking into the bag at the wrapped gifts. "What are they?"

"Toys, a journal. Nothing major. Can you at least try? Even if you have to take the wrapping paper off and give them to them as a gift from you in front of Debbie. Can you at least tell Tamia that I miss her? That's all I want. Can you do that for me, please?"

He rested his free hand on his hip contemplatively. Looked up at the ceiling, then back at me. "Yeah, okay. I'll give it to them."

"Thank you, Will. You're a godsend." I gave him a big hug while planting a kiss on his cheek and left.

I spotted Will's car about four cars past mine, so I looked down at my phone as I walked; pretending to be so distracted by it that I passed my own car in case anybody was looking. I glanced around and didn't see anyone though, so I quickly stuck the tracker in the right front wheel well and hurried back to my truck.

Mission accomplished.

I stopped by Subway to get some sandwiches and pulled up to Tat Life about 40 minutes later. All eyes were on me when I walked in looking pretty in my pink joggers. It was a good hair day, so I let my curly tresses loose and only wore eyeliner and lip gloss. Race's favorite look on me from what he's said.

I nodded at Donnella, the receptionist, who recognized me, and few of the other artists looking my way. There was one in particular, Jade, that I didn't like. She was too giggly and touchy feely for my taste. Every time I saw her, she was in Race's face.

"Hi Baby," I greeted as he looked up from inking what looked like some sort of cathedral on a man's back.

"Hey. What you doin' here?"

I followed up his huge grin with a lingering kiss, making sure to make eye contact with Jade, who was already looking, afterwards. Holding up the Subway bag I said, "I brought you some lunch."

Jade pursed her lips and went back to piercing her client. Jealous bitch. I would be sure to show her how much I appreciated her disrespecting my relationship with a hole in one of the tires of her Mustang.

"Aww that's sweet. I'm not gonna be able to stop and eat for at least another hour though. Were you planning to eat with me?"

"Naw, it's cool Dog," his Hispanic looking client assured. "I need a break for a minute anyway. I gotta take a leak and I'm hungry myself."

"I hear you, but I got another client after you at 4 o'clock. This could end up being a two-day job if we take too many breaks."

The guy already seemed to have made up his mind. "Aiight well, if it does, what time you got tomorrow where I can come back and get it finished? Cause if I don't put somethin' in my stomach right quick, I might pass out anyway. I was just about to say somethin' before your girl came in."

He eyed me licentiously and Race's face tensed. "It's New Year's Eve, Bruh. I'm booked up."

"Damn. What about New Year's Day?"

"I ain't workin'. Donella, what's my schedule on the 2nd?"

"Hold up, let me check," she hollered back, typing on the computer.

"I'm only need like 30 minutes to regroup, eat and piss. Hopefully, we can knock it out today."

Race didn't reply and Donnella let him know he had a 1 o'clock and a 5 o'clock opening.

"One. One is good for me," his client confirmed. "Can I look at it?"

"Yeah. Let me wrap it up for you too before you go out there, so it won't get infected."

The guy stood up, walked to one of the many long mirrors on the walls in between booths, and grinned as he turned to see his back.

"*Yeeeeahhhhh.* This is gonna be fire."

Race smirked, placed what looked like saran wrap over the unfinished tattoo and taped it down. "Be back in 30?"

"Be back in 30," Hispanic man agreed.

Race took the Subway bag from my hands and walked towards his office as I made a b-line towards the sink and soap station. There was no way I was about to eat without washing my hands first.

He was by my side doing the same thing shortly afterwards and we both went to his office when done. I took the Clorox wipes from my bag and wiped down the surface of his desk before plucking our sandwiches from the bag and sitting in a chair on the other side of his desk.

"Double turkey, American cheese, lettuce, light mayo, vinegar and oil," I said handing him his sandwich.

"Let me find out you pay attention to what I like."

"I do. I didn't get any drinks. I figured you had some here."

He rolled his swivel chair across the floor to a small floor refrigerator and opened it so I could see inside. "What you want?"

"Sprite."

He took two cans out, handing me one and placing the other beside his sandwich. We didn't say much for the first few minutes. Both of us choosing to feed our appetites over talking.

"What made you bring me lunch?" he asked after one half of his sandwich was devoured.

"I had an appointment and some errands to run. Since I was out already, I thought it would be nice to have lunch with you."

"It's good to know you're thinking about me."

"Of course. Where's Geo? I didn't see him out there."

"Doing some wedding shit with Lisa. He's not coming in today." He sat back with his hands clasped together in his lap staring at me. "I like this."

"What?" I asked after swallowing a bite of food.

"This. You, starting to look and act like yourself again. Bringing me food at lunch. I like it."

"Tuh! Me bringing you food at lunch on a weekday is not, and will not, be the norm once I start back to work in two weeks. This is too far for all of that."

He smirked. "I like that you're thinking about me as much during the day as I think about you. Seeing your pretty face is gonna help me get through the rest of this crap day."

I blushed, feeling the warmth of his words in my soul. "I'm glad I can assist. But, why's it a crap day? Fussy clients?"

He shook his head, turning the corners of his mouth down. "Not really. I just got a lot of other shit on my mind that's distracting me from wanting to be here."

"Like what?"

"Psssh. Family."

I took another bite of my sandwich and gave him a perplexed look. I wasn't in the mood for 20 questions. I wished he would spit it out.

"Everybody keeps saying I'm an enabler when it comes to Carmen, and I keep trying to cut her off, but I can't. I give advice to people to cut toxic folks out of their lives and try to convince myself I can do that with her, but I can't. I want her to get better and if I gotta be the one to help her, I'm willing to do that.

"I mean… look at you and your dad. I can't believe y'all made up. I don't know if I could forgive somebody who shot me, no matter who it is. You didn't voice it much, I could see how angry and hurt you were about that whole thing, and now here y'all are trying to move past it.

"That's what I keep wanting to happen with Carmen. Seems like as soon as she gets clean and I start believing in her again, she goes right back down the rabbit hole.

"I can't shake the feeling that the next time we see her, she's gonna be in a casket. Like, maybe instead of beating that dude's ass and kicking them both out, we should've beat his ass, kicked him out and made her stay.

"I don't know what keeps making her relapse, but she's come out of it before. I feel like, with the right motivation, she could come out of it for good."

I conjured up an empathetic sigh for the hype-headed heathen. She had never been any kind of mother for him to feel guilty about letting her pick her own poison.

"I don't know Honey. I don't want you to set yourself up for disappointment again. She's been addicted for most if not all of your life. You're not the reason why she started, and you might not be able to make her stop."

He looked ruefully out of the office window. "I think I'm gonna go look for her when I'm done here tonight. I've heard some things about places she might be, and I want to check them out."

"Are you going alone or with Geo?"

"I can't see him wanting to come, but I'll ask."

"So, I probably won't see you tonight then?"

"I don't know how late I'll be out bu—"

"Don't worry about me. I'm going to have you all to myself for the next two or three days. I can spare you for tonight if I must. She's your family, and there's nothing more important than family."

He leaned across his desk and I leaned in to meet his puckered lips in the middle. I wasn't disappointed. I wasn't planning to be home tonight anyway.

19

Greer

Even with gloves over my latex ones, a hat, and thermal underwear on under my thick joggers, I was still freezing. Don't ever let anybody tell you it doesn't get cold in Georgia.

I was going to wait in the shadows of Ms. Nina's backyard for her to leave, but after how sick I got the night after I went to Angie's, I wasn't up for a repeat. Not when I was planning to turn up with my man and my bestie for the weekend.

I parked about three houses down from Ms. Nina's, in the opposite direction she would travel towards the church. She rarely missed Wednesday night bible study and I knew she'd be gone at least three hours, counting travel time.

I spied her house in full disguise from a crouched position in the passenger's seat of my Corolla. Her home was on the right and I didn't want to be within the eyesight of her neighbors for too long. It was dark enough that I thought I would be able to move stealthily, but at only 6:40pm, some people were still out.

Finally, she emerged from the house with one of her signature hats on and a thick shall like scarf draped over her coat. I was already creeping out of the car when she pulled out of her parking spot.

Hustling through the yard between her house and a neighbor's, I rushed to the back door with a backpack on my back and my means to entry in my hands. Once inside, I went straight to her home office. I didn't see her computer in there, but Ms. Nina was real old school. She was all about the paper. She often referenced how successful she was as an accountant before computers became necessities. She took a certain level of pride in it.

I hunted through her desk draws, bookshelves and cabinets with haste. Just when I was becoming frustrated, I found a folder in a separate file cabinet in her closet. JB Investigations.

Inside was a contract between her and the agency laying out exactly what services she was paying for. It was signed December 19th, 2015, and I was the target.

I scoffed at the revelation and read what they were supposed to be doing for their coin. Surveilling my home, investigating my finances, and looking into my whereabouts during the time Michael was killed. This bitch.

There were other things in the folder too. Apparently, they emailed progress reports, which she chose to print out and put in this folder. I was so glad I made it look like I was going to bed early from the street the night I crept out to Angie's. It seems they were monitoring me that day too but had no view from the front of my exit from the back.

I was lucky to have made my trip to SC before she put the bloodhounds on me. Judging from the reports, Ms. Nina was bluffing about having anything even remotely incriminating on me. These investigators were either sleeping on the job or I was just that good, and lucky.

They mentioned the investigation into Kendrick's death and that I was dating him at one point, but they didn't have anything eluding to me seeing him while Michael was alive. She was grasping for straws.

One thing caught my eye though. A report she printed out this morning referenced a video of me going to Will's shop and colluding with Daddy. I hoped the cunt hadn't told Debbie any of this, and I needed to see what video they had. What if they had me on film putting the bug under Will's car? And seeing Daddy at all was a violation of my bail agreement.

I put the entire folder in my backpack and frowned. Where the hell was her laptop? Must be in her bedroom. I doubted she watched the videos they sent on her phone. All I had to do was find it and I could see what they sent her. The chances of it being password protected were slim. Michael used to get on her about it being open to thieves and always argued that it never left her house and nobody lived in her house, but her. So, she didn't need to put a password on it. Hmph.

I eyed her mundane, wood paneled abode with an affronted snicker. I always hated this place. For someone who takes such pride in her appearance, her home showed no personality. The pictures on the walls were basic family portraits and cheaply framed store-bought paintings.

The furniture was newer than it looked, in drab earth tones with mismatched designs on the throw pillows on the couch. It was old ass wood and late 70's décor suffocating me from every angle, and I hated it.

I knew that even if I took or deleted everything, she could get it all again from JB Investigations, but I still needed to know what she knew. The idea of somebody, anybody, especially my ex-mother in law, having the upper hand did not set well with me. I couldn't let anything that could affect me or my budding love with Race be jeopardized.

I spotted the laptop on the nightstand as soon as I entered her room. I was barely two feet in when I heard the front door opening downstairs. Oh shit!

"May God rest her soul. I tell you, stress can be a killer… The older we get, the harder it is to get through it… Right… I don't think she ever recovered after Darren died. I lost my Michael more than a year ago and I'm still not over it. I think about him every day still," Ms. Nina's voice startled me upstairs.

What was she doing home so soon? I bounced back and forth trying to think what to do and where to go. I hadn't planned to kill Ms. Nina. Well… not tonight anyway. But I would if I had to. She wasn't supposed to be home!

She maneuvered around the downstairs talking to whomever was on the other end of the phone as I debated between the closet or rushing into one of the other upstairs rooms. I hoped she was only back because she left something and would be heading out again before it became an issue for me.

When I heard her slow foot falls on the stairs, my heart thumped with trepidation as I quietly retrieved my taser from my backpack and crept behind the bedroom door.

"I guess if you're gonna die anywhere, the church isn't the worst place to go home to glory… she was a faithful servant of the lord and died doing what she loved best. Worshipping him… No. The ambulance was there when I pulled up… Sister Ellis said Sister Reba was complaining of chest pains in the car and then she collapsed on their way in… Yes Lord… Alright then… Be blessed."

I prayed in my head that she would pass by her room and go to the bathroom since her house was an older build with no master bath inside. If she did, I could probably sneak out of the house undetected, but God must've been busy.

The huge mirror atop her dresser allowed me to see her set her phone down, take her hat off, and begin removing her jewelry. My taser tightly in my grip, I attempted to quiet my breathing and stand perfectly still; careful not to brush up against the dry-cleaned dress in a bag hanging on the back of the door.

The moment her eyes met mine through the mirror, her fate was sealed. She turned to face me just as I shoved the door and thrust the taser into her torso, sending 35,000,000 volts into her body.

Her orbs stretched to capacity and the words she was going to speak caught in her throat as her convulse and her body hit the floor with a thud. I couldn't let her live now that she'd seen my face. There was no way in hell she would let me get away with breaking into her home and tasering her. Ms. Nina was about to finally be with the son she claimed to miss so much.

"N-no. Please," she begged in a fetal position when I let up.

Quickly scanning the room, I spotted the nylon bowling ball bag in the corner by the dresser. She was part of a bowling league named "Biblical Bowling Broads", which I found hilarious when I was first told the name.

I tased her again for good measure as I reached for the handle of the oblong bag and was pleased to feel the weight of the ball inside. I put the taser down on the dresser and prepared to strike her with the ball bag in both hands when a sharp pain caused my right leg to buckle.

Shrieking, I fell to one knee as Ms. Nina kicked at me again before attempting to crawl closer to the threshold. Her hand gripped the bottom side of the door catching the plastic from the dry-cleaning bag in her grip at the same time.

The dress fell to the floor as I yanked her back by one leg and slung the bowling bag down on her thigh. She yelped, flipping her body over, and reaching to claw my face. I dodged her feeble attempt, bringing the bag down again on her chest.

She instantly folded like a picnic chair, crying out. "Please Jesus," and rolling to her side.

"Jesus can't help you," I growled, grabbing the bottom of the dry-cleaning bag, and dragging it toward me. I pulled the bag off the dress as Ms. Nina lurched over on her stomach and I squatted on her back.

Pinning her down, I plunged the bag over her inflated head and twisted it around her neck. Her hands immediately shot up to grab at my glove covered hands as I tugged and tightened it to cut off her air supply. She was a lot stronger than I thought she would be at her age. The slowing sound of her inhaling and exhaling the bag while I strangled the life out of her was music to my ears.

"Die bitch! Die!" I grit, pulling on the bag like reins as she tried bucking me off her. "Die already!"

I planted my feet on both sides of her body, tugging with all my might until she stopped inhaling inside the bag and the struggling ceased. Heavily breathing myself, I maintained the vice grip I had on the bag for an additional 60 second count, just to be sure she was fully expired.

My hands hurt when I finally released the bag and let her face hit the hardwood with a thump. Standing, I straightened my wig and swiped the taser from her dresser. Partially removing my backpack, I placed my taser inside it so I wouldn't forget.

Exhaling, I looked down at her corpse with disdain. I was going to have to make this look like a robbery. I guess it didn't matter what was on her laptop anymore since she wasn't going to be using it.

I went to her kitchen and took three black garbage bags out from under the sink. Putting two in my backpack, I opened the third one and intended to go through her downstairs shoveling everything of value into it. Amusingly, other than discovering I would need two bags to encase the 32-inch standing flatscreen in the family room, there wasn't much to steal.

I tried to think like a burglar as I bypassed the kitchen drawers and cabinets, taking her purse from the counter, the cable box and standing flat screen television from her living room. Upstairs, I took all the jewelry she'd just removed and the rings and bracelets still on her person.

I dumped the contents of her jewelry box in and went through her drawers, finding nothing of value or worth in there. Some of this felt like déjà vu. The flatscreen in her bedroom was mounted on the wall, and I was not about to try to take that down right now.

What I did do was find a screwdriver and remove some of the screws from the brackets and pull at it until it was tilting away from the wall. I wanted it to look like she interrupted the robbery in progress.

Unfortunately, there was very little else I thought a thief would want from this place. I searched her closets for safes or money in shoeboxes but came up with nada. That was my cue to leave.

Limping down the stairs, thanks Ms. Nina, I lugged the spoils of my robbery to the backdoor. A hand to my temple, I tried to think of where she, or rather Michael, would have kept his tools.

He was her Mr. Fix It and he I remembered when he bought a full set of tools and a red box to keep it in, just to leave it over here. I searched all through the kitchen, and then one by one, I searched the two spare bedrooms.

Bingo! It was in the closet of the second spare. Inside, I took the hammer out went back to the back door. Dragging the bags outside, I locked and closed the door, then placed Michael's spare key in the lock.

I learned a lot about picking locks from Daddy when he was still operating his locksmith company. I'd gone out with him on a few calls before and listened to countless stories about the profession and techniques thieves used to break in sometimes.

Some used what's known as a "bump key" to do it but I used Michael's spare instead. To make it look like break in, I was literally going to have to… break in. I used the hammer to thwack at the key in the lock to scratch it up as much as possible.

The door opened easily, since the actual key in the lock was the one to the door, but I continued banging on it until I was satisfied the lock looked frayed enough.

When the mission was accomplished, I hauled the bags with both hands to my car and put them and the hammer in the trunk. Just doing that had me breathing hard and I was enormously thankful that I didn't have to exhaust myself by having to move Ms. Nina's body anywhere.

It was pointless to look around for witnesses. If they were there, it was too late to hide. The fact was, they probably wouldn't even notice me if I didn't act suspicious or do anything to bring attention to myself.

I must've been too deep in thought to notice how fast I was driving. The flashing red, white and blue lights in my rearview were exactly the unwelcomed surprise I didn't want. I didn't even have my driver's license with me, and I was totally fucking up by getting stopped.

I pulled over to the shoulder on the side of a residential road under a streetlight and immediately started concocting a story to feed the officer as I rolled my window down.

"Good evening Ma'am. Do you know why I stopped you tonight?"

I barely looked at the officer as I answered. "No sir."

"You were doing 60 in a 45. Can I see your license and registration please?"

"Uh… Officer, I…" I paused when I saw the last face I expected to see looking back at me. "I left my license at home."

He studied my face for a beat. Recognition registering quickly as it did. I could tell he knew who I was even through my disguise.

"Greer?" Officer Ratcliff peered sardonically at me.

"Yeah."

"What's this look you got going on?"

"Just trying not to get recognized. With my face back in the news again recently, I've been getting' noticed by a lot of people."

"Hmph. I wouldn't have known it was you if not for that southern twang. You still look good with dark hair though. Are your eyes a different color too?" he shined a flashlight in the window at me. "You went all in."

"Yeah," I tittered, hoping this was the beginning of my being able to talk my way out of a ticket.

"You're on the wrong side of town, aren't you? You live in Dekalb County. What are you doin' back here in my jurisdiction?"

I smiled. "Visiting my father."

He looked stupefied. "The one that shot you? Or you got another one?"

"Same one. We made up."

"Well good for you. Maybe he can bail you out. Step out of the vehicle please."

"Wait. What?"

"You said you don't have your license, right? And I'm pretty sure the tags on this car, don't belong to *this* car. Which means I'm gonna have to bring you in." his grin was unmistakable.

"Officer Ratcliff. Nick. Please don't."

"Oh, now I'm Nick? Don't try to be friendly now after ignoring my calls. Get out the car, *Ms. Patterson*," he emphasized dryly with one hand on his holster.

"Nick. Hold on. Please. Can you hear me out a minute," I was panicking. God damn it, it wasn't like me to panic. "I left my wallet in my other bag on accident. This *is* my car, but I'm in the process of selling it. I didn't renew the tags because I knew I wa—"

"Save it. I don't care about all that. Tell it to somebody whose phone calls you answer."

"I'm not ignoring your calls. Is that what you think? *Nooo*. No. I haven't been ignoring your calls. I lost my phone. I had to get a new one."

"A new phone and a new number?"

"Y-yeah," I stuttered, remembering I had my burner phone with me. "I told you, the media has really been bombarding me. So, I changed my phone number too. I can give it to you now if you still want it."

"How's your voicemail still picking up if you changed your number?"

"I-I didn't think to turn it off yet. I just haven't gotten around to it. You know how it can ge—"

"Greer, I'm not stupid. As soon as you found out about my girl and my son, you started dodging my calls. It's not like you need to be lookin' for steady dick this soon after your husband was killed. What was it, the top of the year?"

"Early last year."

"Whatever. Neither one of us were looking for a relationship, but you wanted to get high and mighty. You think pretty high of yourself for somebody up on attempted murder charges."

"It's not that. I just don't want to add any trouble to my life. What if your girlfriend found out?"

"That's not for you to worry your pretty little head about," he licked his lips lecherously and darted his eyes left and right. "You know, I can let you make it up to me if you want? And maybe you could go home tonight instead of to the Cobb County jail.

"Make it up to you how?"

"How do you think? Don't play coy with me. I'm no sucker."

"Okay. When? Now?"

"Not now. I don't play around when I'm on duty. I'll let you know when I'm free and I can swing by your crib."

"By my crib? No. I think we should go somewhere else."

"I don't. I'm not paying for a hotel," he looked me up and down like I was the scum of the earth. This negro had more nerve than he deserved. "I'll call you on your *new* phone and let you know what time. What's the number?"

It wasn't the time to argue with him while I still had stolen property in the trunk of my car. I rattled off the phone number and waited for him to tell me I could go. There was no way I was going to violate my relationship and sleep with this dickhead, but I would determine how to duck that later.

Relieved when he let me go, I stopped at three different store dumpsters on the way home and unloaded Ms. Nina's stuff. If any of it was ever discovered, I didn't want them to be discovered together. I even took extra care to dig a hole by a pond in the park by my home and bury her wallet in it. The ground being cold, I couldn't bury it too deep, but it was deep enough not to be randomly uncovered.

I'm glad my phone holds a good charge. It was still playing videos on the Beyonce YouTube channel. I learned that a lot of times if you're watching something on there, it will keep playing additional videos until you stop it. That made the perfect way for me to not only show I was home if my cell was tracked, but to show engagement through my Wifi usage.

Entering my backdoor, all I wanted was a long hot shower and a good night's sleep.

"Where were you?"

I almost fell back down the basement steps as I was startled by Race's instant interrogation.

"Oh my God! What are you doing here?"

"Waiting for you. Where were you?" he asked again, drinking in my appearance from head to toe.

"I went out for a run. How long have you been here?"

"Why are you dressed like that?" he was leaning against the island drinking one of the Corona's he kept in my refrigerator. He was calm and collected. Not accusatory, but I was on the defense.

"Why are you interrogating me?" I stormed past him. Pissed that I couldn't see my driveway from the backyard, and thus hadn't seen his car parked in it.

"I'm asking questions. Not interrogating you. Since when do you go out for runs dressed like somebody else? And when it's this cold?"

"Since I've been having panic attacks and going for jogs started helping. What the fuck is your problem?"

"Whoa, whoa," he grabbed my arm before I could head up the stairs. "Why are you cussin' at me? You come in here dressed like a cat burglar with a wig and contacts talkin' about you went for a run, after ignoring my phone calls for an hour, and you're mad at me? Naw, fuck that, Greer."

An hour. So, he had only been here an hour. I hoped.

"I thought you were going to be searching for Carmen tonight."

"Don't deflect damn it," he barked, clutching my bicep harder.

"You're hurting me," I snarled looking from my arm to his angry face.

He let go. "Why are you dressed like that?"

"Because I'm tired of people feeling like they can say whatever they want to me in the streets! Because my face has been plastered on the news *again*! Because people think I'm some crazy bitch who can't keep a husband whose, own father wants her dead! And those people…they want to talk to me about it! That's why!"

I was screaming at the top of my lungs. Pouring all the anger I felt towards Nick and the pain in my leg from fighting with Ms. Nina, into my dramatics. My vexation was misdirected, but when you corner a cobra, you must expect it to strike.

I left him looking dumbfounded at the bottom as I stomped up to my bedroom with tears in my eyes. Things were falling apart. I was losing control.

20

Greer

December 31th 2015

He never came upstairs last night. I thought he was giving me some space as I stalked around my room pulling out pajamas and went to take a shower. I rehearsed what I would say to him in my head while in there. I planned to apologize for my reaction and give him a BS story about someone approaching me disrespectfully in public. But he was gone.

He left without a single word. As much as I wanted to call him and make up, I was too exhausted to do so last night. When I woke up, every muscle in my arms ached, right along with my right leg that now had a blue and purple bruise on it. Thank goodness the dress I was going to wear tonight was nearly floor length.

So many thoughts were running through my head. Oddly enough, the main one was actually a question. Was I a serial killer now? Is it the number of people you kill or the way you kill them that determines that? I killed, Michael, The Reckless Driver, Kendrick, Angie, and Ms. Nina, made five people I ushered into early graves. Six if you counted Race's cat, Juney.

I know it's great. Nobody's more surprised that I ended up this way than I am. I'm a full 180 different than I have been the majority of my life. But after you get away with murder once, you sort of… develop a taste for it. Or at least I have. It's not like I'm out here taking random people out for frivolous reasons. Besides, I knew I would have to stop before my luck ran out.

The thing about murder, is there's no statute of limitations on it. No matter how long a person can get away with it, some cold case expert could always open it back up 20 years down the line if they wanted to and put you under the jail. *My* goal is to get away with it the first time and leave no reason for anyone to open the case a second.

Granted, it *had* only been a day since my last kill and weeks since the others, but I was optimistic. Improvising Ms. Nina's death put me in a bit of a conundrum as far as Officer Nick Ratcliff was concerned, but I would handle it. It was getting easier, and I'm smart.

With Daddy no longer on my hit list, there was only one, maybe two people left before I was going to turn off my new propensity for murder. For good. It's the people who don't know when to stop that always get caught, and if I was caught, my happily ever after with Race would disappear.

Practically everything I was doing was for us or for the better good of our relationship and future together. For love. Even if he didn't know it. Speaking of Race, I would smooth things over with *him* as soon as I could get all my faculties together.

Right now, I was too giddy about my BFF coming in town to worry about his attitude. I found my phone on the nightstand and called Shan as soon as I realized it was after 9am.

"Hey, girl. I was just gonna call you. We're in an Uber to the hotel," she answered.

"Hey, Greer," Jahari greeted me in the background.

"Tell him I said, 'Hey'. What are y'all about to get into once you're settled in the hotel?" I asked rising from the bed to start my morning bathroom routine.

"I gotta run to the mall to get some shoes for tonight. The strap broke on one of the ones I was going to bring, so now I'm assed out."

"Awww damn. Those were so cute too."

"I know. I was already imagining how I was gonna look in my outfit and now I gotta scramble last minute for shoes. I was supposed to go with Jahari to his cousin's, but if I go, I know I'm not gonna have enough time to hit the mall before we have to start getting ready for the party."

"Oh my God, you're the slowest shopper ever," I quipped.

"I'm not *slow*. I just don't make hasty decisions about what I wear."

I chuckled. "You want me to come with you?"

"Of course. It'll save me Uber money and I'll get to see my bestie for more hours."

I smiled while putting toothpaste onto my brush. "We're at the W Atlanta in Buckhead. What time?"

"Umm… give me till 11."

"Bet."

Forty minutes later, I was dressed in jeans, a chocolate-colored turtleneck sweater, brown calf boots and no coat. The temp was in the high 50's and sunny.

Dark sunglasses on my face, hair piled high in a clip, and a slight limp on my right side, me and my crossbody bag were in route to the W. I called Race's phone and he let me go to voicemail. I sent a short apology text at the next red light and turned up Jidenna's new song "Classic Man" on the radio.

Jahari was gone by the time I got to the hotel, so I just had Shan come downstairs to my truck. We squealed like piglets when we saw each other; leaning over the console to hug.

Her hair was cut even shorter than it was the last time I saw her. Reminiscent of Toni Braxton's style in the 90's. As expected, it complimented her mahogany complexion. She was dressed in black leather pants and a matching jacket with an orange fleece shirt and black booties. My bestie was a baddie.

"You look so cute!" I exclaimed when our hug broke.

"You like?" she grinned touching the nape of her neck. "Something new for the new year."

"Yeah, I love it. Lenox or Phipps Plaza?"

"Phipps. I need to hit Nordstrom up first."

"Phipps it is," I agreed, weaving into traffic.

"I gotta pick up Bri's birthday gift while I'm there too. I couldn't squeeze one more thing in my carryon."

"Can whatever you get be from both of us? I forgot it was her bougie ass birthday too."

"No you didn't," she cut her eyes playfully at me.

I laughed. "You know I wouldn't be going if you weren't in town. Hell, she wouldn't have even invited me if you weren't going. She doesn't like me."

"I don't know why you think that. She's hasn't said a bad word about you around me since college. She's not the same person, G. Actually, I think almost dying has changed her."

"Snakes only shed their skin. They don't stop being snakes."

"You're so unforgiving."

"No more than anybody else. I'm just tired of being disrespected. She's a bully. I know she's your friend, and I deal with her because you love her, but I don't."

"I *don't* love her. She is my friend, and I like her, but I *love* you."

I probably grinned wide enough to see my molars. "I love you too. Speaking of *loooove*… you're glowing. Is that just from the baby, or are you and Jahari back on track?"

She pursed her lips kittenishly. "A little of both. He's been more attentive and affectionate since he found out about the baby, and I like that. he understands what he almost lost and he's been trying to make up for it. Oh! I didn't tell you!"

"Tell me what?"

"Jahari's mom said Wendy is in the ICU."

I frowned. "How does she know? I thought she was supposed to stop watching the bitch's kids?"

"She did. But Wendy's mom popped up asking her to watch the kids so she could go back to the hospital. Said they were there all night and the kids were restless, whiny, and scared. She paid her double to keep them until Wendy's sister could pick them up."

"What happened to her? Somebody else's wife put a bullet in her?" I hadn't checked my emails or my Craig's list inbox lately. I guessed somebody finally put on their big boy drawers and did the deed.

"You're trying to be funny, but she *was* attacked," her eyes stretched with shock. "Her mom didn't give Evelyn all the details, probably because she didn't know them yet, but she was brutally raped and tied to the bed. I caught the tail end of them talking about it on the nightly news. I just didn't know they were talking about *Wendy*."

"They're saying he got in through the fire escape. You know damn near everybody living in an apartment in the Bronx has a fire escape. It's crazy."

I was dancing the Stanky Leg inside. "Sounds like karma to me."

"Greer, that's cold. No. Fucking another woman's husband in her bed is cold. Maybe the word got out that her pussy's *sooooo* good, somebody wanted to sample it for themself."

Shan shook her head chidingly.

"What did you think I was gonna to say? I'll pray for her?" I snickered. "Listen. Whatever punishment God gave her is what she deserved. I'm nobody to be questioning God."

"When did you get to be so mean? I can't believe you just said that. She's in ICU."

"ICU have a lot of sympathy for somebody who didn't have any respect for you."

"Ha ha. Very funny. It's not that I have sympathy for her, but that's a terrible thing to happen to anybody."

"Umm hmm. Anyway, I'm starving. I didn't eat breakfast. Can we eat before you use up half my life shopping for one pair of shoes?"

"Shut up," she shoved me playfully. "Just for that, you're buying."

"Whatever."

"We'll see how nonchalant you are about it after you see how much me and my daughter eat. I'm hungry all the time these days."

"Daughter? You didn't tell me you found out the sex."

"I didn't. I just know this is a little girl I'm carrying. Totally different than when I had Shamari. I'm not as sick, but I'm twice as hungry."

"*Awww.* Little Greer is a hungry girl."

She squinted comically. "Jahari has not agreed to name her Greer yet."

"Yet, being the key word. I'll get him on board before y'all leave. Mark my words."

In the food court, I got a gyro and she got two burgers, fries and a 10-piece nugget from McDonald's. She was *not* kidding about that appetite. Something in the gyro didn't agree with me though, because less than a half an hour after I ate it, I was tossing my cookies back up in the bathroom.

Once the contents of my stomach were empty and I washed my mouth out in the ladies' room, I was ready to shop. A little under two hours of shopping, and Shan finally bought a pair of shoes. I got some haughty diamond earrings to match my new tennis bracelet and a gold rhinestone clip for my hair.

My phone rang as Shan and I walked through the mall towards the parking lot.

"Hello."

"Hey," a monotone Race replied.

"Hey," I looked at Shan and she knew instantly who I was talking to by my expression.

I gave her the same BS story I was planning to feed Race about my outburst, whenever he gave me the opportunity. His silence spoke volumes. He must've called to let me know he still wasn't speaking to me.

"I know I'm supposed to pick you up tonight at 8 o'clock. I didn't forget. I'll be there."

"Uh… okay. I take it you're still mad at me?" He huffed in response and I nodded at Shan to let her know he was. "I tried to call you to apologize but you didn't pick up."

"Listen, I gotta get back to work if I'm gonna be to your house on time."

"Seriously? You're just gonna brush me off? I had a bad night. I—"

"No. *I* had a bad night. You didn't know that though, because you bit my head off. You've been through some shit. I know. We *all* know, Greer. You use that excuse for everything. But you're not the only one God damn it," he growled into the phone. "Now like I said, I'm at work right now. This isn't the time or the place to talk about it. I'll come by a little earlier if that's what you want to do, but I'm not about to do that shit now. Understood?"

I balked and frowned at Shan as we went through the exit doors. Was he crazy? Who the hell was he talking to like this?

"Greer?"

"I heard you. I don't like how you're talking to me, but I heard you."

"Yeah well, tell me about it later. Bye."

My mouth agape, I looked at the phone and then to Shan, "Girl, he hung up on me."

She shrugged, "He must be upset. What did he say?"

"He had a bad night too and I didn't know it because I bit his head off, and it's not all about me. He was too busy to talk about it and he'll come by earlier to talk about it if that's what I want. Then he hung up."

"Is he right?"

"Right about what?" I asked opening the locks to the truck as we reached it.

"Look. We've been friends over a decade now. I told you before, you can be all about what's going on with you sometimes without thinking about what might be happening with someone else. Now, granted, you have been dealing with a lot more than the average person.

"I'm not saying you don't have a right to expect some compassion from the people who know you best. I'm just reminding you that, we have things we might need to lean on your bruised shoulder for too.

"What did he say happened to him to make his night bad?"

"He didn't say. And I resent you saying I'm self-centered."

"Those are your words. Not mine."

"Hmph," I rolled my eyes at her as we drove out of the lot. "I'm not perfect. I never claimed to be."

"I don't think he's wanting you to be. Just be a little more compassionate about his circumstances and what he's going through. You said he went to go look for his crackhead momma—"

"She's not a crackhead. She's a heroin addict."

"Same thing," she waved me off. "That's his mother. It can't be easy loving somebody hooked on drugs. Then y'all have the added stress of you getting shot, your injuries, your court case, his ex-girl trying to keep one boot in the game, and then social media.

"Y'all been together less than a year. He runs two businesses with other people and is responsible for his grandma who almost died. Greer. It – is – a – lot. Especially if he's the kind of man who likes to take care of his woman."

I nodded and merged into traffic with regret on my mind. I was going to need to make this the best New Year's Eve he's ever had. There was no way in hell I was going to go through all this stuff to keep my relationship safe from outside interference, to lose him.

I spent over an hour in Shan's hotel room helping her choose between different things to wear for the night, girl talking, and texting back and forth with Lisa about bridesmaid dress shopping on Saturday. As much as I really didn't want to be a part of the wedding, I agreed to it, and now I had to participate in it. Yay me!

By the time I got home, I had two hours to get ready, which isn't a lot when you're a woman with a shoulder injury that keeps getting aggravated, trying to apply makeup.

Luckily, other things were going my way. My limp improved, my dress was covering the bruise on my leg, and my shoes, though high, didn't feel like they would hurt too bad after a few hours of wear.

I was checking out my handywork in the bathroom mirror when I heard the front door alarm and Race punching in the code on the pad. Butterflies swarmed my stomach as he ascended the steps. I hoped my more attractive than usual appearance would work in my favor.

"Hey," he said appearing the bathroom door behind me.

"Hey," I turned wearing only my gold lace bra, panties, and furry bedroom slippers. If he could overlook my ugly scars, I thought I looked sexy.

He looked like a chocolate Adonis in the black button up Armani shirt I helped him pick out and black slacks.

"You cut your hair."

"Yeah," he ran a hand over his freshly cropped low fade.

"Listen. Before you say anything else, I want to apologize for my behavior last night and probably in general. Some people said some things to me when I was out. I was surprised to see you in the house when I got home and… it's not an excuse. I'm not making an excuse. I was wrong.

"I'm sorry I didn't bother to ask why you were here or what happened. I'm sorry I've been so self-involved. I'm gonna do better. I swear. I'm gonna do better."

He looked at me with the blankest stare I'd ever seen. His seeming indifference to my whole spiel had me fidgeting and nervous.

"Do you feel like we had this conversation before?"

"No."

"Maybe not exactly, but I feel like we've had this conversation before."

I looked away and swiped some curls behind my ear.

"I didn't come here to argue. I don't want to argue with you. I was mad at how you came at me last night, but like you said, I wasn't supposed to be here.

"After thinkin' about it and talkin' to my brother, I guess I could understand how somebody whose house just got broken into might not like surprise pop ups so much," he smirked, showing the one dimple in his left cheek. "Even though I have a key."

"True. But on another note, please, tell me what happened last night. I care."

"I mean… it doesn't really matter now. I'm past it."

"It *does* matter," I reached out, placing a hand on his chest.

He licked his bottom lip and rubbed his chin as if debating on whether to divulge whatever this bad thing was that foiled my discreet return home.

"I found Carmen. Long story short, she didn't want to come with me. She was high as a fuckin' kite. She cussed me out. *Spit* on me and told me to leave her alone."

"Spit on you?"

"Honestly, I don't even wanna talk about it. It's about to be a new year. I don't wanna take this old shit into 2016," he pulled me in by the waist and looked into my eyes. "Can we do that? Can we kill everything toxic in our lives and start fresh?"

"Kill everything toxic." I couldn't agree more.

21

Greer

January 2nd 2016

I got white girl wasted. As much as I can't stand Bri, her birthday, slash New Year's Eve party, was the best one I've ever been to. Everyone was dressed to the nines and Bri and Cameron's seven-bedroom, Sandy Springs mansion, was decorated like a celebrity pad.

A vomitous amount of Christmas lights were on the house and every tree in the yard. Their entire basement level was set up like a 200-capacity night club with two bars, lounge areas and everything. Cameron managed to get one of Atlanta's iconic singers, Monica to perform three songs. I guess with them both being doctors, Bri and Cameron could afford it.

Jahari and Race hit it off like gangbusters and the four of us drank, danced, took pictures, and canoodled with our significant others like newlyweds. Correction. Shan didn't drink, because she was carrying a little one, but we partied long after the 'Happy New Year's' were shouted.

Race and I had *amaaaaaaaazing* sex when we got home and the next morning, I was praying to the porcelain god like it was the sabbath. I stayed in bed most of the day with Race, who was also overserved.

We watched movies, ordered food, and slept in each other's arms, like the married couple I hoped we would someday become. Shan and Jahari took the day to spend with other people, but come Saturday, I was happy to be feeling like myself again, where I could spend most of their last day in town with Shan.

Around 2 o'clock, I was summoned to a downtown bridal shop by the bride to be, so Shan came with me. From my understanding, Race and the other groomsmen were dragged to a tuxedo shop as well. Jahari was not a part of the crew. He was off with whomever he wanted to visit without his wife.

"I hope she doesn't pick that one," Shan whispered as we walked up on Lisa's sister Lana wearing a long, purple, metallic, off the shoulder dress. I nodded.

"Greer!" Lisa chirped scurrying from a chair to hug me. "Shan!" she went to hug my bestie and was met with resistance.

"Hey. Good to see you again. I'm not a hugger," Shan's face twisted with a strained smile.

"Oh. Okay. Umm... we're only on the second dress. Lora and Aaliyah are in the fitting rooms trying on other ones. Here. These are the last two I like," Lisa held up two dresses trying to mask her dejected feelings. One, a hideous purple, ruffled monstrosity, the other another purple, multilayered chiffon strapless number. "They're on the rack over there if neither of these are your size."

I looked at the tags, and they were both too big, so I went to the rack to select the ugly multilayered one. There were other patrons scattered in the store, but I guessed Lisa had this area reserved because her group seemed to be the only ones in the fitting rooms.

"Hello, ladies!" Song came strutting in, grinning like she owned the place.

I noticed her red, stiletto, thigh high boots before anything else. She wore a short, red leather jacket over a winter white jumper that hugged her curves for dear life. A big C, Chanel belt cinched her already tiny waist as she held a red clutch and her honey blonde locks draped over her shoulders. She must have missed the memo that she wasn't going to be a featured runway model here.

Shan scanned her slowly from head to toe, folding her arms across her chest to relay how unimpressed she was. The two of us exchanged catty glances.

"Song, girl, you slay everywhere you go," Lisa kissed ass.

By this time, all Lisa's sisters were out of the dressing room. They all appeared to be underwhelmed by Song's sudden appearance as well, and Lora was the only one who opened her mouth to speak.

"Oh no," Song's face screwed up. "I hate all of them except the purple one she has on." She wiggled an index finger towards Aaliyah in a one shoulder, chiffon, asymmetrical style.

"I can agree with that," Shan mumbled.

Song turned toward her with an arched brow. "Are you with us?"

"She's with Greer," Lisa confirmed as Song looked passed Shan to see me by the racks."

"Oh. I didn't even see Greer over there." She turned back around without speaking. Bitch. "Well, I'm not here to try the dresses on. After so many years modeling, I know what looks good on me and what doesn't. I'll just help you choose from what they try on."

I nodded to the ladies, bypassing Song, and went in a fitting room to try on the dress. I could still hear them chatting clearly.

"Lisa, this thing is *oooogly*. Are you trying to be funny by making us try on these thangs. I thought your taste was way better than this," one of her sister's joked.

"Sometimes things look better on than on a rack," Lisa defended.

"This thing, isn't one of them."

I heard the other ladies laughing along as I emerged wearing the dress. Wide eyes took in my appearance and of course, Song was the first to comment.

"Looks like a cheap knockoff of something better," she smirked.

"Song, I didn't even see you there in your Christmas hooker outfit."

"My ensemble probably costs more than everything you wore here."

"Maybe if the beautiful tennis bracelet Race gave me for Christmas wasn't included in that."

"So, I know y'all have seen pictures of each other, but haven't met before," Lisa broke in. "Lora, Lana, Aaliyah, this is Greer, and that's her friend Shantel, visiting from New York." She waved a hand in front of each woman as she named them.

They verbally greeted Shan and I in unison and we spoke back while Song crossed her legs and looked disinterestedly off. All of the women bore a strong resemblance to each other. Dark hair cut in various styles and lengths, with various shades of caramel complexions, but their cognac-colored eyes and button noses were dead giveaways.

"Greer, you…" Lora shook her head "… are stunning. Those eyes. Gorgeous."

"Thank you."

"Which one of these ugly dresses do you like? My vote's for the purple one."

"Mine too," Aaliyah said admiring herself in the large floor length mirrors as she stood on the platform. "I just don't know about the color."

"Purple is my favorite color. The dress is going to be purple no matter what. I just want the maid of honor and bridesmaid's dresses to be different shades of it."

"Alright. Can mine be lavender instead of this dark purple?" Aaliyah asked with a hand on her hip.

"Violet. It's violet. And yes. So, you ladies like this dress?" Lisa asked us all.

Lana shrugged, Lora nodded, Shan gave an indifferent shrug and the rest of us answered yes.

"I heard you might have to do jail time. Are you sure you're going to be able to full fill your bridesmaid duties?" Song taunted.

Lisa's sisters looked both confused and surprised.

"Jail?" Lana questioned.

"What is your damn problem?" Shan asked approaching Song with her arms still crossed. "I heard you were jealous, but this shit is ridiculous."

Song looked unphased. "Is she not up on charges?"

"Song, you said you were gonna behave," Lisa said with a disappointed hand to her forehead.

"I guess some bitches have never been properly trained on how to behave," I mocked with a tilted head. "You spend a lot of time in my business Ms. Harmon."

"Your business has been in the news, Sweetheart."

"Has it? What's your last name again?" Lora asked ready to type my name in the google search bar of her phone.

"You know who she is. The wife in the "Sleeping with the Enemy" case," Aaliyah murmured to her as my head swiveled around to look at them. Aaliyah clammed up abruptly and ran a nervous hand down the side of her neck.

"Is that the best you've got Song?" I looked back at her. Her husband was killed by the mistress. "You don't know anything about me that Race and most of Atlanta doesn't already know. If your intention is to embarrass me, you're wasting your time.

Race doesn't want your "open legs for everybody" self, whether he's with or without me. I think he's made that as clear to you as he has to me. So, let's act like mature adults in public. Shall we?"

She laughed satirically, picking up her clutch and standing. We were maybe a foot apart, with the other ladies surrounding us.

"He'll get over, Sweetheart."

"I'm not your Sweetheart," I checked her.

"Darling, he may be angry with me now, but he'll get over it. Maybe not today or tomorrow, but whenever he does, no matter how long it takes, these legs you claim stay open for everybody, will be open for him too."

My fist connected with her face before my mind had time to register what I was doing. Her hands were instantly in my hair and we were fighting like alley cats before Lisa's sisters and Shan pulled us apart. One of the store's salespeople appeared in the middle of the disturbance, frantically yelling for us to stop, and strongly encouraging us to leave.

The messy ponytail I arrived with was transformed into a rat's nest and the ugly dress I was supposed to be modeling for Lisa, was ripped on the side. Song didn't get any notable licks in on me, but I was certain her right eye was going to have a story to tell in the next 24 hours, among other things.

After everything calmed, we were asked to leave, but the store manager let Lisa order the dresses anyway on her card, which we would reimburse her for later; and made me pay for the ripped dress in the process. I was pissed to say the least, to have to pay for a dress I didn't want, but I appreciated the fact that they didn't call the police on us. I think if the store manager hadn't been a black woman, things might have turned out differently.

"I can't believe we were fighting!" Shan shrieked with a laugh when we got inside the Yukon. "I haven't had a fight in years."

"I know. I'm sorry. I didn't think you would hit her too."

"Are you kidding me? Of course, I was gonna sneak in a couple of licks on the bitch that's been giving my bestie hell. We always have each other's back. Stuck up, Beyoncé reject.

"I was expecting her to be more of a bad bitch than the tramp that showed up. She's pretty, but you can tell that airhead uses her looks and her body to get ahead. No wonder she's a flight attendant. Flighty bitch."

We laughed.

"We're too old to be fighting. You're pregnant and my chest hurts."

"She didn't hit me at all, and you were shot in your chest. It should hurt. I still have them hands though. I pulled that bitch off you like a bouncer," Shan joked, jabbing the air a few times, and falling back in her seat with laughter.

"I'm glad she couldn't fight. A punch in the chest might've taken me out. Even worse, now I had to pay for my bridesmaid dress and buy that damn ugly one too!" I gestured towards the bagged dress hanging in the backseat.

"Real talk, y'all are gonna have to work something out if you're both going to be in Lisa's wedding. Y'all can't be arguing and fighting every time you're in each other's presence. Her weak ass should've made that clear before putting you both in it in the first place."

"I was prepared to be civil. She's the one who can't stop showing her insecurities."

"I hear you, but that's not my point."

"What's your point?"

"My point is, y'all need to work it out before you start doing other wedding stuff. Bridesmaids have to plan together and spend a lot of time together. You sure you wanna be in this girl's wedding?"

"I'm not gonna let Race be in the wedding with her while I sit it out when she just confirmed she's not gonna stop throwing it at him."

"I hate whores," she pulled her phone out.

"Me too."

Shan convinced me to stop at Olive Garden to eat, and although I enjoyed the food, it didn't agree with my stomach on the way home. I had to pull over on the side of the road to earl the evening's intake.

"We need to stop by a CVS," Shan said when I was finished emptying my stomach.

"I'm okay. I think I can make it home. I have Tums, crackers, a toothbrush, and toothpaste, all in the same place. I don't need to get anything."

"You need to get a pregnancy test."

I frowned. "I'm not pregnant."

"You have been throwing up at the drop of a hat. More than me. When I was pregnant with Shamari, everything made me sick."

"I haven't been throwing up a lot."

"Every day I've been here."

"You didn't even see me yesterday."

"But I bet you threw up."

I rolled my eyes at her, but the more I thought about it, the more I feared her suspicions could be true. I hadn't had my cycle in December at all, and Race and I were having plenty of sex.

Shan took my silence as confirmation and pursed her lips smugly. I stopped at a Walgreens and got two tests. I was supposed to drop Shan off at the W before going home, so I took the tests in her hotel bathroom instead. Two, just in case one was faulty.

"How cool would it be if we had kids at the same time?" she asked leaning against the door frame as I sat on the closed toilet seat, waiting for the results.

"Yeah."

Noticing my lack of enthusiasm, she asked, "What's wrong?"

"I don't know if I'm ready for a baby. I have no idea what kind of mother I would be."

"Why? You're a good auntie and god mommy. Why wouldn't you be a great mommy too?"

"What if Race doesn't want to have a child with me?"

"I think you're too much in your own head. Has he said he doesn't want kids before?"

"No."

"Have y'all ever talked about having kids together?"

"Not a lot."

"A little is enough to get an idea of how somebody feels about kids, Greer. From everything you've told me about Race, and from what I've witnessed myself, that man loves you. It doesn't make sense that he wouldn't love to have a baby with you too."

I ran both hands down my face and looked over at the test on the edge of the bathroom sink.

"What does it say?" Shan questioned, entering the bathroom to get a better look as my teary eyes stayed glued to the symbols displayed on both long white sticks. Positive.

The entire drive home, my thoughts were consumed with plans for the future. I had to do things differently now that I would be acting for two. The more I talked to Shan, the more I became convinced that I could be the mother to my child I wasn't able to experience myself.

Unable to keep the news to myself I called Race through my car system.

"Hey, what's up Baby?" his baritone voice appeared in good spirits.

"Hey. On my way home from dropping Shan off."

"How did the fitting go?"

I sighed, remembering that there were other less jolly details I needed to relay. "Umm… it was eventful."

"Eventful? What does that mean?"

"Well, you know Song was there."

He exhaled a breath that already sounded disappointed. "And?"

"And, she came in ready to start. You can ask Shan and Lisa. I was minding my business, trying on the dress Lisa asked me to, and Song just kept coming for me."

"Coming for you how?"

"Calling me a cheap knock off, saying her legs would always be open for you and asking if I really thought I could fulfill my bridesmaid duties from jail. I just couldn't take her shit anymore."

"Fuck. I knew it was a bad idea to have both of you in the wedding. So, what happened?"

"We, sort of got kicked out."

"They kicked y'all out just for arguing?"

I swallowed hard. "For fighting."

"Fighting! C'mon Baby! You can't afford to get arrested with your case coming up in four days. Are you kidding me? She hit you first, right? Tell me she hit you first."

I remained silent while merging onto the ramp to I20. It may have been better for a police report if she had thrown the first punch, but for my ego, there was no way I would have felt better knowing she snuck me.

"Greer!"

"I hear you. Why are you talking so loud?"

"Don't get cute. Why do you keep letting her get under your skin when you know that's exactly what she's trying to do?"

"Because she needs to learn to stop doing it."

"And what if you would've opened up one of your wounds or got arrested? Then what? Song isn't a fighter so there's no telling how she's gonna handle this. She might still press charges just to hem you up."

I hadn't thought about that. I had decided succinctly, in the best interest of my unborn, to only tie up *two* more loose ends. However, if Song insisted on making herself a liability, a police report would be just the thing to make me finish the list with a third.

"I wasn't thinking about all that when it happened. I was just angry and… you know I've had a lot of built up frustrations that I've been trying to jog off lately. She just pushed me too far and I snapped."

"Shit," he huffed. "Are you hurt?"

"No. Besides pulling my hair, she barely touched me. There may be a bruise or two on my legs where she kicked me, but that's probably all," I exaggerated, doubting he'd noticed the bruise on my leg from Ms. Nina. I always had something long on covering it up, or his attention was focused elsewhere when it was exposed.

"What about her?"

"I don't know. She might have a black eye or two. Listen, that's not why I was calling you."

"Oh, it's not?" he asked indignantly.

"No. I was calling because I wanted you to meet me at the house. I have something I need to show you and it's very important."

"Something you need to show me?" he replied skeptically. "Something good or bad?"

"Well, that will depend on how you look at it."

"Greer, I don't like riddles. And lately, I don't like surprises either."

"I'm almost home now. Can you meet me there?"

"Yeah. Give me 20 minutes."

"Okay. I love you."

"I love you too," he replied before hanging up.

As expected, I made it home before Race arrived. Nervously pacing my bedroom floor, I held one of the tissue-wrapped tests inside the box my tennis bracelet came in. I rehearsed aloud the words I would use to present it to him as if I were trying out for the lead role in a play.

Butterflies fluttered in my stomach the moment I heard him enter the house, as they often did; but this time was different. This news would change our lives forever.

By the time he entered my room, I had decided to sit on the bed instead. His face was muted. Not angry, happy, or sad. It was simply a blank canvas, ready to transform into whatever emotion my news elicited.

Resting his keys on the top of my dresser and leaning against it, he addressed me.

"Alright, Miss Mike Tyson. Lisa called to tell me about your bout tonight too," he shook his head looking slightly amused. "I don't know what I'm gonna do with you. But anyway, I'm here. What do you need to show me?" He glanced around the room once before looking back to me.

I handed him the gold box without reply and apprehensively watched his countenance.

"I see you're wearing the bracelet that came in this box, so what's in it?" He jiggled it with a small frown. "Did you get me a matching one?"

"Just open it."

He removed the top of the box, glanced at its contents, then back to me with a bigger frown before focusing back on his gift. Opening the tissue, his frown turned dumbstruck as he gawked down at the positive test.

It seemed like an eternity was passing before I broke the silence to appease my own anxiety.

"I'm pregnant."

When his head lifted, his eyes were glistening, a smile gradually stretching his lips.

"We're having a baby," he uttered lowly.

"We're having a baby."

"We're having a baby!" he yelled scooping me up from the bed and spinning me around.

22

Greer

January 4th 2016

Thank God for back to school. Today was the last day I would have to venture outside of my home to exact vengeance on an offender. The tracking device on Will's car let me know that he was on the move at 6:00am, as it had been every weekday like clockwork.

Although Race and I spent the rest of Saturday night and most of Sunday together, fawning over the expectancy of our unborn, he spent the night over Granny's. She had three back-to-back doctor appointments today that started at 7:00am. Being her designated chauffer, he thought it best to stay the night over there.

I certainly wasn't going to protest, as his absence allowed me to readily do what I'd planned to do on Thursday, this Monday instead. Debbie would be out of the house no more than a half hour after Will left, to drop Tamia off at school, then baby Willow off at Will's parents.

Debbie was the laziest stay at home mom with small children that I knew. To my knowledge her days were spent being an unproductive, drinking, shopping, television watching, do nothing, waste of flesh, while Will was working hard to support his family. She was known to feed them microwaveable dinners way more than cooked ones, even though she'd been home all day, with plenty of time to prepare a meal.

Tamia might miss her simply because any kid that loses a child would probably miss their mother, but I doubted her absence would break any bonds a loving mom and daughter would share. In my presence, Debbie always made it seem like the children were a burden for her, and I felt like the only reason she had them was because of Will.

Today I would do us all a favor. Will deserved so much more from a wife, and she deserved to die. I hustled through their yard in another one of my disguises, bypassing her car in the driveway and let myself into their backyard through the fence.

Pressed up against the back of the house, I stayed silently hidden, waiting to hear Debbie's car pull off. The sound of my niece chirping as she exited the front door to the car brought a warm smile to my face. I missed her so.

"Are you going to come back up to the school to see me today?"

"Come back up to the school for what?" Debbie replied annoyedly.

"It's show-and-tell day. Remember? They sent a note home before Christmas. All the kids got to make a collage of all our favorite things that happened last year. We brought pictures, cut out stuff from magazines, and got to use glitter, clay, and all kinds of stuff! Mines is *reeeally* pretty, Mom. So pretty!" she squeaked with joy.

"I don't know Tamia. I got a lot of stuff of my own to do today. Do you get to bring the collage home, or does it have to stay at school?"

"We get to bring it home..." she answered defeatedly as I heard multiple car doors opening. I assumed that most of the holdup was due to Willow and Tamia being strapped into their car seats. "...but I want you to see me show it in front of the whole class. Daddy said he's coming."

"Well, if Daddy's gonna be there, it won't matter if I come too. I got a lot of stuff to do. I don't think I'm gonna be able to make it. Maybe next time. You can show it to me when you bring it home."

"Okay," Tamia replied somberly as a car door shut.

I wondered what was so important that this unemployed pigeon brained cunt, couldn't reschedule to go see her daughter at the school. Probably nothing.

As quick as they drove off, I was letting myself into the backdoor with the key I stole from Daddy. The place was a slightly neater version of a pigsty.

The backdoor lead straight into the kitchen, where dirty dishes lay in the sink, two recently used frying pans sat on the stove and the remains of whatever cereal Willow had in her highchair were scattered on the tray and floor nearby.

I peeked into the family room as I passed it on my way to the front door, only to see toys scattered about and cups on end tables with no cupholders under them.

Everywhere except the kitchen was carpeted, so the various stains from spills and tracked in dirt were evident in many places. I hadn't been to Debbie's house in a couple of years, but looking at the condition of it, I hoped she wasn't entertaining other people with it looking this slovenly either.

Taser in one hand, I placed the hypodermic needle I brought on the floor beside me and sat with my back against the wall by the front door. Thank goodness I intended to get rid of these clothes too. I had to psyche myself out to ignore the urge to jump up and run after the view from the floor allowed me to see all the dust balls gawking at me from every corner.

She took longer than I expected to come back, but the adrenaline running through me kept me alert. Rising to my feet when I heard the car in the driveway, I waited behind the door, ready to pounce the moment she closed it behind herself.

The keys on her ring jingled as she stuck the housekey in the lock and entered. Mail in hand, she paused inside with the door ajar, her back to me, sifting through what she deemed important or not. The moment she closed the door with her foot, I emerged from my hiding place and tased her in the back at the highest voltage.

Screaming in shock and pain, she reflexively spun around and knocked the taser from my hand before eating carpet and balling up. I dashed for the taser just as an arm shot out from under her to grab my right ankle.

"You bitch!" she hollered as slobber trickled down the sides of her mouth.

Damn it! She didn't go down as easily as Ms. Nina or the girl at the roller-skating rink had. Retrieving the taser, I turned to shock her foulmouthed ass again, but she grabbed my wrist and tried wrestling the taser from me as I bent to jolt her. I palmed her face with my other hand and shoved it down into the carpet while wrenching from her grasp.

I wanted to kick and punch her, but extreme force could only be used as a last resort, less any unexplained contusions on her body jeopardize everything.

"Stay down!" I roared, managing to tase her in the shoulder.

"F-f-fuck you!" she grunted, getting halfway to her feet and headbutt me in the stomach, driving me fully down onto the carpet.

She left me no choice. I punched her repeatedly with one hand while tasing her with the other. Despite how many times I shocked her, she got some licks in before tasing her in the neck straightened her out like an ironing board; the volts coursing through her body demanding she surrender to their power.

I didn't let up after that. This bitch was going to suffer for all the years of torture she put me through. The best part of it all was knowing that she was rendered helpless under my thumb, fully aware that I was the one doing this to her. Crawling around her to reach the syringe on the floor, I kept tasing her in different places on her neck. Groaned through clenched teeth, her eyes rolled into the back of her head.

Only then did I stop. Stilled from exhaustion, this was the best time for me to inject the needle. I couldn't hold the taser and hold her down while I stuck her at the same time. So I put the taser down.

Two years as a medical assistant in college taught me the skill I needed to seamless draw blood without leaving a mark. In this case, however; I wasn't drawing blood. I was injecting air.

I moved swiftly, inserting the empty syringe into the carotid artery in her neck, the one people touch to check your pulse, and injected 3mL of simple H2O. As soon as I withdrew the needle, the sting of a smack to the side of my head, knocked me back making my right ear, ring with pain.

She still didn't have full control of her faculties though. That smack was a last-ditch effort to save herself. Unfortunately for her, her limbs were not totally functioning on her command. I almost admired her refusal to stop fighting. One thing she wasn't, was a coward.

"What... what did you do? B-b-bitch."

I leered at her. She never had a nice thing to say to me and she was going to die how she lived. I exercised my finger on the trigger of the taser again, waiting for the effects to kick in. Air bubbles would soon cause an embolism and travel to her brain; quickly resulting in a loss of consciousness, which thank God, occurred even faster than anticipated.

It was only a matter of time before a fatal stroke, respiratory failure, or both, transpired. Because we fought, my scheme to seamlessly cause her death by embolism, was coming undone. Since the volts from the taser were only expelled via surface contact, little to no bruising typically appeared after use. But punches... they could show at any time. I needed to neutralize that threat now too.

It also didn't escape me that I was a pregnant woman. I was lucky that the previous scuffles I had didn't result in a miscarriage. I couldn't afford for a brawl with this barracuda to result in me unwittingly leaving my DNA on something or losing my child.

I wasn't prepared to drag a body this time. I didn't have my backpack with me because I carried everything I needed in my pockets. Even if I had, the runner I used to move Angie was no longer in it. Entering the living room, I pulled the area rug by the coffee table out into the hallway in front of Debbie's unconscious body. Grabbing her by both arms I dragged her onto it, then bent down, clenching the edges of the rug, and towed her into the kitchen.

I rolled Debbie off the rug onto the linoleum by the stove, then marched the rug back into the living room to make sure I didn't forget to do it later. Returning to the kitchen, I struggled to pick her fat ass up. Placing one arm over my shoulder to get her on her feet.

Hoisting her up three fourths of the way, I realized I didn't actually *need* her to stand up. She only needed to be high enough from the floor to make a fall impactful. Letting her body drop, her face smacked the linoleum with a loud, "Thwack!"

I cringed with a combination of laughter at the sight and sound of it as I looked down at her still form. Blood, from what was probably a broken nose began to pool beneath her head.

Placing two latex gloved covered fingers to her neck, I felt for the pulse I hoped was still present. And it was. Looking up to the heavens, I said a prayer, thanking the almighty for the strength to do what I had to do, and hopefully, the blessing to get away with it.

Opening the refrigerator, I took out two eggs and two slices of bacon. I found a bowl in a cabinet and cracked both eggs into it, tossing the shells in the trash beside the stove. I placed both pieces of bacon on one of the frying pans. Both pans still had the remnants of whatever was cooked in them before, but it wouldn't matter in the scheme of things.

I turned the burner on medium high and watched the bacon cook. Searching for a whisk, I located it in the dishwasher and used it to mix the eggs. Pouring them into the other frying pan on the stove, I turned the eye on that to medium high and moved them around with a spatula once. Just in case the fire didn't burn everything up, I needed it to look believably like she suffered a stroke while making breakfast.

Next, I stood by the back door, impatiently watching as the food charred and smoke began billowing around us. Minutes passed like a snail in quicksand before flames rose from the burning pan of bacon. Once I was sure the fire was burning strong, I bustled out, trying to walk nonchalantly down the block to the car while discretely coughing the smoke from my lungs.

I didn't need the entire house to burn down, just the kitchen with her in it. If enough of her flesh was seared to mask any visible contusions or marks from the taser or our fight, I was Scott free.

In the car, I couldn't stop smiling. I felt like the burden of nearly 15 years of torture lifted from me as I imagined Debbie's wretched life evaporating into thin air.

This would be my last time driving dear old Rolly before it's final ride to a place where I could have it crushed into a compact heap of metal. Her use had expired and the last person on my list to eliminate, would not require her services.

I got home before 10am and immediately returned a missed call from Race.

"Hey, Baby," I sang into the phone on my way to the shower. "I'm sorry I missed your call. I'm just getting up. I have been so sleepy."

"Maybe it's my little man or princess in there making you tired."

"I don't know," I forced a yawn. "How are Granny's appointments going?"

"Pretty good. She has one more at noon."

"Did you tell her yet?"

"Naw. I haven't told anybody yet. I'm still lettin' it sink in. They say you're supposed to wait until after the first trimester to tell people about a pregnancy, don't they? Just in case there's complications or something?"

I rolled my eyes, knowing he was probably thinking about Song's miscarriage. Hers wasn't a natural loss, so I wasn't worried about mine. If I stopped doing things that could jeopardize it, like wrestling with people before murdering them, I was sure my little bundle of joy was safe.

"Please don't give me something else to worry about, when I'm already nervous about it," I scolded.

"My bad. That's not my intention at all, Sweetheart. Anyway, they're bringing her to the front. I'll call you back later when I'm on my way to the gun range. I haven't been up there for a while. I think I'm gonna put in some work there before I head over to the shop."

"Alright. I love you."

"Love you too."

Hanging up with him, I took a shower, got dressed in a long T-shirt and sweats, and coiled my hair up into a tight bun. I made an early morning appointment for the 7th to see Dr. Selleck, the OBGYN at FFP and went downstairs to make myself a cup of coffee.

A cup of coffee turned into coffee, and a bacon, egg, and cheese sandwich. I grabbed a throw blanket from the hall closet and took it with me into the living room, where I sat in the recliner and draped myself with it. Flicking on the television, I placed another phone call.

"Hi, Daddy. Did I catch you at a bad time?"

"Nah, nah. I'm just settin' here watchin' a movie."

"What movie?"

"I'on know. Somethin' 'bout a free black man bein' treated like a slave."

"Is it "12 Years A Slave"?"

"I thank that's it. That guy Chewbacca somebody."

I chuckled. "His name's Chiwetel Ejiofor, Daddy."

"*Ahhh*, I can't pronounce that mess. Anyhow, I'm surprised to hear from ya'. Checkin' to see ifin' I'ma show up tomorrow like I said I would?"

"No. I'm calling to share some news with you that I recently found out."

"Must be good news from how you sound."

"It is. At least, we think it is. I'm pregnant."

"Pregnant? Well I'll be!" he exclaimed.

"We're not really telling a lot of people yet. You know because it's still early. But I wanted to tell you," his excitement brought me joy. It was exactly how I hoped he would react.

"How far along is ya'?"

"I don't go to the doctor until Thursday, but it can't be more than two or three weeks," I a real yawn followed that time. "Oh. Excuse me."

"Don't tell me ya' sleepy in the middle of the day? You 'bout to go back to work next week ain't ya'? You can't be takin' no naps in the middle of the day no'mo."

"I can until I have to actually *be* back to work. This is the last week I can do what I want on a weekday. I just woke up a few hours ago. I think this baby is making me sleepy," I made a point to say. I wanted as many people as possible to know that I had been asleep during the time Debbie was killed. Just in case.

In fact, I was texting Shan back and forth while talking to Daddy on the phone. Just making small talk to see how she was doing. Asking random questions about being pregnant that I didn't really have a need to know.

"Well, you go'on and get some sleep. I'm 'bout to nap too."

"How have you been feeling?"

"No worse today than I was yesterday. Happy fo' every day I'm breathin'."

"Me too." There was a long lull in conversation, so I decided to let him go. "Okay," I yawned again. "I think I am gonna go ahead and take that nap. I'll see you Wednesday."

"Alright, Baby Girl."

"Bye, Daddy."

I had a genuine smile on my face when we hung up. No matter what, I don't think I could ever shake the need for my father's love and approval. It was in my DNA. *He* was in my DNA.

I slept a few hours, talked to my attorney, and cooked baked chicken, rice, and asparagus for dinner. I hadn't been cooking as much as usual since I got home from the hospital, but knowing Race would be coming over after work, I cooked tonight.

I finally got around to checking my Craig's List inbox and saw the explicit pictures of Wendy's rape. Someone with the username Jet New York sent them. Of course, he was looking for the promised pay, which he would never get. I quickly deleted the ad, my account, and washed my hands of it. What was he going to do? Tell on me?

As I lay across the bottom of my bed, half watching an old episode of "Martin", my phone dinged with a text message. I flipped it over, swiping the screen to see that my sister Donna was the sender. Checking the time, 8:34pm, I had a good idea what it was about. I opened the message to three sentences.

Donna: Not sure if anybody told you. Thought you would want to know. Debbie died in a house fire.

"Tuh!" I exclaimed. I wasn't even worthy of a phone call? The whole family had probably been dealing with the aftermath of the fire and her death all day. But they were just *now* getting around to telling *me*. I texted back:

Me: Wow. Are Will and the kids okay?

Donna: Yes. They weren't home.

Me: Thank God. Thanks for telling me.

She didn't reply and I didn't care. It was no secret that I hated Debbie, so there was no need to pretend. I called Daddy but got his voicemail.

"Hi Daddy. Donna just texted me about Debbie. I'm just calling to see if you're okay. Regardless of how I felt about her, I know you loved her. I'm here if you, Will or the kids need me. Love you. Bye."

Ding Dong the witch is dead!

23

Greer

January 6th 2016

Today was bittersweet. Court went much the way Sylvia said it would, and although Daddy hadn't answered or returned my calls, he came as promised. Sylvia argued that the charges were essentially for victimless crimes and that I was under an inordinate amount of stress on the day.

Judge Renfro was lenient on everything but the DUI. He didn't cut me much slack, short of sending me to jail. He gave me 40 hours community service, I have to attend a DUI Risk Reduction Class, and pay $1000 plus court costs.

Surprisingly, all gun related charges were dismissed. It was a huge weight lifted off my shoulders to know I wouldn't have jail time or attempted murder charges hanging over my head anymore. When I approached Daddy afterwards, he wasn't as warm as I thought he would be.

"Daddy!" I called behind him, separating from my attorney as he walked towards the courthouse doors.

He stopped, and looked over his shoulder at me, but didn't turn all the way around. I touched his arm when I reached him, and he motioned as if he was debating on snatching away.

"Daddy… uh, I wanted to thank you for coming. I know you haven't really bee—"

"I don't want to talk to you right nah, girl. Just leave me be," he glared at me.

I reared back with a hand to my chest in shock. "Why not?"

"Cause, I know what you did, and I ain't no better cause I still showed up to help ya'." His eyes were glassy with… was it anger?

"I don't understand. I thought we talked about that already and ca—"

"I ain't talkin' 'bout that," he cut me off again, in a hushed tone. "I'm talkin' 'bout Debbie."

"What? What about Debbie?"

"I know y' took the key of my rang. I don't know what ya' did fo'sho. The po'lice say it take three days for the report to come back, but I know it wasn't no accident. You did somethin' to her," he jabbed an elderly finger at me.

"Daddy, I didn't do anything to her."

He stepped closer to me, looking at the other people in the distance before speaking in a low, angry growl. "She was still my daughter. She wasn't always good, but she didn't deserve to die and my grandbabies don't deserve to grow up wit' out a momma. I cain't stomach ya' right nah. Don't know if I ever can again."

The mixture of disgust and sorrow in his expression speared my heart as I watched him look me up and down, then continue out of the courthouse. His disdain for me was palpable. I wanted to cry but refused to.

He was just angry now. Grieving men say crazy things and I was convinced that he would change his mind as time passed. I didn't expect the coroner's report to indicate foul play, and then I could explain away my taking the key as something else.

"Is everything okay?" Sylvia asked placing a hand on my shoulder and startling me.

"Oh! Yes," I forced a smile. "Everything is fine. You know my sister died a couple of days ago. My father's taking it pretty hard."

She nodded. "Right. How are you holding up?"

"I'm fine. We weren't close, but I hate to see him suffering like that. And she had a husband and kids so... it's just a rough time."

"My condolences to you and your family. I hate to run, but I have another case to represent in an hour," she checked her watch. "You've got a ride home?"

"Yes. I drove myself. Thank you for what you did for me."

"Just doing my job. Call my office to make sure we have all our ducks in a row. Judge Renfro is strict about following his orders."

"Understood."

We shared a brief, friendly embrace, and strut quickly off down the hallway. I came to court alone. Race wanted to come with me, but I insisted that he didn't. He had businesses to tend to and since neither side was going to call him to testify, he didn't need to. I was consuming enough of his time with my personal issues. He was probably on pins and needles waiting for me to let him know the verdict.

I called to tell him what happened but left out my conversation with Daddy afterwards. We chatted on the phone as I walked to the parking deck.

"Ms. Patterson! Ms. Patterson!" a trotting, long haired Asian woman in heels and a pants suit chased behind me.

"Yes?" I didn't even notice the microphone in her hand and the lone camera man jogging behind her until she was right up on me.

"Loni Chang with Court TV. How does it feel to have the aggravated assault charges dismissed against you, but no charges brought against your father for the murder of your mother?"

I frowned and thrust a hand between the microphone and my face. "Listen, I'm not talking to the press," I walked faster.

"We just want to know if you're okay. A lot of our viewers were in support of you through your husband's murder trial an—"

"Thank you," I fumbled with my keys and unlocked the truck, getting in as she continued to talk by my window. "Oh my God I hate them," I told Race. "They were bombarding me before trial too."

"Hopefully, this will all die down soon. What are you about to get into?"

"Nothing. Same boring stuff as usual. You know me. If I'm not home, I'm probably somewhere with you."

"Okay. It's Stevo at the shop's birthday. We're gonna hit a bar real quick after close and then I'll be on my way to you."

"So, I don't need to cook?"

"Not unless you just want to make a plate for me. It'll probably be around 10 when I get there."

"Umph. Are the girls from the shop going too?"

"A couple of them."

"Jade?"

"Yeah."

"Well, where are y'all going? Can I come or is it only for coworkers?"

"Babe, you can't drink."

"I don't have to drink to go, do I? And who's gonna be driving? Don't you need a designated driver?"

He let out an aggravated breath. "Greer, I got it covered."

"Just make sure you don't cover it with Jade. I don't like her."

"Okay, Babe. I love you. I'll see you tonight."

"Are you brushing me off?"

"I'm going back to work. Love you." He hung up before I could respond, and that type of shit made my temperature boil.

I trusted my man, but I didn't trust that big busted, green wig wearing hoe. I debated on driving up there and inviting myself to their little outing anyway, but decided against it when my car suddenly started slowing as I drove.

"The hell?" I complained aloud as my car suddenly cut off and began coasting to a full stop. Luckily, I was driving through a fairly low traffic area, but there were still cars honking and pulling around me with attitude.

I banged the steering wheel, mad that my Yukon was giving me yet another problem. I was gonna trade this damn thing in ASAP. I doubted Will would be there, but I prayed he hadn't shut the shop down completely because of Debbie's death.

"Will's Auto Experts," a man answered the phone.

"Hi, this is Greer Patterson. My Yukon just cut off in the middle of the street while I was driving. Can I have it towed there?"

"We're a little shorthanded here today Ms. Patterson. We might… huh?" he spoke to someone in the background. "Hold on a moment please." There was a brief silence, then another voice came on the phone.

"Hey, Greer. It's Rodger. We a little backed up today, what with Will being out and everything, but I can make sure we get you in. How you holdin' up?"

"My truck literally just stopped while I was driving. If I have AAA tow it, how long do you think it will be before you can tell me what the problem is and fix it? I feel like y'all keep fixing it and it keeps getting worse.

"I don't have the money or the time to keep spending on this truck like that. If it turns out to be related to the ignition or whatever the last thing was I just paid to get fixed, is this gonna be free?"

"Let's cross that bridge when we come to it. I stand behind the work we do and I personally worked on your truck. It could be as simple as you needing a new battery."

"That doesn't sound simple to me. That sounds expensive. I tell you what. Have it towed here, leave the keys in the glove compartment and you can call a friend or a rideshare and go on home.

"I'll have a full diagnostic done on it, and I'll call you with what we find. If we can fix it today, I'll personally see to it that it gets done, and I'll even drop it to your house for you. No matter what time it is. I know you're grieving and everything. It's the least I can do."

As creepy as Rodger was, I appreciated his willingness to accommodate me. Debbie's death was making life easier for me already.

"What if you can't fix it today?"

"We'll cross that bridge when we get to it. Okay?"

"Okay. Thank you. I appreciate it."

"Alright. I'll call you later. You just take care of yourself and get home safe."

His syrupy tone made my skin crawl, but I needed to be nice to him since he was, essentially, doing me a favor.

"Thank you."

I waited for almost an hour AAA to arrive, then stood outside of a QuikTrip gas station to wait for my Uber driver. Thanks to too much product in the AAA driver's hair triggering my gag reflexes, I had to buy mouthwash, a toothbrush and toothpaste to get the taste of bile from my mouth.

While I waited, my burner phone rang. There was only one person with the number, so I knew who it was without looking.

"Hello."

"Green eyes. How are you doing today pretty lady?"

"Fine."

"I heard your pretrial went good."

"Word must travel fast."

"They do when you have connections."

"Umph."

"Today must be your lucky day."

"Why's that?" I asked dryly.

"I'm gonna be available for you to repay that debt you owe me," he replied smarmily. "I can swing by your place about 8pm tonight. And FYI, I like lingerie. Feel free to open the door in your sexiest."

"Nick, this isn't a good night," I groused.

"Make – it – a – good – night. Don't think just because I let you go, that I can't still find a way to violate you, Greer. You don't want to play with me."

Damn if he didn't pick the worse night possible for this shit. I'd carved out how I was going to handle him already, but his timing was throwing a monkey wrench in my plans. Especially since I didn't have my car. Still, I would improvise. I could always improvise. He was the last person on my list anyway. Once he was out of the way, I was going to be home free.

"Okay," I relented. "Eight o'clock."

"Don't be like that, Baby girl," he said, making me cringe at his use of the same nickname Daddy gave me. "I promise to make sure you'll enjoy it as much as I will." When I didn't respond, he snickered and hung up.

The entire Uber drive home, I thought about Nick and the details of how I was going to handle him. The last thing I wanted to do, was have sex with him, but to carry out my objective, I might just have to.

A stress migraine pounded at my temples like the police with a "no knock" warrant. Not wanting to take any medications now that I knew I was pregnant, I opted to sleep it off. After a shower and changing into more comfortable clothes that is.

I was just about to fall asleep when my cell rang with the number from Will's Auto Experts.

"Hello?"

"Greer, this is Rodger."

"Hi."

"Yeah, so, I was right. It was your battery. Most battery's only last between three and five years anyway. When was the last time you got a new one?"

"I don't know. This was Michael's truck."

"Oh, okay. Well, I can order it from AutoZone and have it here within an hour to install. The cheapest battery for your truck is $280, and I'll give you $45 on labor instead of $80 for a total of $328.67 with tax.

"I can have the work done today and have your truck back to you tonight. We got a lot of repairs today though, so it's gonna be the last one out since I'm driving it out anyway. Is that okay with you?"

"That price isn't okay with me."

"I know, and I'm sorry. I wish I could discount the battery, but we gotta pay AutoZone for it."

"Hold on a minute while I get my card," I told him, not feeling the need to listen to his apologies. It wasn't going to change the cost. I retrieved my purse from my dresser and gave him the credit card information from my wallet.

"Alright, Pretty Lady. You're all set. I'll bring the paperwork with me when I bring the truck to you."

"How are you going to get home if you drive my truck to me?" I asked, hoping he wasn't foolish enough to think I was going to drive him anywhere.

"Oh, I'll just Uber back to my car. We've done it before for other clients. It's a business expense," he assured me.

"Alright. Sounds good. Thank you. Goodbye."

I ran a hand through my mane and laid back on the bed, staring up at the ceiling in thought. I know I've been doing a lot of bad lately, but I was ready to turn over a new leaf. After tonight.

Loose ends are the key to a crime's unraveling. Nick was my final loose end. He could possibly be a link between me and Ms. Nina's death or at the very least, continue being a blackmailing, rapey police officer.

I called him from the burner, hoping he would pick up since I never attempted to call him before.

"Somebody must be anxious to see me," he answered.

"Something like that. I've been thinking about our little... arrangement, and I was wondering if you could do something for me," I spoke kittenishly.

"Do something for you. Something like what?"

"Well, I kinda have this fantasy. You might think I'm weird."

"Weird or freaky?"

"I guess it depends on whether or not you want to participate in it or not."

"I see. So, what is it?"

"Are you going to be coming straight from work when you get here?"

"Yeah."

"So, you'll be in uniform?"

"Yeah."

I tittered. "Alright. This is awkward for me to say, but I have this fantasy. There's a knock at the door, it's a handsome police officer, he's looking for an escaped convict and he thinks they're in my house. When I open the door, he's pointing a gun at me and forces his way in.

While he's looking for the fugitive, he sees how sexy I am and forces me upstairs to the bedroom where he ravishes my body." I let out a nervous giggle.

He chuckled. "I knew you were a freak. The pretty ones always are. So, you want me to pull my piece on you when you answer the door?"

"I mean… you do know how to use it don't you? I would assume you'd have the safety on or something to make sure you don't accidentally shoot me, during our little role play."

"Of course, I know how to use it," he scoffed. "I wouldn't think a woman who was recently shot would have a fantasy involving cops and police though."

"I had that fantasy loooong before I was shot. And let me be clear. My fantasy isn't about being shot. So, the goal is to make sure that the only shots being made come out of your schlong. Not your gun," I joked.

"I think we can arrange that."

"Also, can you bring condoms? I don't have any."

"I'm always strapped. You didn't even have to ask. The last thing I need is to bring something home to my girl."

Was this bastard implying that I'm not clean? The hell? I tried to keep the resentment from seeping into my voice.

"Since we've gotten that out of the way, I'm going to get off this phone and figure out what style of lingerie to wear when Officer Hard Knock comes to my door tonight."

He laughed mischievously and I phonily joined in.

"Alright. Tonight then, Pretty Red. I'm on duty."

"Tonight."

I smiled sinisterly from ear to ear as the call ended. Little did Officer Ratcliff know, my security cameras were going to catch him in the act. I would have proof of his harassment via phone calls and nasty messages on my cellphone, and I'd claim he popped up unexpectedly, forcing his way in at gunpoint.

Unbeknownst to him, I would also have a half-eaten plate of steak, green beans, and mashed potatoes on my bedside table too. You can't properly eat steak without a steak knife, now can you? Unfortunately for Nick, while "raping" me, that steak knife is going to be buried deep in his throat before the night is over.

24

Greer

I cooked, ate, and set up my bedroom as planned. I absolutely was not going to be wearing lingerie. At least, not the type he was expecting. I put on my pink, long, silk pajama pants with a matching spaghetti strapped top.

It was nothing Race hadn't seen me in before. I didn't want my actions to seem suspicious upon investigation. I hated that he would arrive to a crime scene when he got in from hanging out with his friends, but it couldn't be avoided.

I was going to move in with him anyway, so I was perfectly fine with one more desecration of the Patterson home. Me and baby Banks were going to move in, mark our territory, and make ourselves comfortable.

I knew it was going to kill Song when she found out I wasn't just living with Race but carrying his baby too. It was only going to be a matter of time before he popped the question and I would revel on the day, in her despair.

My baby was barely a pebble in my tummy, yet I already felt connected to it. Him or her. I wasn't sure I even wanted kids, but now that I knew I was carrying one, I felt, maternal. I placed a hand on my belly and rubbed it in a circular motion.

"It's okay little one. I'll make sure you're protected. I'll stab him as many times as I can to make sure you're not in harm's way."

The bell rang, and I switched the television to see who was at the door. Rodger. It was after 7:18pm. The shop closes at 5pm so he must've been working on my car pretty late.

I put on my robe, tying it at the waist as my feet slid into my slippers. He rang the bell a second time before I got to the door. Opening the door, his bulky figure rocked from side to side like he was cole. He wore a skull cap, a big coat with work pants and boots. Both hands were jammed into his coat pockets until he removed one to adjust the bifocals on his face.

"Hi," I greeted, looking passed him at my truck parked in the driveway.

"Hey, Greer. I got your car back to you fixed and in one piece," his other hand presented paperwork with a stapled receipt on it and my keys on top. "Here you go."

"Thank you."

"Hey, would it be okay if I waited for my Uber inside? It's cold as a witch's titty out here."

"Uh… yeah. Sure," I agreed, stepping aside to let him in. He smelled of cigarettes and sweat, making me breathe through my mouth to stave off the urge to vomit. "How long till they get here?"

He pulled his phone from his pocket and looked down at it as I lead him into the living room. "Says they'll be here in 17 minutes."

I huffed under my breath as he sat on the couch and I sat in the recliner. What the hell were *we* going to talk about for 17 minutes?

"Nice place."

"Thank you."

"How long have you lived here?"

"Eight years."

He surveyed the room until his eyes rested back on me. "Doesn't bother you to keep livin' where your husband was killed?"

I tongued the inside of my cheek. "Sometimes. I'm moving soon."

"I hate to bother you, but do you mind if I have something to drink? Some water maybe?"

"Sure," I rose with an accommodating smile. "Ice?"

"Too cold for ice. You wouldn't have any tea, would you?"

"No. Sorry I don't."

A frown briefly etched his face, as if he knew I was lying, before disappearing. "Water's fine then. I'll even take tap if you want me to."

I pivoted towards the kitchen without response. I just needed him to leave. If Nick showed up early, Rodger was going to mess everything up.

I took a plastic cup from the cabinet and placed it under the water dispenser on the fridge.

"So, why won't you go out wit' me?"

I nearly jumped out of my skin, spinning with cup in hand, spilling water on the floor.

"Because I have a boyfriend. I told you." I abruptly handed him the half-filled cup, turning to snatch a paper towel from the countertop roller. I wiped up the spill in frustrated strokes. Who told him to get up?

The depraved look in his eyes as I rose to throw the paper away caused me to tighten the belt on my robe. Suddenly, being alone with him seemed like a bad idea. He'd taken the cup from me but hadn't taken a sip.

"I thought you were thirsty?"

"How long have you and your… *boyfriend*, been together?" he spat "boyfriend" out like a dirty word. "I just think you should keep your options open. I'm a good guy when you get to know me. I know I look a little rough around the edges, and I might not be able to afford some of the luxuries you're used to…," he scanned the room. "…but it ain't always about money. You know?"

I began slowly pacing backwards around the island. I wasn't comfortable standing in such close proximity to him anymore.

"Let's go back into the living room," I suggested.

His eyes narrowed. His voice growing harsh. "Why won't you tell me what the problem is? Am I too fat? Too ugly? Too poor? What is it? Even before you got your, so called...*boyfriend...*" he hooked his fingers into quotes. "... you avoided me. You look at me like I got a booger on my forehead. Tell me."

He put the cup down and placed both palms flat on the island. His face was reddening with anger and my heart was beginning to beat with fear.

Making direct eye contact with him instead of looking at the knife rack I planned to patronize on the countertop, I answered.

"I was either married, grieving or already in a relationship like now whenever we've been around each other. There's nothing wrong with you," I lied like a rug. "I'm sorry. I just never looked at you that way. Hey... how far away is your Uber?"

He didn't return my labored smile. In fact, his expression grew more frightening.

"Anxious to see me leave, huh? Don't matter how nice I am to you, does it?"

I silently thought of my exit strategy. Grab the biggest knife I could from the rack, dodge around the island and head to the door. I cursed myself for leaving my phone upstairs. I could easily have set off the silent alarm from the app.

"I could've had you that night you know. If I really wanted to."

"What night?"

"The night you came home. Will said he didn't think you would get released for another week, but he was wrong. Them cars always been in the driveway. I ain't know you was here till I heard the music playing upstairs."

My jaw dropped. *Rodger* was the burglar in my house? "Why were you here?"

"I needed a place to stay and I knew you was in the hospital. Relax. I only stayed two days. I kept it respectful. I ain't even sleep in your bed. I only laid in it a couple times. I was in the middle of reading that diary when you came home. Hope you don't mind that I kept it. I'm a slow reader," he smirked.

Oh my God! Rodger had the diary!

"Y-you should probably check your phone to see where your Uber driver is."

"Probably in the house watching T.V." He laughed ominously. "I never called a Uber. I didn't need nobody shortening the time we had together."

On that note, I lunged for the knife rack, toppling it over, and grabbing the handle of the first blade I could. I used the island as a barrier between us. Pointing the knife at him threateningly.

"Leave," I snarled.

"I don't think so," he replied calmly.

"Leave! Or I'll gut you like a fish. I swear to God I will."

"I'm sure you'll try," he began moving towards me at a frighteningly slow pace.

He was twice my size, his big coat would make it hard for my knife to penetrate, and he'd said too much. People who planned to leave their victims alive, didn't talk so much.

"Why are you doing this? What do you want from me?"

"I want what every man wants from you, and I'm tired of you holdin' out." Without warning, he rushed me.

Screaming and trying to run, I stabbed at him ferociously before I was tackled to the floor. I landed hard on my left side, still screaming and slashing with all my strength. I managed to knock his glasses off, but it did little to deter his motion.

Slamming my face repeatedly into the floor, he laid his full weight on me. Rodger twisted my wrist with the strength of a barbarian. I tried to hold on, but resistance was futile once I heard and felt the muscles in my wrist snap. The knife fell with a clang to the floor once my hand was rendered useless.

"Please! Stop!" I cried out as he flipped me on my stomach.

"Shut up!" he ordered slamming my face into the floor again.

My front teeth cut into my bottom lip and a throbbing in my face blurred my thoughts. Temporarily dazed and struggling to breathe with him on top of me, I was at his mercy.

I prayed Nick was close. This time as my savior instead of a victim. I was in over my head.

"Please," I begged weakly. "I'll do whatever you want."

"I know you will," he whispered in my ear.

I felt his grimy hands ripping down my pajama bottoms as helpless tears flooded my face. I debated on whether to fight or let him have his way. I tried to buck him off, but I had little energy to move and I was hurting all over. The cracked rib in my back had been healing well, but now, it felt like it was about to pierce my flesh with Rodger's body crushing me. It was at that point that I tried to check out.

He somehow worked his pants down and I felt his unwelcomed penis barging through the delicate lips of my womanhood. My body jerked beneath him with every thrust. It wasn't until his oil caked palm cupped my mouth that I realized I was still screaming.

His grunts were like nails on a chalkboard as his crusty lips suckled my left earlobe. I vomited through his fingers, causing him to snatch his hand away and lift enough to allow my left arm, previously pinned down, movement.

I knew the knife was within reach and he was temporarily distracted by the disgust at his puke covered hand. I had to take the chance. For myself and my unborn child.

The moment my fingers wrapped around the handle, I lifted the knife and thrust the blade backwards over my head, hoping to stab him in the face or neck.

The howl he released let me know the metal struck him somewhere, but he didn't lift up from me as I anticipated. Instead, his large fingers wrapped around the back of my neck, pressing me harder down into the floor before I felt a deafening blow to the head.

"You bitch! You stupid bitch!" His punches rained down on me like boulders thrown from a mountain top. I felt them on my head, my neck, and my back with such speed that I wondered if he was hitting me with both hands.

It wasn't until I saw the spirts of blood landing onto the floor in the growing puddle beneath me that I realized he wasn't punching me at all. He was stabbing me.

"You – stupid – cunt – bitch! You think you're too good for somebody? Now – you – ain't – good – enough – for – nobody!" he mocked with every blow.

I could do nothing but gasp for air. Stare at the plasma seeping from my body as my life and that of my child's drained from my person.

Pain faded into numbness by the time I heard the faint chime of the doorbell. Officer Ratcliff was here to save me. I tried to scream, but no sound escaped my gaping mouth. Tears raced from one eye, over the bridge of my nose and onto the floor as the desire to sleep beckoned me.

I heard the doorbell ring once more and...

25

Epilogue

"Devastation struck this Lithonia neighborhood last night Greer Patterson, whom some of you might remember from the "Sleeping with the Enemy" case in 2014, was assaulted and killed in her home off Bay Ridge Drive.

"We're told the assailant has been identified as 36-year-old Rodger Clemente Gaines of Marietta. Mr. Gaines worked as a mechanic at Ms. Patterson's brother in-law's Auto shop in Marietta. He was supposed to be dropping off Ms. Patterson's Yukon, which you see here behind me, after repair.

"Police say Mr. Gaines gained entry to Ms. Patterson's home under the guise of waiting on an Uber car to arrive. It's unclear what took place to insight the brutal attack that occurred inside, but it has been confirmed that Ms. Patterson was raped and stabbed over 40 times.

"An officer, whom has not yet been identified, is responsible for arresting Mr. Gaines at the scene. We're told the officer befriended Ms. Patterson during her stay at the hospital after her most recently publicized case with her father. The officer made an impromptu stop at her home and interrupted Mr. Gaines in the act.

"Reports say Mr. Gaines was the one who opened the door, covered in Ms. Patterson's blood, immediately surrendering himself and saying, I quote, 'She was too good for this world.'

"It seems Ms. Patterson's life has been plagued with bad news these past two years, and tragically, we're told she may have been pregnant with her first child.

"Neighbors were stunned by the news and as you can see behind me, mourners have already begun leaving flowers by the sidewalk here at her home.

"It's an unfortunate end to a beautiful life. This is Marlo Prentice with Channel 7 News."

Enjoy This Book?

Please leave a review on Amazon or Goodreads to share!

Other releases by K.F. Johnson:

BEHIND CLOSED DOORS: LOVE HURTS
LIAR'S BALL: BEHIND CLOSED DOORS 2
WHEN I'M BAD I'M BETTER
WHEN I'M BAD I'M BETTER 2
WHAT I'D DO FOR LOVE
LOVE HURTS: SERIES COMPILATION
WHEN I'M BAD I'M BETTER FOREVER: SERIES COMPILA-
TION
STABBED THIS CHRISTMAS: A NOVELLA

Join my mailing list and be the first to get sneak peeks, give-aways, contests, new release info, learn event appearances and more!
https://www.kfjohnsonbooks.com

"The Empress of romantic, murder, suspense", **K.F. Johnson** is a Queens, New York native residing in Atlanta, Georgia. As a child, habitually failing to make curfew before the streetlights lit, earned her numerous occasions on restriction where reading & writing became her main form of escape. Later, K.F continued to develop her talent while obtaining a B.A. in Psychology at Spelman College & acquiring an MBA. In 2012, she published her 1st book for her social media friends & family to see. To her delight, it went viral, repeatedly reaching #1 on Amazon's top 100 for its genre. Since then, K.F. has published multiple books, started One Ironwoman Publishing, been featured in magazines & nominated for numerous awards, both for her books & as an author. With her fan base cheering for more, this mother & wife has blossomed into a witty & cunning author, penning spicy, realistic & deadly tales of African American life to remember.